THIS BOOK IS TO DIE FOR

When I thought about it, the whole process now felt odd. As a favor to my publisher, Lane Barfield, I had agreed to read *The Affair*, give him my honest thoughts about it, and offer a blurb in the event he wanted one. I wished I'd had the opportunity to validate his decision—to tell him that if this wasn't the next big thing in the publishing world, I didn't know what was. Instead, I had ended up cracking open the manuscript to see if it might yield some clue as to the circumstances behind his death. If it was suicide, so be it. If it was someone trying to provide that impression, though, this book, or something contained within it, might hold the motive for his killing.

I rose from my seat and tried to stretch the stiffness from my neck and shoulders, the result of being stuck in one position while I read. My eyes drifted backward and I froze.

Manuscript for Murder

A *Murder, She Wrote* Mystery

A Novel by Jessica Fletcher & Jon Land

Based on the Universal Television series created by
Peter S. Fischer, Richard Levinson & William Link

BERKLEY PRIME CRIME
New York

BERKLEY PRIME CRIME
Published by Berkley
An imprint of Penguin Random House LLC
1745 Broadway, New York, NY 10019

ISBN: 9780451489326

Berkley Prime Crime hardcover edition / November 2018
Berkley Prime Crime mass-market edition / April 2019

Printed in the United States of America
1   3   5   7   9   10   8   6   4   2

Cover photographs: bookstore by Johann Helgason/Shutterstock Images;
book stacks by Africa Studios/Shutterstock Images
Cover design by Katie Anderson

For Michelle Vega, Tara O'Connor, Jen Monroe,
Tom Colgan, and everyone at Berkley.
Thanks for making me part of a great team!

And a special acknowledgment to Zach Bain Shippee for
helping me carry the torch so brilliantly lit by his grandfather,
the great Donald Bain.

The world is full of obvious things which nobody
by any chance ever observes.
—SHERLOCK HOLMES IN
THE HOUND OF THE BASKERVILLES
BY SIR ARTHUR CONAN DOYLE

Chapter One

"*What's the most fun you ever had killing someone?*"

I've been asked just about everything at book events, but that question was a first. I looked out from behind the podium at the woman who posed it, and found it wasn't a woman at all but a girl who looked to be in her teens. She was chomping on some gum and holding one of those energy drinks, this one colored aquamarine of all things. What flavor was that exactly? Maybe I'd ask her later.

"Well, I've written so many books," I said, still forming the rest of my response. "Let's see. . . ." Drawing a blank, I thought I'd try a different approach. "The first thing that comes to mind isn't actually from one of my books at all. It's from a story written by Roald Dahl called 'Lamb to the Slaughter.'"

In the back row, Seth Hazlitt and Mort Metzger, who'd made the trip from Cabot Cove to New York to help celebrate the release of my latest book, started bowing invisible violins, knowing what happened sometimes when I got off on a tangent at these things. I pried my eyes off them and returned my focus to the teenage girl who'd posed the question.

"A woman murders her husband with a frozen leg of lamb," I continued, "then cooks and serves it to the police investigating the case. It was adapted for an old TV show called *Alfred Hitchcock Presents*, and the last line, spoken by the lead detective as he bites into the lamb, is something to the effect of 'I'm sure the solution is right under our noses.'"

Seth and Mort were feigning yawns now, leaving me contemplating ways I might be able to get even. Maybe I'd invite them over for dinner; maybe I'd even serve lamb. Then again, given my reputation as a cook, they probably wouldn't show up.

The teenage girl was jotting down notes on a pad, something I was hardly used to at a book signing. It was rare even for press people to take notes these days, preferring to just switch on their cell phones to record the interview. Not that I did a lot of interviews. Writers are famous only to those who read our books and I've never been comfortable with the whole nature of celebrity. It was something that belonged to film and television stars, not authors, and particularly not me.

"Anyone else?" I asked those assembled at Otto Penzler's fabulous Mysterious Book Shop, located on Warren Street in Manhattan's Tribeca neighborhood.

It had been in business for about the same length of time I'd been a published author, and I so loved cramming in people for an event like this, surrounded by books by the true legends of our craft, any number of them signed first editions. There was something about being inside a place with such a sense of history, with so many titles and authors that have stood the test of time, that made me appreciate my career and whatever level of success I'd managed to achieve. Many of those whose work was prominently featured were no longer with us, but their books always would be.

I watched a few hands rise into the air, and was about to call on a man this time when I spotted a figure weaving his way to a chair in a row toward the back. I recognized Thomas Rudd immediately, even though the years had not treated him well since the last time we'd met. He'd been an author of some repute, a master of noir whose work had regularly appeared on the *New York Times* paperback bestseller list, until that list went away a few years back. We shared the same publisher and I'd heard that publication of Rudd's latest effort had been canceled, mostly because the head of the imprint we shared deemed it unpublishable. I'd also heard that he'd quit writing after a brazen display at our publisher's office in which he'd flung the pages of his rejected manuscript into the face of an assistant.

Looking at Rudd now, I could see why he wasn't writing. He was one of those people who'd looked old even when he was young, and now that he was older, he looked wan, worn, and much the worse for wear. The tweed suit I never saw him out of was draped over his emaciated frame and made for a perfect match with Rudd's sallow, hollow cheeks mottled with several days of stubble. His eyes were drawn and rheumy, with bags the size of orange slices sagging beneath them. He took a seat but didn't look settled at all, fidgeting with his knees as they knocked this way and that.

"Mrs. Fletcher," started the man I'd forgotten I'd called upon, "which do you find more interesting: the mysteries you make up or the very real ones you often end up involved in?"

"That's quite a question," I said, glad it had distracted me from the presence of Thomas Rudd, though my gaze drifted back his way to find him picking at his fingernails. "I like to be in control, and I also like it when good triumphs in the end and everything gets wrapped up in a nice, satisfying package. So I'd have to go with the real ones."

I waited for the smattering of laughter to die down before continuing. "The truth is, writing is about organization and predictability, neither of which comes into play much with reality. I seem to stumble into the mysteries I do mostly to help people, and let me say this to answer your question," I told the man. "I think that kind of experience in the real world has made me a better writer, because it's brought me a great appreciation of the cost of crime. How many people are affected and hurt when someone is killed. I guess you could call that collateral damage, and I believe it's what reality is all about yet what fiction usually pays little attention to."

The man nodded, smiling. In the back row, Seth and Mort were now pretending to be asleep. Thomas Rudd was studying me intently, as if something I'd just said resonated with him somehow. Before I could continue, Otto stepped out in his typically stately fashion.

"That's all the time we have, but Jessica will be staying with us to sign books for you, backlist included. Right, Mrs. Fletcher?"

"Of course." I smiled, already moving to take my chair behind the signing table before a sea of Sharpies and a bottle of water.

Many writers will tell you they detest these things, and while some do, the vast majority of us revel in the opportunity to meet and greet our readers. After all, they made the effort to come out and spend their hard-earned money for a brand-new hardcover just to have me sign it. I've never been able to accurately express how much that means to me, especially given the fact that the only book signings I've ever attended have been my own.

Based on the depletion of the pile, I probably signed around forty as the store's staff assisted me and while Seth and Mort busied themselves at the wine and cheese station, doing their best to take advantage of Otto's hospitality. It wasn't until the line neared its end that I recalled Thomas Rudd's tardy appearance and gazed out past the chairs more of the staff were folding up, but he was nowhere to be found.

Once I'd finished signing, Seth, Mort, and I walked the short distance to Le Pain Quotidien, just up the street from the Mysterious Book Shop. I'd invited Otto to join us but he'd declined, saying he had a prior engagement with Lee Child and David Morrell.

"Reacher and Rambo," he said, a bit guiltily. "How could I say no?"

"Well, you're buying next time," I told him.

"Deal!"

Le Pain Quotidien might've been a chain, but each LPQ I'd eaten at felt like a stand-alone. Even the pastries tasted different, as if each store added its own wrinkle to the mix. It was the perfect place to go when you wanted more than a snack but less than a full meal, and it featured a bright, airy atmosphere populated mostly by patrons comparable to the teenage girl who'd asked me my favorite way to murder someone.

"That was a great answer you gave that girl," Mort commented, "about that episode from Alfred Hitchcock. I remember seeing it."

"Never realized it was based on a story, ayuh," noted Seth. "I was always more partial to *The Twilight Zone*, anyway."

"Plenty of those were based on short stories, too, some by the likes of Richard Matheson."

"Who?"

"He wrote the episode 'Nightmare at 20,000 Feet.'"

"What?"

"William Shatner starred in it."

"Oh yeah." Seth nodded. "That was a good one. I'm thinking of picking up some Ronald Dahl now, thanks to you, Jessica."

"It's *Roald* Dahl, Seth."

"Isn't that what I just said?"

We were about to laugh, all three of us, when the disheveled Thomas Rudd entered Le Pain Quotidien and shambled toward our table like a scarecrow walking away from its perch.

"Mind if I join you?" he asked as he reached our table.

Without waiting for our answer, Rudd spun the lone empty chair around and shoved it forward, forcing Seth and Mort to shift their chairs aside. Rudd straddled his chair, his worn tweed suit smelling damp and musty. At least, I thought it was the suit. His appearance suggested a general lack of hygiene, as if he'd given up caring about more than just his writing. I couldn't tell whether the second scent I detected was stale hair gel rising from his unwashed mane. The fingernails I'd noticed him picking at inside the Mysterious Book Shop were yellowed at the base, a sign of ill health to go with his teeth, which gave him the look of a man who'd lived on coffee and cigarettes for much too long.

"I'm here to do you a favor, Jessica," he said in a hoarse voice that pushed out breath that stank of whiskey. "You're going to be thanking me a whole lot. Oh, Mrs. Fletcher, you have no idea."

Seth and Mort looked at each other and then at me, as if for a cue. I'd seen that look on Mort's face plenty of times before: his cop look, his eyes fixed on Thomas Rudd as if he were studying a lottery ticket to see if he had a winner. Had he been allowed to carry his gun in New York City, I imagine one of his hands would have instinctively strayed toward it.

"Is everything all right, Thomas?" I asked, my lame question originating from the fact that I didn't know what else to say.

"No, it most certainly isn't. I'm being robbed."

I nodded, trying to show as much compassion as I could, given all that I'd heard about Rudd's plight. Looking at him now, it was hard to reconcile this disheveled man with the cult figure whose picture had graced the back cover of dozens of bestselling paperbacks and who had been proclaimed the King of Noir once by none other than the *New York Times Book Review*.

"And so are you," Rudd continued, his eyes seeking me out and fighting to focus. "You're being robbed, too."

I could tell how increasingly uneasy Seth and Mort were becoming with the whole scene. "I'm staying overnight, Thomas. Why don't we meet up to talk in the morning? As you can see, I have company. I'm sure this can wait."

"Just like you're sure you're not being ripped off by our mutual publisher. And you're wrong there, too, because no, this can't wait. It's waited long enough, dollars being stolen from us by the moment. *Ching, ching, ching!*" he added, doing his best impersonation of an old-fashioned cash register.

"Thomas—"

His voice plowed right over my words. "It's the royalty statements, Jessica! Or should I say the lack thereof."

"Thomas," I said, loudly enough to keep him from interrupting me again, "there's a time and a place to discuss this, but here and now isn't it."

Rudd picked up a roll from the basket in the center of the table, put it back, and plucked another. I wondered if his financial ills had reached a point where that would pass for dinner.

"Do you still live in the area?" I continued. "Your apartment's just a few blocks from here, isn't it?"

"For now, anyway." He frowned. "Only thanks to rent control." He seemed to be settling down before his hollow cheeks went flush again. "He's a crook, Jessica. You may think he's your friend, but he's not."

"Who are we talking about?"

"Lane Barfield, our publisher—who else?"

"Barfield's stealing our royalties *personally*?"

"Head of the snake." He nodded. "I can explain it all to you, tell your accountant what to look for. I'm going to sue him for everything he's worth. I'm going to sue the whole damn company. I'm going to get the rights back to every single book they've let lapse and publish them myself and make a killing. Then I'm going to write new books that sell even better."

I didn't know what to say. What can you say to someone who's clearly delusional, his judgment clouded by failure and temperament spoiled by booze?

"I heard things didn't work out for your latest book—"

"Good thing, since there'll be less for Barfield to steal, the jackass."

"You didn't let me finish, Thomas," I said, putting an edge in my voice. "I was going to say maybe I can help find you a replacement publisher. I've got contacts around town from all the endorsements I get asked to give. It'll be nice to finally call in one of those favors. How about breakfast tomorrow?"

Rudd rocked backward. "You think I'm a charity case?"

"I think you need a publisher."

Before Rudd could respond, Mort stood up, slowly and menacingly, his torso angled forward to make himself appear closer to Thomas Rudd. Within range, whatever that meant. Mort might have left his hardened days as a vice detective with the New York Police Department behind when he settled in Cabot Cove as sheriff, but he could still bring it when he wanted to.

"I think you should leave," he said to Thomas Rudd in a tone that left no room for doubt. "You can take the rolls to go."

Whoa, I'd never heard Mort talk like that, couldn't recall a time when he'd stood up for me so demonstratively. Sure, Thomas Rudd was an easy target, but I was still impressed by Mort's boldness and I could tell Dr. Seth Hazlitt was, too, based on his expression.

Rudd looked up at Mort, trying to appear tough while pretending to know who he was. "You're the police chief."

"Not here, I'm not."

"This isn't any of your business."

"Maybe not. But it's my table—mine, Jessica's, and Dr. Hazlitt's here. Notice I left you out."

Rudd stumbled out of his chair and fixed his gaze as best he could on me. "Tomorrow morning, nine o'clock right here?"

"That sounds fine, Thomas."

"I've got the proof. I'll bring it with me."

I nodded.

"And don't say anything to Lane Barfield. He has no idea I figured his little scam out, getting rich on our backs. You're not going to believe it, Jessica. I can still barely believe it myself."

"Mr. Rudd?" Mort said, leaving it there.

Rudd started to back away from the table. "I've said what I came here to say. And if you're smart, you'll listen."

"Tomorrow morning, Thomas," I told him. "I'll meet you here at nine o'clock."

He nodded and finally turned around, retracing his faltering steps to the door as if the floor were slick with ice.

Chapter Two

Thomas Rudd didn't show by nine o'clock the following morning and still was nowhere to be seen a half hour later. I'd just started working on my third hot tea at Le Pain Quotidien when I figured he wasn't showing at all. Not that I was surprised. I've done plenty of research into alcoholism to properly cast some of the side characters in my books, enough to know that Rudd had all the unfortunate traits of a full-fledged alcoholic. His poor hygiene and complete disregard for any semblance of etiquette were the most prevailing characteristics, closely followed by paranoia.

He's a crook, Jessica. You may think he's your friend, but he's not. . . . I can explain it all to you, tell your accountant what to look for. I'm going to sue him for everything he's worth. I'm going to sue the whole damn company.

Rudd had to blame his failed career, and subsequent lack of income, on something or someone. So why not on Lane Barfield, our mutual longtime publisher, being a crook? Rudd's paperback originals were no longer selling through no fault of his own, meaning he had to cast responsibility in a way that at the very least allowed him to tolerate himself. I'd suggested we meet this morning not only to get rid of him the previous day but also because I held him and his work in genuine regard. Still, I had to admit I was glad when he didn't show, as I wouldn't have felt nearly as confident in his presence without Seth and Mort there to back me up if Rudd flew off the handle again.

I felt guilty almost as soon as I formed that thought, thinking how lucky I was to have a career that had withstood all the changes in the publishing industry. My hardcovers continued to sell and the transition to a digital world had served my books surprisingly well. Sure, my paperback sales were down like everyone else's, and my royalties had suffered to some extent, though nothing like Thomas Rudd's. So upon exiting Le Pain Quotidien, I walked the six blocks through the cool spring air to his rent-controlled apartment in Tribeca. I recalled the address because of the cab we'd shared following a Christmas party at the Mysterious Book Shop a few years before.

I smelled the smoke a good two blocks from his building, and a block later a coarse wave of it wafted through the air, well ahead of the dark cloud rising behind a cordoned-off police and fire line. I knew it was Thomas Rudd's building before I drew close enough to possibly be sure. Once the building came within view, it was clear from the blown-out windows that the fire had started on the old building's fourth floor, spreading up as well as down.

Rudd lived on the fourth floor, I thought, as I continued to approach.

I pictured him going to bed drunk with a cigarette dangling from his lips. One that must have ultimately slipped to the sheets and ignited the inferno that had likely consumed him long before the fire department could arrive. They were still here in force, hosing down the building to guard against the chance of flare-ups and probably inspecting the building's integrity to see if it was still habitable. I saw a pair of red SUVs that likely belonged to the city fire marshal and a member of the arson squad. Then I turned my gaze upward, curious as to the fourth-floor windows that were gone and the windows on the third and fifth, which had all shattered.

Before I could contemplate that further, I caught a glimpse of my old friend NYPD lieutenant Artie Gelber inside the police line, and waved to get his attention. When that effort failed, I ducked under the waist-high length of tape strung across the street and made my way toward him without any of the uniformed cops making a move to stop me.

"Please tell me this is for research," he said, coming over as soon as he spotted me.

"I wish it were," I said, casting my gaze up toward the fourth floor and the fire's origins. "But I had a friend—well, an acquaintance—who lived here. We were supposed to meet for breakfast."

"Hopefully not the tenant in 4-A."

"I'm not sure."

Artie checked his memo pad, which was a twin of the one Mort Metzger carried, making me wonder if they were standard-issue for cops. "Thomas Rudd?"

I nodded, gazing upward again.

"You don't look surprised, Jessica."

"We ran into each other yesterday," I told Artie, not really wanting to go into detail. "He seemed to be in a very bad way."

That grabbed Artie's attention. "How's that?"

"He'd fallen on hard times, both financially and creatively," I told him, leaving it there.

"Suicidal?"

"Is that what your preliminary report suggests?"

"You tell me, Jessica."

I didn't have to regard the blown-out windows on the fourth floor again, because I'd snapped a mental picture. "I'd say the fire was caused by an explosion. That would explain the shattering of the windows on the adjacent floors, as well as the scoring on the exterior of the brick. I recognize the pattern."

Artie nodded. "I remember that book of yours. One of my favorites."

"It was one of my early ones. Thomas Rudd gave me a blurb for it. That's how we first met."

"I'm sorry, Jessica," Artie said, squeezing my arm tenderly.

"Was it a gas explosion?"

He nodded again. "What was left of him was found in the kitchen, where the gas stove was open and on. Initial assessment is he set off the explosion while trying to light the pilot. My guess is his blood alcohol level will be over point-three-oh."

"Was anyone else hurt?"

"Minor injuries, some rattled eardrums, and lots of property damage, but nothing lasting."

I looked again at the smoldering building. "Unless you count a whole bunch of people losing their homes."

"There is that." Artie frowned. "So you would agree with our preliminary assessment?"

"Based on what I saw yesterday I would agree he was angry."

Artie's eyes flashed like a cop's, not a friend's. "What was he angry about?"

"His next book had been canceled and his career seemed to be over, or at a crossroads at the very least," I said, not wanting to lend credence to Rudd's claims or cast aspersions on my publisher.

Artie was making notes on his pad, which, like Mort's, seemed to have an inexhaustible supply of pages. This time it was he who turned his gaze back on the charred building ahead of me.

"Not a good way to check out, is it?" he said matter-of-factly.

"Is there any, Artie?"

My publisher's offices were located closer to the East Side in an iconic building on Fifth Avenue. Lane Barfield had started the company as little more than a one-man operation, but it had sprouted into a boutique legend in publishing's heyday. It was still a boutique imprint, though now owned by a massive corporate interest, one of what was known in the industry as the Big Five: the five companies that had pretty much gobbled up all the smaller and medium-sized houses in a massive consolidation. Our industry was hardly unique there, but it seemed to hurt more as men like Lane Barfield lost more and more control. Lane, though, had managed to retain complete management of his company even after it had been swallowed.

The imprint was squeezed onto a single cluttered floor space in the twenty-one-story Manhattan icon. But Lane's corner office, looking out toward the Empire State Building, offered an amazing view of the city.

I didn't have an appointment but Lane saw me right away, which was a good thing since the imprint's limited space no longer allowed for even a modest seating area. Where a single couch had long resided, a cubicle had been erected.

"I'd like to say, *What a nice surprise*," he said, greeting me at the door to his office, "but the look on your face suggests otherwise."

"Thomas Rudd is dead."

He didn't look sad; he didn't look shocked; he didn't look, well, anything. "How?"

"A fire in his building."

"Suicide?"

"What makes you ask that?"

Lane cast me a frown I'd seen a thousand times in our nearly thirty-year relationship. He was as dapper as ever, tall and lean and wearing one of his customary three-piece suits. If not for the thinning hair and a face that drooped a bit instead of hugging his skull, he might've been the same man I'd first met a lifetime ago.

"Had you seen him lately?"

"Yesterday," I said, nodding, "at the Mysterious Book Shop."

"Yes," he said, taking my arm lightly and steering me toward a couch set against a wall-length bookcase crammed with volumes wherever the slightest space allowed. "I'm so sorry I missed that."

"Was it because you were afraid you might run into Rudd?"

Lane sat back and sighed. "I had no choice, Jessica. His books just aren't selling. We can't get the distributor to even stock him anymore, and the arms we've been able to twist have resulted in massive returns. I had no choice," he repeated, perhaps a bit guiltily.

After all, Lane had discovered Thomas Rudd, just as he'd discovered me. There but for the grace of God, right?

"The answer's no, by the way," Lane said abruptly.

"What was the question?"

"Did I avoid Otto's event for your release because I was afraid Rudd would be there? Something came up—something, well, incredibly exciting."

"What?"

He curled a single knee atop the couch and leaned a bit closer. "I've been in this business my entire working life, started out on the loading docks and came up through sales."

"I'm familiar with the company bio, Lane."

"Then I'll skip ahead. A manuscript has come in that's one of the best I've ever read."

"Better than mine?" I joked.

He grinned. "I passed on *The Da Vinci Code*, you know."

"Actually, I didn't."

"The books that were the basis of *Game of Thrones*, too. Just couldn't afford to bid on them when they were auctioned. But this one—this one I own outright. No auction, no rival bidders. The next big thing, huge thing, has fallen into my lap."

"Definitely not mine." I nodded. "So, what is it?"

Lane rose, moved to his desk, and slid open one of his cavernous bottom drawers, which I'd always taken for some magical closet that contained every manuscript he'd ever published. But he produced only one, a voluminous ream of pages held together by criss-crossing rubber bands. He brought it to the couch and laid it between us.

"It's the best political thriller I've ever read," he pronounced. "I don't even know what to compare it to. I offered the absolute most I could for it and am so far out on a limb, I'm holding on for dear life."

I ran a finger across the title page, noticing the book was called *The Affair*, written by someone I'd never heard of.

"Benjamin Tally," I said, reading his name out loud. "A first novel?"

Lane nodded. "Very first. And I wasn't going to let this one slip away."

"Congratulations."

His expression turned reflective, maybe even a little sad. "I remember how I felt reading your first manuscript."

"Clearly not this excited."

"I remember reading the first thing Thomas Rudd ever wrote as well," Lane told me. "The pages came in curled because they'd gotten wet on the way over here, and there was a coffee stain on the title page. But I remember realizing his brilliance from the first page, the first paragraph really. I knew he was going to be a star."

"Stars fall sometimes, Lane, through nobody's fault at all."

"He refused to change his style, refused to write longer books, refused to make even the slightest attempt to expand his audience. They were tough books, Jessica, but that didn't matter so long as there were enough male fans to buy them. Can I confide something to you?"

"Of course."

Lane lowered his voice, as if afraid somebody else might be listening. "I think Thomas had issues with the women in his life. He married three times and believed they took all his money. I think he blamed them for his failures even more than he blamed me."

"So the two of you talked about that," I said, my interest piquing again.

"He showed up a few days ago without an appointment."

"Like I just did, you mean."

"Except you didn't drag a whole barroom in with you."

"Oh."

"He was drunk when you saw him yesterday, too, wasn't he?"

I nodded.

"He barged in here ranting and raving," Lane continued. "It was all I could do not to call security. I'd actually picked up the phone, and then I remembered our history and that first manuscript of his I'd read, the star he almost became." Lane shook his head, his eyes moistening. "I lied to him, Jessica."

"What'd you say?"

"That I had a project for him, one of those 'Written with' series we publish."

"A ghostwriting job."

He shook his head. "No, I lied and said I wanted to team him with a bestselling author to start a fresh series that was right in his wheelhouse. I told him I couldn't tell him which one because the deal wasn't final yet. But I asked him if he was interested."

"What did he say?"

"That he'd think about it." Lane shook his head again, as much angry as sad. "Here I am offering him a lifeline and he didn't even say yes."

"It was a lie."

"But he didn't know that. The head of sales popped in with a report I needed to initial, and that's when he must've done it."

"Done what?"

"There was a thumb drive on top of my desk. It was there when Thomas came into my office and it was gone when he stormed out."

"You think he stole it," I said, reconciling that with Rudd's claims that Lane was cheating him out of money, the possibility that he was desperate enough to clip something he thought might contain some evidence.

"The man was utterly unhinged, Jessica. In retrospect, you're right: I never should've lied, never should've looked at him and made myself see the raw talent I'd discovered over thirty years ago but was long, long gone. I should've made that call to security and had him tossed."

"I'm not sure about that, Lane."

He dabbed his eyes with a sleeve. "What would you have done, Jessica?"

"I've never run a publishing house."

"We're not a house anymore, just a small imprint nobody recognizes and plenty think went out of business years ago."

"Well, I'm living proof that's not true."

Something changed in Lane's expression, back briefly to the youthful excitement that had characterized our early years together. "Can I ask you a favor?"

"Anything."

He picked up the manuscript and placed it on my lap. "Tell me what you think of *The Affair.*"

"For a blurb?"

"And your thoughts. To see if I'm way off base on this one, if I'm just an old man still chasing a dream." Lane's gaze locked on the stack of pages. "And that's the actual original manuscript sent by the author himself. He e-mailed the file after I requested it, but it felt good to receive an actual manuscript, like in the old days." He shook his head reflectively. "An old man talking again."

"You're only a few years older than me, Lane, and I do dreams for a living."

That got him to smile. "You'll read it?"

"Of course. On one condition."

"Anything," he said, throwing my word back at me.

I leaned a little closer to him. "When I told you Thomas was dead, first I thought you looked indifferent. Then I realized it was more like . . . relieved. Right or wrong?"

Lane nodded just once, looking like he'd just swallowed something bitter. "That flash drive he swiped from my desk . . ."

"Yes?"

"*The Affair* was copied onto it."

Chapter Three

"You're kidding," Herb Mason said to me from behind his old-fashioned steel desk.

"Have you ever known me to kid about money, Herb?"

"I've never known you to even talk about money, Jessica. I want you to repeat what you said," he added, adjusting both his hearing aids, "just to make sure I heard it right."

Herb had been my accountant for almost as long as I'd had Lane Barfield as a publisher. His office was downtown, a fifteen-minute cab ride away. He'd had his own shop for years before he gave up the space and rented an office inside a larger firm on the occasion of his seventy-fifth birthday a few years back. A few of us, I guess, are meant to work forever. Like Herb Mason—and me, for that matter.

Lane had given me a tote bag, culled from his endless collection of bags given out at writers' conferences, to haul the manuscript around. I couldn't blame
him for how he felt about Rudd's passing, given how
much he had tied up in the manuscript on the flash
drive that Rudd had swiped and the disaster that
would have resulted if Rudd had leaked the book
around town to gain a measure of revenge. Swiping
the flash drive had been a clear act of desperation by
a man who'd turned to alcohol to numb all the tor-
ment he was feeling from his failed career.

No surprise, I guess, given the type of character
Thomas Rudd excelled at writing. Men with sallow
souls who loved to inflict pain on others. They populated tough, hard books that provided no hope for the
world, a world without redemption. Bad men wiped
away like bugs on a windshield by men who were not
quite as bad. You'd read his work and know it could
only have been written by an angry man.

Except I've never really believed that. I don't think
characters come from the dark pits of our souls; I think
they come from the bright proving grounds of our
imaginations. Thomas Rudd had lost control of himself and, in the process, had lost control of his characters. They became living embodiments of his own
frustrations and inadequacies, his own id running
rampant and roughshod over his life. He'd never been
happy, even while enjoying a modicum of both commercial and critical success. He won awards, was invited to speak at conferences, but I once heard he'd
passed out drunk before a packed audience that had

waited in line for hours to see him. Part of his mystique, his tough-guy aura, and an act that had ultimately consumed him.

Thomas Rudd had died friendless. Hard to envision who might attend his funeral, save for Lane Barfield and me, and I wasn't so sure about Lane anymore. Come to think of it, who exactly was going to make the funeral arrangements, given Rudd's estrangement from whatever family he had? He'd shut himself off from the world and now the world would neither miss nor remember him. I didn't know if there was a sadder story to tell, and I resolved to make the funeral arrangements myself if there was no one else to do it.

I had no reason to suspect foul play in the case of Thomas Rudd's death, but I couldn't get his claims of being robbed out of my head. And while I had no reason to suspect Lane Barfield of such malfeasance, I felt I owed it to Thomas to at least look into it. Call it lingering guilt over being relieved, even happy, he hadn't shown up for breakfast that morning and then learning it was because he was dead.

If I were back home in Cabot Cove, I'd meet up with Seth Hazlitt at Mara's Luncheonette to sort through all this. Smell the sea air while cruising the streets on my bicycle. Today I would be missing the monthly meeting of the Friends of the Cabot Cove Library, something that shouldn't have bothered me but suddenly left me wondering if there was any chance I could get there in time by plane. I'd already called our librarian, Doris Ann, three times to remind her of things that needed to be placed on the agenda, learning they already had on each occasion.

Cabot Cove, I supposed, was one of the main things that separated me from Thomas Rudd. Who was it who said home was the place that, when you go there, they have to take you in? Rudd had lost any semblance of a place like that. But I had this bucolic town where, except during the cluttered summer months, people smiled and addressed you by name. I was Jessica Fletcher, a resident who happened to be a mystery writer, instead of a mystery writer who happened to be a resident. Whenever I went back there, they took me in, even Sheriff Mort Metzger, no matter how much my pushing my nose into this crime or that left him questioning his decision to seek a quieter life in Cabot Cove.

"You believe," Herb was saying, behind his gray steel desk, "that your publisher may be stealing from you by skimming some of the royalties."

"It's what another writer believes and made known to me. I have no evidence beyond that."

"If you had nothing beyond that, Jessica, you wouldn't have bothered to stop by."

"Well, my statements have been showing less income."

"I imagine that's the case for almost all writers, and I've never noticed anything awry in your statements."

"How closely have you looked at them?"

"Not very," Herb admitted with a shrug. "Not at all, really, other than to make sure your taxes are prepared properly. To be honest, my interest hasn't extended beyond the bottom line."

"And if it did?"

"What do you mean?" Herb asked me.

I eased aside the tote bag containing *The Affair* to push my chair closer to his desk. "If a publisher wanted to skim off an author's royalty income, how might they do it?"

"Any number of ways, but the process is all computerized now. It's not like the old days when someone like me would hammer out typed statements to accompany the checks."

"I don't recall anyone complaining about such things in the old days. Writers complained about not being paid enough, not about being cheated."

"And there are plenty of ways writers *are* being cheated today, all of them legal. Like holding back reserves against returns, even when no more returns can possibly come in. I can go on, if you like."

I sighed. "Not necessary. You made your point."

His expression grew even more serious. "Then let me make another, Jessica. The only way to have a chance at finding something specific, provable, and actionable would be to commission a forensic audit of the publisher's books. No one does them anymore because a publisher that's corrupt enough to steal their authors' money would be smart enough to hide it. And, while a good forensic audit can reveal where all the bodies are buried, they're prohibitively expensive and come with no guarantees and no decent upshot."

"What about peace of mind? And since his imprint was bought out, Lane's insisted on generating his own financial statements instead of trusting the conglomerate owners to handle them."

"Because he was looking out for his authors' best interests, you once told me." Herb nodded. "Because he was trying to avoid exactly what Thomas Rudd was accusing him of. The height of irony, Jessica."

"Or hypocrisy. Can you take a look at my statements for the last few years and see what you can find, just to allay my fears?"

Herb frowned, his cheeks and jowls seeming to expand from the gesture. "I'll probably find nothing."

"Then I'll be satisfied."

"And if I do find something, it probably won't lead very far."

"A chance I'm willing to take. And please, Herb, bill me at your regular rate."

The man who'd been my accountant since I earned my first dollar as a writer grinned at that. "I don't have a regular rate. Last time I did, and worked in an office like this, I think it was something like seventy cents per hour. But I date myself."

"You're dating both of us, Herb."

He nodded, still looking none too happy about what I was asking him to do. "Another thing about such detailed audits is that they tend to ruin relationships. It would be a shame to savage those thirty years you've been with Lane Barfield because of the claims of an old drunk."

"Who was once a great writer."

"I know." Herb nodded. "It's the books that got smaller."

"Actually, it's the marketplace that shrank, as well as changed, and it left Thomas Rudd behind."

"Sad."

"I'll say."

Herb gazed about his cramped, windowless office,

seeming to genuinely appreciate his surroundings. "I don't know what I'd do if I couldn't work anymore. Even if it's only for a few hours a day, it still helps define who I am."

"Rudd got hit by a double whammy: Not only could he not write anymore; his backlist was only paying pennies."

"Not exactly a persuasive argument for him being ripped off by a major publisher. Publishers already have a whole other name for stealing: They call it accounting."

I was about to respond when my cell phone rang. I drew it from my bag, hoping it was Cabot Cove librarian Doris Ann calling to conference me into the Friends meeting.

"Are you still in New York, Jessica?" Detective Artie Gelber's voice greeted me.

"Yes."

"Good. Are you free? I need to see you."

"Does this have something to do with the fire, Artie?"

"Let's talk in person."

I'm no stranger to crime scenes, having examined more than my share either as research for my books or during the course of the real-life investigations that seemed to follow me around like a stray cat. Most of the time, the process started with me trying to help somebody out, and things proceeded to get out of hand from there. You'd think I'd learn my lesson.

That is, if I wanted to.

When it comes to crime scenes, fires tend to be the

worst. Fire destroys not only lives but also pretty much everything those lives held dear. And I could never get used to the stench of smoldering refuse, burned-up walls, and even the mold and mildew already rising from soaked upholstery or carpeting where the water firefighters had used to douse the flames collected.

Thomas Rudd's apartment building made for no exception there. The smell of scorched, charred wood hit me first when Artie Gelber led me through the front door, followed by the stink of the rancid water that had soaked the walls, pooled on the lobby carpeting, and dripped down from the first-floor ceiling. Based on the absence of the armada of police and rescue vehicles outside, I assumed Rudd's body had been taken away, and that at least the preliminary stages of the investigation were likely wrapping up.

Although I was right about that much, I cringed as soon as Artie led me inside Thomas Rudd's apartment. The combination of bitter, acrid odors was overbearing. It always amazed me how powerful scents can cling to the air over ridiculously long periods, as if that air itself can't vanquish the memories of what transpired.

Artie led me to the remnants of the kitchen, ground zero for the original gas explosion and fire that had turned much of the building into an inferno. All that remained of the walls were peeled, blackened swaths of wallpaper. The major appliances I could still recognize were charred black. The refrigerator was missing its door and the explosion had shattered every bottle and jar stored inside it, leaving a mixture of glass and unrecognizable liquids. What I'd first taken for blood staining the walls in patches was actually some kind of preserve or jelly.

"We were able to get a DNA match on the remains of the corpse and confirmed it was Thomas Rudd," Artie reported. "Now, tell me what you see, Detective."

Artie handed me a pair of plastic evidence gloves I promptly squeezed over my hands.

"Look around and tell me what's amiss."

"I'm not a detective," I told him instead, "which explains why I'm not seeing anything."

"Really? This coming from a woman who's solved almost as many crimes as she's made up."

"I wouldn't go that far."

Artie pointed to his eyes, sign language for "Get on with it." I gazed about the stench-riddled refuse, the waterlogged floor still marred with puddles, and the walls shredded or burned through to expose the building's hidden hodgepodge of wiring, which looked as if Thomas Edison may have installed it himself. The floor was an obstacle course of yet-to-be-collected evidence that was innocuous at first glance.

On second glance, something drew my eye to what looked like the wooden arm of a chair that likely went with the room's small kitchen table, the laminated top of which seemed to have melted in the heat of the fire. The finish on the object I took to be a chair arm wasn't in great shape, either, but something caught my attention down where someone might lay their hand, if I had my bearings right.

"The discoloration in the wood isn't consistent," I

said, tracing a fingernail along the length of the chair arm through the plastic glove Artie Gelber had provided.

"Okay." Artie nodded as if he had noticed the same thing and was waiting for me to explain further.

"Why are you asking me, if you've already formed your own opinion?"

"Because I want to see if another professional sees it the same way I do."

"Now I'm a pro?"

"You've solved more murders than any detective on my squad, Jessica. Now, how would you explain this apparent discoloration?"

I turned my attention back to the charred wood. "Well, Thomas Rudd's arms being tied to the chair arms would explain it. But you'd already figured that out before you called me back here."

"I needed a second pair of eyes. And what does that second pair of eyes think?"

"This wasn't an accident, Artie. Thomas Rudd was murdered."

Until that moment, those words were the last thing I ever expected to say. I ran the fingers contained in that plastic glove about the contours of the chair arm.

"The scoring pattern's entirely different on the side here that looks like the top of the arm," I told Artie. "Picture a man's arm tied to it. The initial blast would have burned the exposed underside, but not the top side covered by Rudd's arm in anywhere near the same pattern. But you already knew that, right?"

"Like I said—"

"I know what you said. But even though we're friends, since when do NYPD homicide detectives consult with mystery authors?"

"Author, *singular*, Jessica," Artie corrected.

"Any way of determining whether Rudd was already dead when the explosion happened?"

"You think someone rigged the gas explosion to cover up the fact they'd murdered him."

"I think someone wanted to make it look like an accident."

"Well," Artie said, "once the autopsy results reveal the condition of the lungs, we'll know a lot more than we do now on that subject. Pity the poor fools for not realizing America's favorite mystery writer would end up on the case."

"I'm far from that and I'm just helping out a friend here."

That comment got Artie's attention. "Me or the victim?"

"Could I get away with saying both?"

Artie looked at me as if I'd finally figured out the substance of something. "That's why you're here, Jessica. If this was in fact murder, do you have any idea why someone would want to kill a failed writer?"

"He wasn't always a failed writer, Artie," I reminded him, persisting with the need to defend Thomas Rudd for reasons I didn't understand. "But he was, by all accounts, having serious financial problems."

"In my experience, financial problems are always serious."

I decided to come clean, didn't see that I had much choice or reason, really, not to. "Rudd thought our publisher was stealing from him. He'd recently confronted Lane Barfield in his office about that."

Artie was jotting in his endless memo pad again. "Barfield's office would be over on Fifth Avenue?"

"Yes. And there's something else," I added, trying to choose my next words carefully. "I was wondering if any of the crime scene technicians found a flash drive."

"Flash drive? I wouldn't know. I haven't seen the full inventory yet and something like that could easily have escaped being recovered and logged. Any idea what this flash drive may have contained, or where it came from?"

"It wasn't Rudd's property. Let's say he 'borrowed' it from Lane Barfield."

"Care to tell me what makes this flash drive so important?" Artie asked, sounding just like Mort Metzger.

"It's probably nothing."

"Not if you bothered to mention it."

"The flash drive contained a book. But Rudd was hoping for something else when he swiped it."

"Like what?"

"Information he needed to prove his royalties were being skimmed."

"I never even heard of the guy."

"A sad and unfortunate condition of time and readers having passed the man by."

Artie weighed the substance of that. "And he still believed somebody at the publisher was stealing his money, when there probably wasn't any money to steal? That doesn't sound like a rational man."

"How about a drunken one, Artie? It was probably the booze doing his thinking for him."

Artie didn't look convinced of that. "Stop there. You've already given me a possible motive for Thomas Rudd's murder."

I went back to the obvious connection he had made. "Lane Barfield wouldn't know how to turn on the gas, never mind ignite it. And there was no reason for him to kill Rudd a second time."

"What's that mean?"

"That his career had already preceded him to the grave."

Chapter Four

I took the opportunity to divert my mind a bit, maybe head over to my apartment to drop off the manuscript Lane Barfield had asked me to read. Everybody had been looking for the next *Da Vinci Code* for years, just like they'd been looking for the next *Valley of the Dolls* back in the sixties. Publishers are always chasing the next trend. The only big bestseller not subject to a huge bidding war was the Bible.

Being in dire financial straits would have sent Thomas Rudd scouring for money wherever he could find it. Living in a rent-controlled apartment still meant he had to pay the rent. With his diminished royalties and lack of advances for new books, and with no family to speak of that held him in any regard at all, Rudd may have turned to shady sources for cash. So I called Lieutenant Artie Gelber and asked him to do a deeper dive into Thomas Rudd's situation to see if there was a way to determine whether he'd been surviving from money off the street. CIs, confidential informants, loved working for Artie because he always treated them with respect and was true to his word when he promised them something.

"This could take some time," he warned me.

"I'll give you the rest of the afternoon."

"So now you're my boss?"

I couldn't help but laugh.

"What's so funny, Jessica?" Artie asked me.

"That's the same thing Mort Metzger always says to me."

"I was thinking of applying for the sheriff's job in Cabot Cove, when Mort retires. It would be nice not to deal with exploding apartment buildings and murdered authors."

"Well, Artie," I told him, "that depends on the day."

I'd called Artie from a coffee shop that was going to be open for only a few more minutes, now that the lunchtime rush had died down. I ordered a tea and a blueberry muffin, which I picked at after lifting the manuscript of *The Affair* from the tote bag Lane Barfield had given me and placing it atop the table. It was heavy enough to rattle the dish, and I decided against removing the rubber bands to better scan the opening pages. It was rare indeed for a publisher like Lane Barfield to land such a book, and I was happy for him, even as I wondered why the author named Benjamin Tally had gone in that direction. Normally, books like this are sold at auction to the highest bidder, who invariably has the kind of deep pockets needed to front an advance stretching into seven figures.

Lane had never been that kind of publisher; he was cut more from the same cloth as the legendary Bennett Cerf or even Max Perkins, since Lane had started as an editor and remained one of the best in the business. He was always about the books and the authors, which explained why he had spoken with such pride that morning about coming upon Thomas Rudd's work in the proverbial slush pile. It also explained how much the similarly proverbial end of Rudd's career must have affected him. He had discovered Rudd and built him into a well-respected, solid-selling name, and truth be told, I think Lane had enjoyed his books far more than he did mine.

Still loath to risk pulling off the rubber bands holding the more than eight hundred manuscript pages together, I peeled back the title page of *The Affair* to see what came next. No dedication or acknowledgments yet—no epigraph, either—Benjamin Tally jumping right into the prologue:

> I'm going to die tonight, maybe in five minutes, maybe in five hours. Inevitable. All of it my fault for not doing what I should have when the chance was there.
>
> It's gone now.
>
> It's all gone now.
>
> I looked in the mirror at the bruises on my face, saw them clearly even though the light was off. Had I locked the door?
>
> What's the difference?
>
> It didn't matter.

That opening made me wonder if *The Affair* might not be my cup of tea. It seemed a bit too hard-boiled to suit my tastes, but the noir-like style was definitely alluring to the point where I could see myself crafting a decent blurb—the writer's catchphrase for an endorsement or paragraph-long love letter—for Lane Barfield. I'd always been hesitant to ask for blurbs myself, while never failing to answer a request made of me for one. The challenge came when I really didn't like a certain book but felt obligated to find something good to say about it anyway. After all, I'd been in that position once and knew how much up-and-coming writers valued such things. If they respected me enough to ask for a blurb, how could I disappoint them, other than to beg off on the feigned excuse that I was too busy?

I resolved to read more when I got back to my apartment across town, enough at least to give Lane Barfield some semblance of the thoughts he'd asked for. I could tell he could use some affirmation, given all he had clearly staked on this manuscript by an utterly unknown author. After all Lane had done for me over the years, I resolved to give him something he could hang his hat on, even if I had to utilize some creative wordplay to manage that task.

After all he had done for me . . .

Had Thomas Rudd been right, though? Was Barfield really stealing from him, me, maybe from all of the authors housed under his imprint?

I could have just shrugged Rudd's comments off, but they amounted to a mystery and I could never resist trying to solve any mystery.

I was so lost in that thought I almost didn't hear my

phone ringing, alerted to it by the fact that my pocketbook was vibrating. I managed to answer it just before the call went to voice mail.

"Can you stop by my office, Jessica?" Herb Mason asked me.

"When?"

"How about now, as in *right away*?"

"I can't be sure about this," Herb said after closing behind him the door to the windowless office and taking a seat at his desk.

I took the same chair I had earlier in the day, realizing the only thing that passed for life in the office was a pair of plants that must be artificial, given the lack of light. Herb's face was grave, more, it seemed, from fatigue than from worry. At seventy-five, he looked like the project I had dumped in his lap had exhausted him.

He forced a smile before resuming. "Guess it will be up to Miss Marple to determine that," he said, using his pet name for me.

"She's a lot older than me," I told him, referring to Agatha Christie's female version of Hercule Poirot. "And I'm a widow, while she never married. But pretend I'm her and tell me what you found."

He pushed his chair closer to his desk, so his legs disappeared beneath the steel. "As I was saying, I may have found some, well, oddities, inconsistencies, in your royalty statements for the past three years."

"Thomas Rudd was right?" I said, having clung to the hope that my trusty accountant would've found nothing amiss at all.

"Bear with me on this. How familiar are you with digital subscription programs?"

"Not very, to tell you the truth."

"They basically entitle anyone who pays around ten bucks per month to download as many books onto their Kindle or comparable device as they wish," Herb explained, "even if they never get around to reading them."

"Well, I get paid when they buy the book, not when they read it," I quipped.

"That's where things begin to get complicated here, because in the case of these programs, that's not entirely true."

"It isn't?"

Herb shook his head. "Theoretically, you get paid by the page."

"What's that mean?"

"Someone downloads a J. B. Fletcher title for free. If he or she never looks at it again, you get nothing. If they read the whole thing, you get close to your regular split. And for anything in the middle, you get paid on a prorated basis."

"For example . . . ," I prodded.

"If they read a page, maybe you get a penny. If they read a fifth of the book, maybe you get a quarter. The digital sites have never been entirely specific about their calculations, and not all traditional publishers make their titles available; in fact, Lane Barfield's is the only imprint in the building that's part of the program."

I nodded. "Part of the deal he struck with the parent company that allowed him to maintain control. You find that strange, Herb?"

"I find it convenient. How long did Thomas Rudd claim this alleged theft of his royalties had been going on?"

"He didn't, not specifically anyway."

Herb Mason's expression was matter-of-fact, the fatigue vanishing from his features as he plunged deeper into the world of numbers, where he was most comfortable. "Then say three years, back to the start of the program. I obviously don't have access to Rudd's statements, and you're the only author I still handle. But the firm I'm housed in here handles several, and they allowed me a peek at their statements for comparison purposes only."

"Okay."

Herb's eyes found mine. "I discovered some discrepancies between your statements and those of these other authors."

"Like what?"

"The numbers, the percentages, don't match. These digital sales sites don't furnish specific figures, so the evidence is strictly anecdotal, but if I had to guess, I'd say your statements are coming up short in the area of fifteen hundred dollars per statement."

I did the math in my head, easy enough even for someone who'd yet to master balancing her checkbook. "Two statements per year for three years would mean nine thousand dollars."

"You must've been an accountant in a past life."

"Enough to know there's a lot I could've done with that amount of money."

"How many authors does Lane Barfield publish? How many books make up his imprint's backlist?"

Herb asked, that "backlist" referring to authors' older titles, often readily available only in digital format these days.

I couldn't even begin to estimate the number. He'd been a publisher for thirty years, and I'd been with him for almost that long. His offer hadn't been the biggest I'd received, but his conviction and passion more than made up for that, and he presented convincing arguments that he could build my career in a way no other publisher could. So I signed with Lane and never regretted it for a minute. He was always way ahead of the curve, including with contracts, since from the beginning his were structured to give him control of a host of rights that included digital. That meant that, unlike others in the industry, his authors couldn't poach their backlists from him and place the digital editions elsewhere. I expected very few, if any, of Lane's authors were bothered by that, given Lane's unfaltering dedication to their work, as his loyalty to them was returned in kind. I don't think I'd ever heard a negative word spoken about him.

Until now.

"I must not have been an accountant in a past life, Herb," I corrected, "because the math of that is impossible for me to calculate."

"Not just you. I took a gander on Amazon, for one, trying to get a count of how many of Barfield's backlist titles are included in Kindle Unlimited. I stopped at a thousand."

"Wow."

"I said *stopped* at a thousand," Herb reiterated. "And there's something else to consider that stuck out,

Jessica. A great number of those books were written by authors who are now deceased, and it appears Lane Barfield had acquired a number of their older titles, in addition to publishing their more recent ones. I don't have to tell you what that means."

"Those authors' royalties become part of their estate, and what heirs, unfamiliar with publishing, would bother to notice a discrepancy?"

"Exactly." He nodded.

"Now for the sixty-four-thousand-dollar question."

"One of my favorite television shows of all time," he reflected, "even though I don't think I ever got the question right."

"You're dating yourself," I told him.

"I'm almost eighty, Jessica. Who else am I supposed to date?"

"So, my question," I said, after chuckling, "is how much in authors' royalties might Lane Barfield have stolen?"

"Ballpark figure?"

"Ballpark figure."

"Between six and seven million dollars," Herb said.

I couldn't shake that figure from my mind. The more I thought about it, the more the pieces fell together, as much as I hated the assembled puzzle.

Thomas Rudd's drunken, fanciful claims.

Now supported in theory by both the anomalies in my royalty statements compared to other authors' and the anomaly of a traditional publisher offering his backlist titles on an unlimited platform.

Explaining why Lane had insisted on control.

So he would be free to use fuzzy math to skim off the top of the royalties of his authors' backlists, books long published and often nearly as long forgotten.

To the tune of millions of dollars.

As I rode in the back of a cab to my apartment, the tote bag containing *The Affair* occupying the seat next to me, my thoughts veered to an oft-reported story that never failed to baffle me. How some simple bookkeeper, bank clerk, teller, or other employee had managed to steal an absurdly large amount of money, stretching into six or even low seven figures, over an equally absurd duration of time. Why hadn't they just quit while they were ahead?

I know in their minds that's what they'd intended. It would be just a onetime thing, they'd tell themselves. It was so easy to get away with, though, it became a second-time thing, and then a third. Before they knew it, they'd lost count of how many times they'd done something they'd honestly intended to do only once. Like an addiction, a fix, part of their normal routine. If they hadn't been caught the first time or the next ninety-eight, why would they be caught on the hundredth?

Except they always did get caught at some point.

Maybe Lane Barfield had started out stealing only from the titles of his deceased authors. Then maybe he'd expanded the practice to include authors who'd left him for other houses. And, finally, he'd added the likes of Thomas Rudd and me. None of Rudd's more recent titles had sold much at all, but his older ones still had value and earned enough on a regular basis for him to at least afford his rent most months and put food on the table and whiskey in the liquor cabinet.

More if Lane Barfield hadn't been stealing from him.

"Here we are, ma'am."

The cabdriver's voice shook me from my trance, and I realized he'd pulled up in front of my apartment building on the East Side. I added a generous tip to the amount on the meter and climbed out, struggling to lug the tote bag containing *The Affair* with me.

"You need some help?" he offered.

Boy, do I ever, I almost quipped but just thanked him instead, my thoughts veering to a more serious matter indeed.

I had to confront a true friend with the knowledge that he was very likely stealing from me.

Chapter Five

I'd hoped to dig further into the manuscript that night but couldn't get past the first page, couldn't watch television, and finally couldn't sleep. Herb Mason's findings, though totally unproven, had rattled me. We want to believe that if you go about your life treating people right and doing the right thing, you'll be treated in kind. The mere possibility that a trusted friend for so many years might well have stolen from me was utterly unthinkable.

Writers live in a bubble of their own making, a fantastical existence where we spend an inordinate amount of time in worlds of our own creation where reality enters in only when we allow it to. The fact that we might be treated unfairly, that the world we trusted with childlike innocence would cheat us, was as difficult to fathom as the thought of writers ourselves being capable of the evil perpetuated by the villains we create.

I remember hearing an interview with a horror author during which he was asked, "Why do you write about things that go bump in the night?"

"Because things really do go bump in the night," was the author's reply.

As a mystery author, I had pondered virtually every crime imaginable for potential plot points in this book or that. And yet I found being a victim of a crime myself, fraud in this case, to be more unsettling than the plots of any of my own books.

Go figure.

Part of me wanted to head back home to Cabot Cove tomorrow and sort this out in more familiar surroundings before confronting Lane Barfield. I thought about retaining the services of private detective Harry McGraw to do some more digging and find me the firm proof Herb Mason had stopped short of discovering. I wanted to sit with Seth Hazlitt and, especially, Mort Metzger at Mara's Luncheonette in the center of town to get their thoughts on what I should do. Then again, given his new John Wayne persona, Mort might head to Manhattan to exact justice himself.

That notion should've made me smile, ordinarily would have.

But not tonight.

My cell phone rang and I grabbed it off the coffee table, noticing a 202 area code for Washington, DC.

"Jessica Fletcher," I answered, glad the offices of the IRS had already closed.

"Mrs. Fletcher, this is Sharon Lerner, director of White House communications. Can you hold for the first lady?"

"Of course."

A few moments passed before I heard the voice of Stephanie Albright. "Jessica, so sorry to be calling so late."

"You can call me anytime, Madam First Lady. You know that."

"Stephanie, please. We're friends, after all."

We were indeed, thanks in large part to my helping her champion the cause of literacy by getting big-name authors to appear at the fund-raising events she sponsored all over the country.

"I just wanted to let you know I've got that updated list of events for you," the first lady continued. "Sharon's sending it over now."

"I'll check it against my calendar and get back to you right away."

"Perfect. And I also wanted to thank you."

"For what?"

"Everything, Jessica. You put this program on your back and have carried it the whole way."

"I believe in the cause, Stephanie," I said, still having a difficult time calling the first lady by her first name. "I believe in everything you're doing."

"I can't tell you how much that means to me. So, what are you up to? Working on a new book?"

"Something like that," I told her.

As had become my routine when staying at my Manhattan apartment, I turned the television on as soon as I woke up the next morning, tuned to NY1. My night's sleep could be generously described as fitful, given that I'm not sure I ever was out all the way. Every time I started to feel myself drifting, thoughts of my looming confrontation with Lane Barfield intruded. How exactly was I going to broach with him the subject of the apparent malfeasance Herb Mason had identified? There was a very good chance that Herb's suspicions, and thus Thomas Rudd's allegations, were well-founded. But there was also a chance that they would turn out not to be credible after all, in which case I would be risking irreparable harm to a relationship thirty years in the making.

I know so many families that have been shattered by squabbles over money, the legitimacy of which often paled in comparison with the effects of an accusation lodged by one relative against another. It was truly tragic, made all the more so by the fact that, with few exceptions, the whole situation had been avoidable. Sometimes the closer people are, the more likely things are to get blown out of proportion. It never ceases to amaze me how reasonable, rational people can act so rashly and without forethought. I've always thought the drafts folder was one of the great things about e-mail, since it allowed you to hold off sending words written in anger and thus tainted by emotion and vitriol.

There was no such folder when it came to the spoken word, though. Once the message was out, it couldn't be delayed or withdrawn. You lived with what you had said because there was no way to take the words back.

I had briefly considered contacting Lane Barfield by e-mail, quickly rejecting the idea since I wasn't sure I could even put these particular thoughts and feelings into type. I owed him the dignity of expressing my concerns in person, open and up front, while affording him every opportunity to respond to and refute Rudd's claims, as well as Herb's preliminary findings.

I lay in bed for a time, putting off starting the day as long as I could—maybe up to a week, given that none of my ruminations had produced anything even approaching a script to use once I reached Lane's office. I wanted to take a soft line with him, maybe even keeping it to Thomas Rudd's accusations and not raising what Herb Mason believed he had uncovered. I thought I might be able to couch my words in that form, from more a theoretical standpoint than a practical one, maybe suggest the potential methodology had come from someone else or through some research I was doing for a book. Anything to keep Lane from getting overly defensive.

It's funny, but back home in Cabot Cove I never turned the television on upon awaking. A sign, I supposed, of the relative comfort of my surroundings. My favorite ritual at my house there was yanking open all the blinds in the house to let the sunlight spill inside. And, except during the winter months, I loved opening all the windows, the sounds of birds singing and the occasional car passing by on my street replacing the sounds of the television.

Putting off the inevitable any longer made no sense, so I decided to try Lane Barfield at home, where he'd still be at this hour, given that he was known for both starting and ending his workday late. I muted the sound on the television and was jogging through the contacts on my phone for Lane's name when something on the television claimed my attention. I wasn't sure what it was until I focused on the screen, where a picture of Lane Barfield was displayed above the banner NOTED PUBLISHER FOUND DEAD OF SUS-PECTED SUICIDE.

I had to remind myself to breathe. Lane Barfield was dead, had killed himself by all accounts. The report was not specific as to how, and I didn't particularly care at this point. Instead I looked down at my phone, where my contact page for Lane Barfield was dis-played, phone numbers I'd never be dialing again, an e-mail address I'd used for the last time.

All thoughts of the financial malfeasance he might have been guilty of vanished. We'd known each other so long, had experienced so much together, celebrated so many momentous benchmarks. We'd shared time at weddings as well as funerals, shared tables at var-ious industry functions, and shared thoughts over any number of late-night phone calls. We'd enjoyed the kind of relationship that extended far beyond red-penciling pages during a nine-to-five workday. Because we were also friends, comfortable calling each other anytime about anything.

And now Lane was gone. The word "irreplaceable" is often clichéd or misused. But it was perfectly appro-priate in this instance. Lane Barfield was an old-school publisher who'd maintained the old ways of doing business while mastering the new ways of conducting it.

My grief over losing such a good friend, as well as a publisher under whose stewardship I'd sold millions and millions of books while building a sizable income that left me wanting for nothing, was palpable. And I hated the fact that the final thought of him I was left with was my intention to confront him about being a crook.

I wanted to be wrong, started trying to convince myself that I was, so as not to soil Lane's memory in my mind.

I let myself consider the obvious: that I might not have been the only author of Lane's Thomas Rudd had alerted to his suspicions. Someone else, perhaps even more than one person, might have been planning to go to the authorities and expose him. If the charges proved true, I saw no way Lane could have avoided jail time. Both his life and his reputation ruined through no one's fault but his own. Suicide might have seemed an acceptable alternative to that, especially if there was no effective defense he could mount. People lied, but numbers didn't. And the numbers Herb Mason had turned up, even on a preliminary basis, definitely indicated that something was wrong.

Maybe Lane Barfield had bit off more than he could chew, overextended himself, and saw the scheme uncovered by Herb as a way to get back to even. Only he hadn't stopped once he got there and had taken his life to spare himself the scandal and ruin inevitably to follow. His suicide could have been a sign of his guilt, that both Thomas Rudd's claims and Herb

Mason's findings rang true. Thinking of that made me recall how he'd mentioned to me how he'd spent so much to buy *The Affair*. And now I knew where the money had likely come from.

But I needed to know more, so I lifted my phone with my trembling hand.

"So sorry about your publisher," Lieutenant Artie Gelber said. "I just heard the news."

"Me, too. What do you know?"

"What I just told you."

"Nothing else, Artie?"

"It was a suicide, Jessica. That's hardly reason to alert the Major Case Squad at One Police Plaza."

I swallowed hard. "What did you hear?"

"Pills," Artie said simply.

"Oh."

"I don't have any more details."

"I understand, Artie."

"Do you? Or is that murder sense of yours acting up again, Jessica?"

"No, it's just that . . ."

"Just what?" he asked when my voice tailed off.

"Remember how I told you yesterday Thomas Rudd was convinced Lane Barfield was stealing from him?"

"Stealing what? I mean, based on his current lifestyle and all the failure he'd encountered in recent years, there couldn't have been much."

"I did some checking. I think the theft involves Rudd's older titles, the ones that are still selling moderately well. I confirmed the methodology with my own accountant, who found some discrepancies in my royalty statements dating back three years."

"Barfield was stealing from *you*, too?"

"I didn't say that, Artie."

"You certainly suggested it. I'd like to hear more. I'd like to speak to this accountant."

I regretted even raising the issue. "I don't have any proof."

"That's what the police are for, especially if it's connected to Barfield's death."

"I thought the Major Case Squad doesn't handle suicides."

"Unless it's a special crime."

I could hear him breathing on the other end through the entire duration of the pause that followed that line.

"Tell me something, Jessica. You were going to confront Barfield with your suspicions, weren't you?"

"What's the difference now?"

"The fact that you could never let this go, any more than I can. The circumstances surrounding the man's death need to be investigated, and if criminal action was involved, the victims need to be informed so they can respond as they see fit."

I thought for a moment. "So you'll need the name of my accountant."

"I will."

"The price being I want to work this case with you."

"Jessica—"

"Don't use that tone, Artie, please."

"What tone?"

"The condescending one that says I've got no place in an active investigation."

"This isn't Cabot Cove," he said, sounding even more condescending. "We've got fifty thousand cops and support personnel on the NYPD force and are perfectly capable of handling an investigation without outside help."

"I'm not outside, in this case. My accountant's doing a deeper dive into this. He can explain his findings, both new and old, to you once he's finished. But not until he's got firm proof."

"You want to believe he won't find it."

"Lane Barfield built my career from the ground up, took a high school English teacher and turned her into a bestselling author."

"You sound like you're defending him now."

I recalled Lane's tone when he'd told me about *The Affair* the day before. He'd sounded like a kid who'd given up on the present he really wanted for Christmas, only to find one more under the tree. He talked about the book with the kind of childlike enthusiasm I recalled from years before, how much he loved talking about building a publishing company from the ground up. I don't think he'd ever wanted to sell, merge, consolidate, or whatever they were calling it these days. His hand had been forced and he was never the same again, no matter how much control his deal allowed him to maintain. It wasn't his company anymore. Not paying to keep the lights turned on meant somebody else could have them turned off at any time.

I realized in that moment what had been plaguing me since I heard Lane's name on NY1. I'd been focusing on his suspected financial malfeasance, skimming off the top of his own authors' royalties. But even six or seven million dollars paled in comparison to what a book as big as *The Affair*, not to mention its inevitable sequels, could yield. So why choose this moment to kill himself? Certainly it wasn't because Thomas Rudd alone had lashed out at him.

"Did he leave a note, Artie?" I asked.

"I don't think so."

"He was a man who spent his career in letters. I can't imagine he wouldn't have left something behind, some explanation."

"Did he have any family?"

"Not that he was close with."

"Most suicide notes are addressed to those the victim was close to. That alone could explain the lack of a note."

I wasn't convinced. There was too much here that didn't seem to add up, starting with the fact that in *The Affair* Lane might have just acquired the biggest book of his entire career.

"There's something else I need to tell you, Artie," I heard myself saying.

Chapter Six

Artie picked me up an hour later outside my apartment building, looking none too happy when I climbed into the passenger seat of his police-issue sedan.

"Would you rather I sit in the back?" I asked, shooting him a look that vented some of the frustration and sadness I was feeling.

On the phone earlier I'd told him about *The Affair* and my thought that the pressures surrounding its acquisition might have contributed to Lane Barfield's taking his own life. He didn't know Lane, had never met him, so I think what I was suggesting went right over his head.

"I'm just trying to sort this out, Jessica. Why murder seems attracted to you like metal to a magnet."

"You sound like Mort Metzger."

He looked at me, frowning, the car still in park.

"I've never felt worse for any man in my life. What's it like picking up after you full-time?"

"I guess you're going to find out, given you'd like to apply to succeed him."

"I'm rethinking my retirement plans." He stopped, glanced out the windshield as his fingers drummed the steering wheel. "I'm sorry. I know how close you were with Barfield, know he was more than just your publisher," he said, voice ringing with compassion.

"Thirty years will do that to you. And . . ." I stopped there, letting my voice tail off.

"And what?"

"I must've been one of the last people to see him. That leaves me thinking maybe I missed something, some sign. That there was something I could have done."

"You accepting the preliminary finding of suicide?"

"I'm not accepting anything at this point. I spent most of last night reviewing our entire conversation, and I keep settling on the fact that this monster of a book he'd acquired had him more excited than I'd seen him in years. I can't reconcile that with him swallowing a boatload of pills."

"Prescription sleep aids, by all accounts," Artie elaborated. "We found the bottle in the bathroom."

That claimed my attention. "Where was the body found?"

"In the living room of his apartment. Television tuned to New York One."

"He was a true New Yorker and it was his favorite station, except in winter, when he was obsessed with the Weather Channel," I said, taking my turn to elaborate, before my mind shifted in midthought. "So he took the pills in 'he bathroom and sat down to watch the news?"

Artie checked his mirror, ready to put the big car in gear. "That raised my eyebrows, too."

"With most suicides by overdose, the pill bottle is found near the body," I said. A statement, not a question.

"That's not evidence, Jessica; it's supposition."

"Whatever you want to call it, it suggests we may not be seeing the whole picture here."

I wished I'd been able to read more of *The Affair* the night before. It had genuinely meant so much to Lane Barfield to get my opinion, as if after all these years in publishing he still needed assurance that he'd made the right call in preempting a potential auction to offer the most money he ever had for a book. He was risking everything by doing so, and I found myself starting to ponder if that had gotten to him, if it had left Lane visualizing the book tanking and his being unceremoniously replaced as head of the company he'd founded as a result of putting his imprint in the red.

That left me wondering whom else he might have given *The Affair* to in order to get a read. What if they had come back with a negative report? What if he began to fear he'd made a terrible misjudgment and jumped the gun in making Benjamin Tally a ridiculous offer for a first novel? Might this have had something to do with Thomas Rudd's theft of the thumb drive containing the manuscript?

I guess I was trying to make sense of Lane's death,

find in all this the kind of order I employed in my mysteries. Life, though, almost never resembles art in that respect. I guess that's why I saw murder in what was almost surely a suicide. So what if he drifted off to NY1 but swallowed the sleeping pills in his bathroom? I wanted it to be murder, because then at least I'd have the opportunity to find some sense in this amid the ultimate motive on the part of his killer. If it had been suicide, that sense might remain forever elusive.

That's why I was glad Artie and I were headed to Lane Barfield's office. Somewhere in the phone and visitor logs there would hopefully be some clue to provide that sense. I guess this was how I did my grieving.

I could feel the somber pallor enveloping the entire floor as soon as Artie and I stepped through the door. I could hear people weeping in the subdued office, ringing phones going unanswered, the company's longtime receptionist, a burly man named Edwin, staring at the blank screen of his computer as if he was watching something only he could see.

I led Artie to Lane's office, where whatever answers I was looking for might be found. Lane went through assistants quickly, not because he was difficult to work for, but because he prided himself on grooming them for sales or editorial jobs as quickly as possible, with an eye to giving them a leg up on their careers. He screened them carefully and seldom chose wrong. I'd sat in on one of his typical "job interviews" once, amazed to hear almost all of it consist of a discussion about books. He wanted no one manning the desk directly outside his spacious office who didn't love reading, love books, and thus find passion in a job that even at the highest editorial levels paid barely enough to make ends meet in Manhattan.

His latest assistant was named Zara, hired fresh out of NYU's creative writing MFA program. He'd told me a few months back she was the best one he'd ever had, to the point where he was giving serious consideration to giving her a raise instead of a reassignment when her typical twelve-month window closed. Lane, after all, had been getting older and had started to dislike continually training new assistants to act as both his shepherd and his sentinel.

Zara wasn't at her desk when we arrived, but the muffled sobs Artie and I detected led us into Lane's office, where she sat on the couch beneath the side window. She dabbed her eyes with what looked like a napkin and cleared her throat upon spotting us.

"I'm sorry," Zara said, straightening her jeans as she stood up. "I was just . . ." Her voice cracked, her eyes filling with puddles of tears. "Oh, Mrs. Fletcher . . ."

I took her in my arms and let her cry it out; I felt she was doing it for both of us. So much passed through my mind during those moments, how much time I'd spent in this and Lane's original office uptown. How we'd toasted my first *New York Times* bestseller with apple cider, since I was no more of a drinker then than I am now. How many times I'd met him here to listen to him rave about some new author he'd discovered. "The next J. B. Fletcher," he'd proudly proclaim, knowing it got under my skin.

As we separated, I felt a profound sadness over the fact that there would be no more lunches, no more future J. B. Fletchers, that Benjamin Tally and *The Affair* marked the last boasting Lane would ever do with me. Sniffling, I turned my gaze on Artie Gelber, who looked a bit uncomfortable standing there alone, as if he'd stumbled into the wrong office.

"Sorry, Artie," I said, wiping my eyes.

"For what?" came his reply, which sounded comforting for some reason.

It drew a smile to my face and I left things there. Having lost my husband, Frank, so many years ago and having precious little family myself exaggerated the impact friends and colleagues had on my life, meaning their loss produced an even more pronounced effect on me. Lane Barfield was both of those and more, a true pillar who'd overseen the growth of my career with the care and concern now almost entirely missing from the publishing industry. He had slaved over every order, every review, whether bad or good, every stop on every book tour. For a time, I thought I was getting special treatment before realizing, several books in, that every author Lane published got the same or similar.

That must've been what was so special to him about *The Affair*. It left him excited again, eager for what he'd been able to do on the book's behalf—before the prospects of that very notion might have terrified him. Benjamin Tally was his latest, and now last, Jessica Fletcher, and that made me realize as well why my approval of the book was so important to him. I found myself wanting to meet this author very much, to see in him the hopes and dreams I'd once seen in the mirror as a beginning writer myself.

Zara had sat back down on the couch, knees pressed together to still their shaking. I sat down next to her.

"Zara, this is Lieutenant Artie Gelber from the Major Case Squad, out of NYPD headquarters. He's looking into Lane's death."

Her expression moved from pained to confused. "I heard it was suicide."

"Artie's also a very good friend of mine," I told the young woman, "and he's here out of respect for that as well. Everything certainly points to suicide, yes, but the lieutenant has agreed to help me sort through whatever led up to this."

Zara nodded as if she understood, even though she clearly didn't.

"Would you mind if I asked you some questions?"

She turned to blow her nose weakly into some balled-up Kleenex. "Anything I can do to help."

"Did Lane appear agitated or depressed lately?"

She shook her head.

"Nothing that stood out, made you take notice?"

"I'm sorry, Mrs. Fletcher, no."

"Don't be sorry, Zara. I know the high regard Lane held you in, how much he wanted to delay your moving on for as long as possible."

She swallowed hard. "He wrote me a letter of recommendation."

"When?"

"Just last week." She tried to swallow again but didn't quite complete it. "He said he wanted to keep me on the desk but understood if I wanted to move on—or move up; I think he said *move up*. Either way, he wanted me to have the letter so I wouldn't have to ask him for it."

"That's Lane," I said through the lump forming in my own throat. "And I'm glad you stayed, Zara, because there's nobody better equipped to help find what led up to this." I stole a glance at Artie before continuing. "I need to ask you about a book Lane had recently acquired entitled *The Affair* by an author named Benjamin Tally. Does that sound familiar?"

She started to shake her head, then simply froze. "He told me to keep it a secret. Not to tell anyone the book existed . . . That was the only conversation we had about the book."

"Had Lane ever done anything like that before?"

"Not to that degree. Sometimes he had titles he wanted to keep under wraps—you know, to avoid questions or challenges from Sales or Corporate."

"Makes sense," I acknowledged, rising from the couch. "Could you check for us? Could you check his personal records to see if he logged *The Affair* in under a different title?"

Zara rose from the couch nodding, looking happy to have the opportunity to help us. As she moved behind Lane's big L-shaped desk, and stood as she logged into his computer because she didn't want to take his chair, I considered the logic of what she had suggested. Lane might have indeed been keeping his acquisition of *The Affair* a secret for as long as he could, at least until the initial edits under his direction were complete. As I had suspected earlier, he probably had the manuscript out with several authors in addition to me, hoping their feedback would validate the risky decision he had made. Endorsements would help him make the case that this book was going to be something big, against the conventional belief that he wasn't that kind of publisher anymore. I wondered if *The Affair* represented a last gasp for Lane Barfield, which made the possibility of suicide all the more plausible.

"You said the title was *The Affair*?" Zara asked me.

"Yes."

"And the author's name?"

"Benjamin Tally."

It was clear from her expression that Zara wasn't having any luck finding either of those on Lane's computer.

"Any idea when Lane might have received it? Normally, I'm responsible for logging in all the manuscripts that get as far as his desk."

I didn't want to hurt Zara's feelings by mentioning that the importance of this book might've led Lane to cut her out of the loop. Still, the fact that there was no mention of it even on his computer seemed strange. A potential mega-bestseller or not, *The Affair* was still just a book, a manuscript, that even Lane wouldn't have gone through such lengths to hide. A thought struck me.

"Do you keep a list of authors' manuscripts that have gone out for blurbs?"

"I redid the entire system myself," Zara said, beaming slightly before reality encroached again.

"Could you check to see if there's a listing somewhere? Look for the kind of names Lane held back for his most important books."

"He called that the Favor Bank," Zara said, stopping just short of a smile. "He said you could only go to it so often."

"Any withdrawals you see on his computer?" I asked, not bothering to mention that my own name would've been among them.

Zara scrolled through the screen for one minute and then another, before she responded. "No. Nothing like that I can find reference to here."

Again, Lane could have been using extreme measures to keep the existence of *The Affair* secret. But he was a man who lived by regimen, routine. He'd been late adapting to a computer, and I can recall index cards lined up all over his desk doing the job he'd finally turned over to the machines.

I looked toward Artie, who took that as his cue to close the door. Then I fixed my gaze back on Zara.

"I'm about to share something with you that Lane must've had good reason to withhold. You shouldn't take any offense at that because I can tell you he'd been secretive, even paranoid, about books he held the greatest hope for. I believe *The Affair* was one of those and that he'd offered a very large amount to purchase it. I'm not sure if the deal had closed yet, but there must be some record, also secret, in the contracts department toward that end. Do you know how to access such records, Zara? And be assured this will remain strictly between us."

She looked toward Artie, who nodded his assent on the subject; then she turned back to me. "He taught me how to access the system. He wasn't supposed to, but he did."

"Then that's it. That will give us a starting point. He may have logged the book in as 'untitled' with a fake author name. Look for a significant advance, paid out over a protracted period of time, or perhaps even a multibook contract."

Zara went back to work behind Lane's computer, and spent a longer stretch tapping the keys this time.

"There's nothing."

"You're sure?"

"Nothing matching that description, not even close. If Lane had a deal in place for this book, Contracts didn't know it."

Which made no sense at all, utterly confounding. If I hadn't started reading the vaunted manuscript myself, I'd be questioning Lane's sanity right now.

I realized Zara was fresh at work again behind his computer, her expression suddenly resolute. "What are you doing?" I asked her, resisting the temptation to check the screen myself.

"You said Lane sent this manuscript, *The Affair*, out for blurbs?"

"Yes," I said, again not bothering to mention that I was one of those he'd passed a copy to. "I'm quite sure of that."

"Then he would have either mailed a manuscript or e-mailed it as an attachment, using either his work or private e-mail address. His private one most likely, because that can be accessed only from his computer and not mine."

"Then . . . ," I started.

"I know his password," Zara said, leaving it there. She returned all of her attention to the screen, clearly mystified at what she was seeing. "This would have all happened recently, right?"

"Within the last month anyway."

She looked up at me across Lane's desk, her face aglow in the light spraying off the monitor. "There's nothing, Mrs. Fletcher. No e-mails or shipping receipt confirmations. Nothing."

I couldn't make any sense of that at all, glancing toward Artie, who looked equally befuddled even though he was hardly privy to the inner workings of the book business.

"It's like," Zara was saying from behind Lane's desk, "this book never existed."

Chapter Seven

I had a copy, of course, so I knew *The Affair* was very real indeed. And the late Thomas Rudd had swiped a flash drive Lane Barfield told me contained the same manuscript.

"We need to ask you to do something you may be uncomfortable doing, Zara," I said, looking over her shoulder at Artie Gelber, who mouthed, *We?* "We need to ask if you'd feel comfortable calling the agents Lane dealt with most often. See if any of them got the book to him in the first place."

"Why wouldn't I?"

I didn't know what to tell her exactly. Something was wrong here; something was off. Lane had somehow come into possession of a book he considered a potential monster that, for all practical purposes, didn't exist. So either he had gone through beyond-extraordinary efforts to hide its existence, or else . . .

Or else *what*?

The fact that his experienced assistant, Zara, whom he'd proclaimed to be the best one he'd ever had, couldn't pick up even an inkling of the manuscript's existence was troubling to say the least. Even if Lane had realized his folly, that he'd made a terrible mistake he intended to erase before taking his own life, there would at the very least be some digital relic left someplace, in the contracts department or elsewhere, that Zara should've been able to find.

I couldn't make any sense of this, because there was no sense to make of it. I still hadn't told Artie I actually had a copy of *The Affair*, because the fact hadn't seemed pertinent until now; it still might not be. I just didn't know.

"I know just who to call. In what order, too," Zara was saying.

"And . . . ," I started.

"I know," she said before I could continue. "Be discreet."

Zara almost smiled. The color had returned to her face and her eyes no longer brimmed with tears. Having something to do, an assignment, had clearly provided purpose, recharging her in the process. The odds were overwhelming that the manuscript had been submitted by an agent. Huge deals being the product of unsolicited manuscripts was the stuff of fiction and legend. It just didn't happen these days, especially when the vast majority of publishers refused to even consider such submissions anymore.

"Can I ask you a question, Mrs. Fletcher?" Zara resumed suddenly, the pain creeping back into her expression, her face currently enveloped by shadows in a patch of Lane's office untouched by the sun.

"Of course."

"Why do you think he did it?"

"I really have no idea," I said truthfully.

"It wasn't like him. He loved his work. You can tell when someone loves his work. There were nights when I couldn't get him to leave the office, even though he kept nodding off at his desk."

"He was lonely, Zara. That might have played a part in it."

Lane had been married once, but it hadn't lasted long and had produced no children. He spoke occasionally about a brother and sister, but I got the impression they were both deceased. He had built an insular world for himself that, at his age, came with a life expectancy that was drawing to a close. And with that end looming, Lane Barfield might've been forced to confront the fact that he had nothing with which to replace his fifty-year career in publishing. It happens to people sometimes when they reach that stage; the dangerous combination of fear and depression sets in over the big, dark void that's coming next. Maybe better that it not come at all and, fearing such ruinous thoughts would become the norm, they opt to swallow a month's supply of sleeping pills or choose another means to slip away to someplace else.

"Anything else I can do?" Zara asked me.

"Benjamin Tally is probably a pseudonym. My thinking is that at some point he's going to call, looking for Lane."

"Lane's cell phone calls were automatically routed

to his private office number. I'll monitor both that and his regular office number. Should I call you if I hear from him?"

"Immediately," I said, not bothering to look at Artie this time, because I didn't care whether he approved of my involvement or not.

With the book apparently stricken from existence here at the publisher, our only chance to learn anything more about the part it might have played in Lane's suicide would be from the author.

"Something more?" Zara asked, reading the change in my expression.

"As a matter of fact, I think you should make subtle calls to all the other major imprints. Ask if they've ever heard of an author named Benjamin Tally or a book called *The Affair*."

"You think Tally may have changed his mind and taken the book elsewhere?"

I shrugged. "It would explain a lot of things."

But it would have needed to happen fast, after I'd left Lane's office yesterday with the manuscript in hand. I pictured him receiving a call with the bad news and flushing every trace of *The Affair* from the company's system in a rage, before he went home and cashed in his chips.

"Check the call log from yesterday afternoon, both his office and personal lines," I told Zara. "Make a list of any number without an ID or that you don't recognize," I added, figuring one of those numbers might have belonged to Benjamin Tally.

"That it?"

"One more thing, Zara: I'd like a list of all the top authors Lane called in the past two weeks."

"Why'd you ask her for that?" Artie asked when we were alone in the elevator.

"Because I figured one of those authors might have penned *The Affair* using a pseudonym."

It was a lie, but a fairly credible one. The truth was, I wanted to find out who else Lane might have sent the manuscript to besides me for an evaluation and potential endorsement. After all these years in publishing, he still needed that kind of affirmation, especially for a book that had so much riding on it. If the response had been negative, I'd have another potential scenario explaining why Lane had killed himself.

Unfortunately, Artie wasn't buying it; maybe the hook and line, but not the sinker. "What is it you're not telling me?"

"How do you know there's something I'm not telling you?"

"Because I work at One Police Plaza now. I'm important."

"And that makes you clairvoyant?"

"No," Artie said, "not clairvoyant—just right, in this case."

"If I'm not telling you something, it's because whatever it is doesn't matter."

Artie gave me a long look as the cab began its descent. "Are you like this in Cabot Cove?"

"Like what?"

"A pain in the ass." He reached out and hit the

emergency stop button, jerking the cab to a sudden halt accompanied by an alarm buzzing just loudly enough to be annoying. "Got any plans for the rest of the day?"

"I was thinking of spending it in a stuck elevator."

He positioned himself between me and the red button. "And it's not going to get unstuck until you explain to me the point of what just happened in Barfield's office."

"He made a huge offer for a book that his own contracts department has no record of. He'd never have done that without checking in with the sales department first, but Sales has no record of the book's existence, either. And every place the manuscript should have been logged in, it wasn't."

"Okay." Artie nodded. "I get most of that, but give it to me short and sweet, the way you pitch your stories."

"I don't pitch my stories."

"Then how do you sell them?"

"I sign multibook contracts, usually three at a time."

"Sight unseen?"

I shrugged. "It's the way things are done."

"And they trust you to keep doing it?"

"Lane did," I told him, leaving it there.

Artie released the emergency stop button. "You think he trusted Benjamin Tally, too, Jessica?"

"That's what we need to find out," I said, still not telling him I had a copy of Tally's manuscript.

From my apartment, after Artie dropped me off, I checked in with Zara twice for updates over the course of the afternoon. So far, her efforts had produced the names of two of the imprint's biggest authors, whom Lane had been in touch with several times over the course of the past two weeks. The call logs, of course, spoke nothing as to the content of those conversations, but a combination of their length, their frequency, and that they'd occurred one after another on several occasions suggested following up on this lead might indeed yield information pertinent to my investigation.

Zara excitedly gave me the names of the writers, both of whom I immediately recognized as major authors who could claim number one *New York Times* bestsellers to their credit, something that had always eluded me. She was a bit more reluctant to pass on their phone numbers, until I said I'd be making the calls on the pretext of ensuring they'd heard of Lane's passing. One of the authors lived in Santa Fe and the other on a ranch in Montana, so it was very possible they had, in fact, not gotten the news about Lane's passing, which had come out only this morning.

I put off making the calls as long as I could, trying to find the right frame of mind. Though I was familiar with both authors, and I was sure we'd crossed paths at some conference or awards ceremony, I couldn't recall actually meeting either of them. A. J. Falcone, a huge action-thriller seller, was a complete recluse on the order of J. D. Salinger. There wasn't another ranch within three hundred miles of where he lived in Montana, and I'd once heard he moved there from his first ranch when a neighbor bought a home a half mile away, destroying his sight line of the wilderness. Alicia Bond, meanwhile, was the pen name for a bestselling romance writer who'd needed a new byline to craft a fantasy series that had become a huge hit on pay cable. Her original series would continue to make Lane's imprint a boatload of cash, but she'd sold her pseudonymous one to another publisher after a bidding war that reached unfathomable numbers. I doubt either one of them ever answered their phones, meaning I'd have to decide between leaving a message and calling back. And I hated leaving a message since it likely meant I'd have to wait who knew how long for them to call me back, if ever. I needed to talk to them, needed them to answer my questions as soon as possible, not next week or next month, not even tomorrow.

Patience might've been a virtue, but it was never my greatest strength, which served me well as a writer, since I couldn't wait to finish a book. Writing feels like an impossible task, unless you're doing it. So my solution has always been not to stop.

I flirted with opening up the manuscript of *The Affair* again and picking up where I'd left off, but my mind was still racing too fast to concentrate. And after doing pretty much everything else I could think of to distract myself, I finally settled down to phone A. J. Falcone and Alicia Bond, starting with A.J.

"Lane?" a gruff, gravelly voice greeted me on the other end of the line.

My thoughts froze, silent for what felt like a much longer duration than it really was. Clearly A. J. Falcone received so few calls on this particular line that he assumed I must be Lane Barfield.

"It's Jessica Fletcher, A.J.," I said finally, sputtering through my words.

"Who?"

"Jessica Fletcher, the mystery writer. We're both published by Lane Barfield's imprint."

"Never heard of you. How'd you get this number? I'm hanging up now."

"No, please don't hang up. I got your number from Lane's office. I'm afraid I've got some bad news to share with you."

"He's dead?" Falcone's gruff voice kind of rolled his words together.

"Then you've heard."

"Nope, haven't heard a thing. When some stranger calls you on a number they shouldn't have, what else could it be? How'd it happen? Accident?"

"Suicide," I told him tersely.

"How'd he do it? Shotgun?"

"Er, no."

"Noose?"

"No again. Sleeping pills."

"Barfield never had any guts. Hemingway had guts, emptied both barrels into his head instead of just one, made sure he got it right."

That final remark made me cringe. I'd seen author photos of Falcone on his book jackets; he was inevitably pictured in a cowboy hat atop, or standing next to, a horse. Leathery skin with lines and deep furrows that made his face look like a cracked windshield. An old-fashioned cowboy look that had served him, and his book sales, well.

"I was calling to let you know."

"And now you have. Nice talking to you, Jennifer."

I switched my cell phone from one hand to the other. "It's Jessica. And I did have one other thing."

"Somebody else die?"

"No."

"Did Barfield die twice?"

"Mr. Falcone," I started, adopting a more formal tone, until he cut me off.

"We got nothing more to talk about."

"Did Lane Barfield send you a manuscript lately?"

"Why would he do that?"

"To get your thoughts."

"Why would he care?"

"Maybe he wanted a blurb for it."

"I don't do blurbs. You didn't call for one, did you? Please tell me you're not a writer."

I decided to keep right on going. "Did Lane send you a manuscript called *The Affair* by an author named Benjamin Tally?"

"Never heard of him, either. Never heard of any of you."

"I'm asking you about *The Affair*."

"Not interested, Jennifer. I'm a married man, most of the time."

"I wasn't talking about that."

"It's what you just said."

"Yes, the title of a book: *The Affair*."

"Oh, that. It sucked. Awful. A waste of time, like all books are, including my own. I write 'em, but I wouldn't be caught dead reading 'em."

I felt my heart flutter in my chest. "Lane Barfield sent you *The Affair* and you read it?"

"What did I just say?"

"Did you tell Lane what you thought of the book?"

"Why bother? He doesn't hear it from me, he'd

figure it out for himself." I could tell A. J. Falcone's patience with me was wearing thin. "I'm sorry Barfield's dead. Would've been sorrier if he'd used a shotgun. Bye."

Click.

My call to Alicia Bond went considerably faster: She didn't answer so I left a voice mail saying I had some bad news to share about Lane Barfield, elaborating no further. Short and sweet. I doubted I'd hear back and began wishing I hadn't left a message at all, as soon as I hung up.

My thoughts turned to the author named Benjamin Tally, who wasn't listed on Amazon or any other book site and didn't have a Web site, a Facebook page, a Twitter handle, or anything else that might ease the task of finding him. I found plenty of Benjamin Tallys online and a few on LinkedIn with full profiles, too. But none of them were, or claimed to be, writers. The name had to be a pseudonym, just like I'd figured, which meant I needed to find Benjamin Tally's real identity.

I jogged my phone to Contacts, jogged the screen to *M*, and touched the name I was looking for.

"You again?" came a voice that sounded like it had been strained through oatmeal.

"Let's get some coffee, Harry. I'm buying."

Chapter Eight

"You said you were buying," said Harry McGraw, rising as I approached the same table he seemed to always be sitting at inside the Tick Tock Diner, located on Thirty-fourth Street not far from Penn Station. "That's why I showed up."

The location was perfect, given that I intended to catch a train to Boston directly from our meeting. Harry looked as rumpled and ragged as ever, a cheap suit with arms and legs hanging out of it and a face that looked like he washed it with coffee grounds. Though he refused to admit it and might not have even known it, he was still the best private investigator in the business, all his self-disparaging remarks aside. He never let me down and hated taking credit for anything he did, as if the persona of a down-on-his-luck, has-been loser suited him better. Call Harry a victim of low expectations.

He was well into his coffee by the time I got there, the usual twisted stack of old-school Sweet'N Low packets nowhere to be seen around the saucer.

"What happened to the Sweet'N Low, Harry?" I asked him, sliding into the chair and tucking my wheeled carry-on bag under the edge of the table.

"Gave it up. I heard it causes cancer."

"That study is twenty years old, Harry."

"What can I say, Jess? I'm still working my way through a pile of old *Reader's Digest*s."

"Twenty years?"

"It's a big pile."

"I need your help with something."

"Of course you do. God forbid you should call just to say hello."

"I call to say hello all the time, Harry. You always hang up when I say I don't need your help with anything."

He took a sip from his cup, his jowls drooping as he swallowed. "I'm raising my rates."

"I didn't know you had rates."

"That's because you don't pay your bills."

"You never send me any."

"That's no excuse," he said and signaled for the server, also the same one he always seemed to get, as if the Tick Tock Diner had only a single table and server so far as Harry was concerned.

The server refilled his cup and took my order for a tea.

"Don't forget my pie," Harry said to him when he started to back away from the table.

"You didn't order any pie, sir," the waiter said, confused.

"I just did. Big slice of whatever looks good. Your choice."

The man nodded and took his leave.

"What do you need, little lady?" Harry asked me, draining a river of sugar from an old-fashioned dispenser into his cup. "I'm going to warn you, though, I now require a twenty percent deposit up front."

"Whatever you say, Harry."

"Okay, fifty percent."

I took out an envelope containing the actual title page from *The Affair* and handed it across the table. "I need you to find the author on this title page."

"Who is he?"

"His name is Benjamin Tally."

Harry opened the envelope and consulted the page. "Never heard of him."

"He's new."

"Never heard of the book, either."

"It hasn't been published yet."

"Lousy title. Any good?" Harry asked, looking back at me across the table.

"I've only just started."

"I heard your new book came out."

"That's why I'm in New York."

"Where's my free copy?"

"I invited you to the launch party at the Mysterious Book Shop."

He tucked the title page back into the envelope and frowned. "Then I'd have to pay. I like getting them for free like a tip. Or, in my case, my entire fee for services rendered."

The server brought my tea and Harry's pie, which looked like a double slice.

"Which flavor is it?" I asked as he took a bite.

"Can't tell," he said, chewing. "Something with fruit. What's the difference?"

I leaned forward, rattling my teacup. "Benjamin Tally, Harry."

"You try the phone book?"

"I don't think they make them anymore."

"They also have this thing called the Internet. Maybe you've heard of it."

"I think the name Benjamin Tally is a pseudonym. I want you to find out who he really is."

"Who's bringing the book out?"

"My publisher."

He nodded as if he'd figured something out. "All right, tell you what I'm going to do. First thing tomorrow, I'm going to call them and ask who Benjamin Tally really is. That ought to keep your bill down."

"You can't."

"Why?"

"Because he's dead, Harry."

"Benjamin Tally?"

"No, my publisher. Lane Barfield."

"How'd that happen?"

"Suicide."

"Uggghhhhh . . ."

"That was my thought."

"Book sales must be pretty bad." He nodded to himself, carving out another bite of pie, a chunk of whatever the fruit was falling onto the envelope that held the title page, Harry making the stain worse when he tried to clean it with his napkin. "I'll bet it was pills."

"How'd you guess?"

"It's always pills with the intellectual types who hit the off switch. Normally, they don't own guns and like dreaming anyway, which your boss will now be doing for eternity."

"He wasn't my boss."

"Then what was he?"

"My publisher."

"That's not the same thing?"

"No more than me paying you makes me your boss."

"Except you don't pay me."

I let him work on his pie for a few moments before resuming. "Can you do it?"

"Finish this whole piece? Absolutely."

"Can you find out who Benjamin Tally really is?"

Harry ran his index finger through the dark smudge on the envelope. "Sure, right after I part the Red Sea and make frogs rain from the sky. Jeez, Jess, do I look like God to you?"

"The Red Sea and the frogs were the work of Moses, Harry."

"But he had help, didn't he? He needed God, just like you need me."

"So you're God now?"

"Only to you, little lady, only to you." Harry passed the halfway point on his pie and, for some reason, spun the remainder around to eat the crust first. "Anything else you can tell me about Benjamin Tally?"

I shrugged. "That's pretty much it."

"A name on the title page of an unpublished manuscript?"

I nodded. "I'm afraid so." I checked my watch and looked at the upside-down check the server had just set down next to Harry. "I need to catch the train. What's the damage?"

Harry looked at the check, so casually he seemed bored. "Two thousand and eleven dollars."

"For a piece of pie?"

"No, my back alimony payments. I thought I'd give it a try."

I walked the short distance to Penn Station and took an Amtrak Northeast Regional train that would get me to Boston just in time to catch another train headed north to Portland, from where I'd make my way home to Cabot Cove. I could have saved time by flying, but I was actually looking forward to all that uninterrupted time alone, if for no other reason than it would give me a chance to read a considerable chunk of *The Affair* during the ride.

I'd forgotten the garish opening, so I started from scratch again. The train wasn't very crowded and I had a double seat all to myself. I'd tucked the tote containing the manuscript into my overnight bag, guarding it as if it might be worth the large sum Lane Barfield had paid for it.

Lane Barfield . . .

Strange how much that simple tote bag he'd mindlessly provided had come to mean to me.

It's what I had to remember him by, a token of the

last time we were ever together. And that got me thinking about the inexplicable oddities surrounding the book itself. Like how could Lane have possibly paid out a huge advance, or at least made the offer, without his own imprint's contracts department knowing about it? Why was there no profit-and-loss statement assembled by Sales on his computer? That was a basic industry standard, and sitting alone under the dome lights I'd switched on as the train sped through the darkness, I let myself consider what I'd been resisting since Artie and I had met with Lane's assistant, Zara:

What if someone had made all reference to *The Affair* in the company's database disappear?

As a mystery writer, I often find the conspiratorial nature of evil creeping into my everyday life. Sometimes with foundation, sometimes without. But Lane's death was very real, as was the fact that a book he had splashed layers of praise upon didn't seem to exist as far as his own imprint was concerned. And that got me back around to the crime scene at Thomas Rudd's apartment.

Yes, I said crime scene. Because someone had bound his arms to a chair before setting off that gas explosion. And that wasn't just my overactive imagination talking, either. I was just about to dig back into the manuscript when Artie Gelber reached me by phone.

"Artie?" I greeted him, afraid of what he might have to tell me this time.

"Just wanted you to know our crime scene unit went over what's left of your friend's apartment building again. Still no sign of that flash drive you asked me to look for."

For some reason, I was glad I hadn't corrected Artie when he called Rudd my friend.

"It could've burned up in the fire, I suppose," he continued, "especially if it was in the kitchen area."

"Or it could have been taken by whoever rigged the explosion," I pointed out.

"I made some calls about Rudd, Jessica. The number of people he was in debt to would fill a book by itself, and plenty of those would make great villains."

"The kind who blow people up?"

"For starters, anyway."

He paused so long I thought he'd hung up. Then his voice returned.

"You on your way home?"

"I'm on the train now."

"Be careful," he warned.

"I'm not driving, remember?"

"Just be careful. I don't know what's going on here, but too much of it doesn't add up to anything I can make sense of."

I should have told him I had the manuscript, should have left *The Affair* with him in the first place. Instead I glanced at the pages piled on the seat next to me and wondered if A. J. Falcone's critique had been accurate:

It sucked. Awful. A waste of time . . .

Then again, Falcone hated his own books, by his own admission.

"Did you hear me, Jessica?" Artie asked me in my ear. "I told you to be careful."

"I heard you."

That was Artie. He was probably the best detective I'd ever known, never giving up the chase no matter how much time had passed or how many roads in an investigation ended up leading nowhere. Harry McGraw wasn't bad, either, was pretty damn good, actually, in spite of what his ruffled persona might have indicated. If anyone could uncover who Benjamin Tally really was, it was Harry, even if all he had to go on was a manuscript title page.

I sat on the aisle so I could lay the manuscript on the seat next to me by the window. It was so voluminous, I wouldn't be surprised if the conductor asked me to purchase an extra ticket. Musing on that, I picked up a stack of the pages, finished the obligatory prologue quickly, and moved on to the first chapter.

Chapter Nine

If I'd known she was the president's daughter, I never would've said yes. No, I'm lying, because I couldn't take my eyes off her, and when she approached through the haze of club-made smoke from dry ice and asked me to dance, well, let's just say my legs melted.

I shouldn't have been drinking that night; she shouldn't have been drinking. That's how it all started, with a fight that separated her from her Secret Service escort team and left Abby under my sole protection.

Her name wasn't really Abby, as I'd quickly learn. But it was how she introduced herself, so, for me, the president's daughter became Abby.

We ended up at a motel that night, but not for the reasons you think. She didn't want to go home, back to the White House in other words. It was a Motel 6 or

Super 8, some chain with a number in its name. A dump, basically, and I've never seen anyone so overjoyed to have all of twenty-four basic cable channels to watch without anyone peering over her shoulder or protesters chanting across the street.

Everything was just fine, until the door to our room shattered and blew open.

I nodded off for a fluttery second there, only to snap alert an instant later. I caught a bald man sitting in a seat facing mine a few rows away easing his gaze away from me and wondered if I'd cried out or something in my half sleep. But he trained his eyes casually out the window and melted back into the scenery.

I could already see what had gotten Lane Barfield so excited about *The Affair*. It was beyond commercial, bestseller written all over it thanks to a simple and exceedingly melodramatic premise. *A young man involved with the president's daughter . . .*

Wondering what that dot-dot-dot might be, I settled myself with a deep breath and went back to reading.

The three men didn't know who I was, where I had come from, what I'd been trained to do. They had no idea the president's daughter wasn't the only fugitive in the room, and it cost them.

They had launched their attack, not anticipating any resistance. That told me something about them before I could catch my breath, because true professionals, special operators, always proceed with that possibility in mind. And their misjudgment of the situation they were walking into cost them. It cost them dearly.

Hating the kind of lurid and graphic descriptions that followed, I skimmed the next few pages, finding myself relating quite well to the president's daughter's reaction to what she'd just witnessed.

Abby had taken refuge in a corner, the roach motel's flashing marquee turning her face jagged with color. I had to step over the bodies to reach her, two of them anyway, avoiding the blood that was already soaking into the cheap carpeting. I felt bad for the maid who would come to clean this room tomorrow.

Abby looked up at me in terror. "Wh-wh-who are you?" she managed.

"You're not the only one with secrets, Abby."

Her eyes fell on the bodies. "But . . ." She left it there, nothing more to say until she was ready again. "The only thing I lied to you about was my name."

"I didn't lie to you at all."

"You're a killer."

"No, I'm not."

"You just killed three men, three men with guns."

"That doesn't make me a killer. And if I'd been somebody else, they'd have you now."

"So, what, you're like a knight in shining armor?"

I shook my head. "Sometimes knights are as dark as those they're protecting the kingdom from."

"The kingdom," Abby repeated behind a trace of a smile, as if she found that funny, maybe ironic. "Who are you?" she asked again.

"Come on," I said instead of answering her question, stretching a hand toward the corner where Abby had taken refuge. "I'd better get you home."

"No," she protested, pulling back against the tug of my hand. "That's who sent them."

Wow!

I could almost feel Lane Barfield reading over my shoulder, pleased to no end that I saw exactly what he had in *The Affair*. It was utterly addicting, a twist or surprise literally to be found on every single page. I couldn't wait to read on to see what was going to happen next. Abby and . . .

I realized I didn't know the narrator's name and flipped back through the pages to see if I'd somehow missed it. Nope. I didn't know his name because it hadn't been provided yet, rendering him anonymous, the lack of a true identity meant to give the reader a glimpse into his life on the run from whoever it was who'd made him what he was. It wasn't a new theme, but it was pretty much tried-and-true when in the right hands. And Benjamin Tally clearly had the right hands, a maestro on the keyboard when it came to this pulp tale of ridiculous connections and coincidences that readers would overlook as the plot spun them along at a breakneck pace.

I needed to use the restroom, wanting nothing to distract me from my reading of *The Affair*. Given all the time remaining on this ride, and the one that would follow between Boston and Portland, I'd have plenty of time to cover a considerable chunk of the manuscript and actually wouldn't mind a delay, since that would give me a chance to read the whole thing.

I realized the bald man I thought I'd caught watching me was gone, likely having detrained at one of the stops that we had passed while I'd been transfixed by the double-spaced pages. New riders had taken seats in the car, and I began to fear I'd have to give up my cherished extra seat, currently occupied by the bulky manuscript.

When I thought about it, the whole process now felt odd. I had agreed to read *The Affair* as a favor to Lane Barfield, to give him my honest thoughts, offer a blurb in the event he wanted one. I wished I'd had the opportunity to validate his decision—to tell him that if this wasn't the next big thing in the publishing world, I didn't know what was. Instead, I had cracked open the manuscript to see if it might yield some clue as to the circumstances behind his death. If it was suicide, so be it. If it was someone trying to provide that impression, though, this book, or something contained within it, might hold the motive for his killing. Nor could I chase from my mind the fact that Thomas Rudd had been murdered. Unpaid street debts aside, murder seemed extreme even for the thugs who held his markers.

I rose from my seat and tried to stretch the stiffness from my neck and shoulders, the result of being stuck in one position while I read. My eyes drifted backward and I froze.

The bald man I remembered from before was now seated three rows behind me.

He appeared to be sleeping. I blinked a few times to make sure it was him and sat back down. I didn't dare leave the manuscript behind, and lugging a clump of pages up the aisle, along with my handbag, would make me feel ridiculous. I'd have to pass the bald man's seat on the way to the restroom, so I resolved to wait as long as I could.

Sitting back down left me feeling anxious and tense, resisting the urge to peer backward over the seat, perhaps to catch the bald man watching me again. I eased the cell phone from my bag for no good reason at all; whom was I going to call and what was I going to tell them? There were at least fifty other passengers in this car and their presence lent a measure of security. I didn't dare fall asleep, though, and resolved to do a better job keeping an eye on my surroundings.

No easy task, given how much I kept slipping into the world of *The Affair*. If nothing else, reading on would keep me awake, as well as distract me from the fact that I'd never gotten to the restroom. And as soon as I plunged back into the manuscript, the president's daughter, Abby, posed the same question I'd been asking myself.

"What's your name?"

"Does it matter?"

"When somebody saves my life, I like to know their name."

"This happens a lot, does it?"

"First time for everything, but not the last. You can rest assured of that."

"What did you do exactly, Abby?"

"Uh-uh. You first, pretty boy."

That stung. "Pretty boy?"

"Nobody ever called you that before?"

"I don't get out much."

Abby watched me drag the first body toward the closet to hide it from view of anyone peering through the thin, flimsy curtains. She wasn't rattled. I found that interesting.

"We need to get going," I said to her.

"Where?"

"I was going to ask you the same question."

"If you don't tell me your name, I'll keep calling you pretty boy."

That did the trick. "Emerson."

"Really?"

"No, it's the name on the television."

She glanced that way, then back at me. "Want to try again?"

"Okay," I said, pretending to relent, "it's Ricoh."

"What's that?"

"Japanese."

She gazed toward a small cluster of appliances. "The microwave?"

I shook my head, stuffing the final man I'd killed into the closet. "Coffee maker."

"I'm going to ask you one more time."

"No," I told her, forcing the closet door closed, "you'll keep asking until you get your answer. But I'll make you a deal. You tell me why somebody from inside the White House wants to kill the president's daughter and I'll tell you my—"

I awoke with a start, not realizing where I was for one brief, breathless moment. An unkempt pile of manuscript pages lay on my lap with a few having slipped to the floor. I looked to my right and breathed easier when I saw the remainder of the manuscript was still there.

I checked my watch and realized nearly an hour had passed since I'd risen from my seat with the intention of going to the restroom. I stood up again, pretending to reach for my carry-on bag, and spotted the bald man still in the same seat, his face aglow from a cell phone screen he must've been watching. He seemed to have no interest in me.

I think maybe the content of *The Affair* was making me paranoid, making me fear I might be attacked just as Abby and the book's unnamed narrator had been in the grungy motel room. The writing was sparse but muscular, Benjamin Tally knowing just how much to say without saying too much. He had an ear for dialogue and had already given me a deep interest in his young heroes, who, I suspected, held many secrets yet to be revealed.

My mouth was dry and I craved a bottled water terribly. But I didn't dare vacate my seat as the train rumbled through Connecticut, hugging the coastline and Route 95, closing in on Rhode Island. Pretty soon, I'd have to use the restroom whether I liked it or not, even if that meant lugging more than eight hundred manuscript pages with me. But for now I shook the weariness from my mind and went back to *The Affair*.

"—name."

I watched her nod, the hair tumbling into her face. I positioned myself so she wouldn't see the blood starting to leak out from beneath the closet door.

"I heard something I wasn't supposed to."

"Involving your father?"

"Uh-huh. Your turn."

"Pace."

Abby nodded as if she was bored. "That's an English company, I think."

"It's also my name. The name they gave me."

"The name who gave you?"

"We should get out of here," I told her, looking back at the closet.

"Don't you want to ask me another question?"

She was right; I did. "What was it that you heard?"

"Something they can't afford me telling my father. They're going to kill my mother and my brother if I do."

I tried not to show how interested I was. "I'm not your father."

"And it's not your turn; it's mine," Abby said, peering through a crack in the drawn curtains to see whether there were any more men I needed to kill.

"Nobody there," I told her. "This was all of them."

"How can you be sure?"

I shrugged. "I just am."

"Ready for my next question?"

"I just answered your next question."

"I haven't asked it yet."

"'How can you be sure?'" I repeated.

"That doesn't count."

"Yes, it does. But because I like you so much I'll give you another. Last one before we have to leave."

"Where are you from?"

"I don't know."

"No fair. I get another: Where are you going?"

"Same answer."

"Then I get a third, and one more for each time you don't answer." She didn't stop to let me argue the point, just asked away. "Who made you this way?"

"They did."

"Who are they?"

"Changing the rules again?"

"Who are they?"

"The Guardians. We call them that because that's what they are to us, and it's the way they see themselves for a lot more than just us."

"I don't know what that means, Pace."

It felt strange to be addressed by as close to a real name as I had.

"What do the Guardians do exactly?"

"Is it still your turn?"

"Answer the question."

I looked toward the closet. "They send men like that. To keep the wrong secrets from ever getting out, among other things."

I could tell the notion of that frightened her. "You think that they . . ."

"I don't know. I do know we need to get moving; we need to get moving now."

I nodded off again right there, exhausted after all that had transpired over the course of the last two days. I tried to go back to the manuscript, but fatigue kept claiming me no matter how hard I fought back.

I stole another glance backward to find the bald man still in place, still caught in the spill of light from his cell phone screen. He'd probably switched seats just to ride in the right direction, so his back wasn't to the engine. He seemed entrenched in whatever he was watching, buds dangling from his ears, no interest in me whatsoever.

We'd just passed into Massachusetts; another forty minutes to go before the train reached Boston, never mind the additional three hours of travel that awaited me after that. I began to regret not flying. I could have been back in Maine now, heading home, instead of on this endless ride with only Abby and Pace to keep me company.

I gathered up the whole stack of pages and tucked them back into the tote I put on my shoulder before heading down the aisle. I regarded the bald man for a single moment while heading for the restroom. I made sure to slide the lock into place. It rattled a few minutes later when someone outside began to jiggle the door latch.

Chapter Ten

"I'm terribly sorry," the man said when I slid the door open. "But the light wasn't on and I thought it was jammed."

I nodded at him, realized I was clutching one of the straps on the tote containing *The Affair*. When I swung round to head back to my seat, I caught the bald man's gaze angled in my direction. Or maybe he was really watching the man who'd jiggled the latch. Or maybe he just happened to turn around.

I didn't do any more reading through the rest of the trip to Boston, trying to sleep but managing to do so only fitfully. Isn't that the worst? You fall asleep when you're trying not to, and when you try to fall asleep, you can't. Every time I managed to nod off, I was struck by strange dreams populated by the likenesses of Pace and Abby, the president's daughter and the mother of all bad boys, off on some crazy adventure.

Whoever Benjamin Tally was, he had a wild imagination, but he also seemed to be a man of letters who'd fallen into this pulpy form of staccato prose and machine-gun dialogue that screamed hard-boiled, and written a thriller framed in the form of a classic mystery of the sort Hammett and Chandler would be proud of.

I wondered what they'd think of me. Probably not very much.

The night wound on forever. I lost track of the bald man when we reached Boston but watched for him when I boarded my train for Portland. I never saw him get on, which I found to be a welcome relief. Of course, he could still be on this train somewhere, but at least he wasn't sitting three rows behind me. I thought he'd gone left in Boston's South Station, while I'd gone right.

So I took more solace in the fact that he didn't seem to be following me.

I hated putting anybody out by asking them to drive such a distance to pick me up so late, even though I could hear Seth Hazlitt saying the same thing he always did when I used Uber or a cab instead.

"Should have called me, Jess. Would have saved you the bother. If it makes you feel better, just pay me next time. Ayuh."

Seth was nothing if not consistent, so tonight, given all the stress and the lateness of the hour, I called him not long after the train had left Boston.

"It's late," he said, feigning displeasure at my request.

"You always tell me to call you when I need a ride."

"Nobody ever means it when they say those things.

I have patients to see tomorrow morning. You know how long a drive it is from Cabot Cove to Portland?"

"It's an even longer walk."

"So, how was the rest of your trip?"

"You wouldn't believe me if I told you, Seth."

"How many bodies?"

"Two."

"You're kidding."

"I only wish I was."

"I'll see you at the station," Seth told me.

When I arrived he was waiting at the track, instead of inside the terminal. I spotted him when I was scanning the crowd for the bald man. We met halfway.

"What's that, the sequel to *Moby-Dick*?" he asked, noticing the stack of pages I was struggling to hold under my arm, having left Lane Barfield's tote bag in my carry-on wheeler.

"It's part of the story."

"The one that has two bodies?"

"The very same." I nodded.

I told Seth everything on the long drive to Cabot Cove, filled him in from soup to nuts, including the presence of the bald man on the train from New York to Boston.

"You didn't see him again after you got off?"

"No."

He shook his head. "I don't know how you do it, Jess."

"Do what exactly?"

"Keep painting a bull's-eye on your forehead."

"Maybe you didn't hear the part about my publisher committing suicide after he paid a boatload for a book that doesn't seem to exist."

"That would be all those pages in the back seat, ayuh. Any good, is it? Worth all that money?"

I nodded. "I think it might have been, yes. It's as commercial as it gets. Lane Barfield always had great instincts."

"I imagine that's how he found you."

"It's going to feel strange working for someone else, Seth."

"What's next?"

"I still need to reach Alicia Bond, the other author I think Lane Barfield asked for a blurb for *The Affair.*"

"Lousy title. About as original as a sale at Macy's."

"Guess Lane was a believer in one of Sam Goldwyn's favorite sayings."

"What's that?"

"Give me the same thing, only different."

Nestled safely in my house, I was afraid my mind was still too much abuzz for me to fall asleep easily, so I figured I'd knock out some more of the manuscript until I finally nodded off.

The problem was I couldn't put it down, couldn't stop recharging the stack of pages I kept pulling from the pile. I kept telling myself just one more batch, just one more batch. I don't know how many times I resolved that, but I couldn't live up to my end of the bargain. Pace and Abby's adventures were outright intoxicating, the book jam-packed with incredible escapes, impossible coincidences, hints at a conspiratorial plot hatched from somewhere within the White

House, and action scenes that rivaled the best I'd ever read. Much too violent for my tastes, but then *The Affair* itself wasn't for my tastes. It wasn't the kind of book I'd probably ever pick up on my own, and yet I couldn't put it down, putting myself in Lane Barfield's shoes the first time he'd read the thing.

The pile of spent pages had at long last risen above those yet to be read when I came to a pivotal point that finally made the stakes, and Abby's plight, clear.

"Who's behind it?" I asked her from the other side of the diner booth.

"I don't know who they are. How many times do I have to tell you that?"

We were the only people in the diner, had made sure to take a table you couldn't see from the road or even the parking lot.

"Tell me who you think they are. Tell me what it is you heard that you weren't supposed to."

"My parents were talking."

Abby stopped. I decided to wait until she started talking again on her own, no pushing. I watched her swallow hard.

"They were talking about me. They weren't sure what to do."

"About what?"

"The truth."

"What truth?"

"The truth about me."

"Which is?"

She swallowed hard again. "I'm not their daughter."

I read that line three more times to make sure I had it right. Abby wasn't the president's daughter? Then whose daughter was she? And what did that have to do with the fate of the country, maybe even the world, hanging in the balance?

Only one way to find out.

"Years before," Abby continued, pulling the words harder than pulling teeth, "when they'd first gotten married, they learned they couldn't have children of their own, so they arranged for an adoption. Everything legitimate, aboveboard."

"Until it wasn't."

"They never knew the truth. It wasn't their fault," Abby insisted, as if trying to convince herself.

"What wasn't?"

"The adoption was anything but legitimate. Because my real mother hadn't given me up. I was stolen. Right out of the hospital. My parents were party to a kidnapping."

I'd lost my appetite, played with my scrambled eggs when the waitress finally brought them. Abby poured syrup on her pancakes but pushed the plate aside.

"What was it you heard them saying?"

"That somebody from all those years back had talked. That my real parents were coming to get me, that they were going to expose my parents as criminals who'd paid some thugs to steal me from my mother, from the hospital, when I was only a few days old."

"They weren't thugs."

"What?"

I hadn't realized I'd spoken the words under my breath. "I said they weren't just thugs."

"How can you know that?"

"Because the same thing happened to me. How do you think I ended up with the Guardians?"

Impossible coincidence, right? I didn't care. There it was, the inevitable connection that strains anything remotely approaching credulity. Both Pace and Abby had been kidnapped. She'd ended up in the White House and he'd ended up being trained as a killer, socialized with an entirely different set of norms and values. The flashback to his escape, intercut by Benjamin Tally with dreamlike snippets and lurid action that was all too real, was as harrowing a scene as I'd ever read. Pace forced to kill the adults he'd spent his entire life with. It was the only way he could get out. The book made a mess of morality but also made points about human strength as well as frailty, the ability of the spirit to survive as Pace's true nature emerged. A good person who'd been trained to do horrible things. Stolen from the hospital, just as Abby had been.

Stop and think about it too closely and the absurdity of it all comes through. You have to hold on tight to something to avoid falling through the plot holes. But the book was written at a rapid-fire clip designed not to give the readers any time to think and to involve us so deeply in the plight of the characters that we wouldn't care about the flaws that should have destroyed the book's integrity but instead came to define it. Who wants to think when there are more pages to flip and more things to make your jaw drop?

I read on.

Abby looked at me like I was stranger, like she was seeing me for the first time.

"Who are they?" she asked in somebody else's voice.

"What's the difference?"

"I want to know. These people who stole me from my real parents, who are they?"

"You already know."

"I know what they do."

"What they do is who they are."

"These . . . Guardians." She had trouble saying the word.

"They fill orders, support and manage their efforts with the money they raise from trafficking drugs, guns, people—pretty much anything. And they do it with people they trained as disciples. Mindless drones who exist to serve, like me."

"Not like you," Abby corrected. "You got away. You killed the men who came for me."

"Everybody makes mistakes, misjudgments, and they made one with me. It was my real parents who got me through the years. Thinking of them. Where they were, what they looked like, what they were doing. Did they still miss me? Was there an empty room in their house for when I finally came home? I promised I'd find them someday. That kept me going."

"My parents hired the Guardians."

"They didn't know who they were hiring."

"But they knew what they were doing, didn't they? They knew I was stolen from somebody else to be given to them."

"Probably." I nodded, circling my fork though my cooling plate of scrambled eggs. "You said your real parents had tracked you down, that they were going to expose the whole thing."

Abby was trembling on the other side of the table, her teeth chattering. This was when people needed to be hugged, comforted, but my training hadn't included that stuff. I just sat there stiffly, might still be sitting there if Abby hadn't resumed.

"That's what my parents were arguing about. How everything could be ruined, the scandal that would result. My mother was panicking and my father tried to calm her down. Told her she had nothing to worry about, that it had all been taken care of."

I knew what was coming next, could hear Abby's words even before she spoke them.

"My father had them killed."

Where had this story come from? It was so ridiculous, so incredible, so absurd, as to test the very limits of the imagination. One impossible revelation piled atop another. Whoever Benjamin Tally turned out to be, I'd never want to be inside his head.

My eyelids were so heavy, I literally had to hold them up, before fetching some eye drops to relieve the strain of reading while so exhausted. If I started to close my eyes, I'd be asleep before I finished. I checked the wall clock to find three hours had passed since I started reading, three hours that felt like three minutes. Just a few more pages, I promised myself, just a few more pages . . .

I had my answer, what Abby had overheard that had set all this off. She knew her father, the president, had first arranged to have her kidnapped from the hospital and then ordered her real parents killed to keep his deadly secret. And her mother had been a conspirator, to at least the original crime, and then one of the major forces behind her father's campaign, leading it, for all intents and purposes. She could expose the president as a criminal and murderer, and clearly his love of power had trumped his love for the daughter he must've wanted very badly.

As a prop.

That's all she was to him, something to wave around at political rallies so he could proclaim himself a true family man who supported the values that term suggested. And once she was killed—murdered, too— he would use the resulting national mourning and sympathy to further enamor the people with himself.

Instead of being led out of the White House in cuffs, he'd likely win reelection as president, a psychopath utterly devoid of feelings for anything but power and the furthering of his own villainous ends. What the Guardians had tried to train me to be, to relinquish my conscience in favor of the parameters of whatever missions they dispatched me on. I wondered if Abby's father might have preceded me in the program, a chill creeping up my spine as I considered the very real fact that his becoming president might have been part of a far more wide-reaching plot. If, effectively, the government of the United States had already been taken over and nobody knew it.

"What are we going to do?" Abby asked me.

I looked at her, my gaze as cold and dispassionate as I felt. "We're going to kill him."

It was the phone ringing that awoke me, the sun streaming upon me curled up on the couch, surrounded by pages of *The Affair*, which had sprayed everywhere when I'd lost my grasp. I'd started to bunch them back together when I heard the phone and snatched the cordless handset up from its cradle, not recognizing the number.

"Hello?" I managed, clearing my throat.

"Mrs. Fletcher?"

"Who is this, please?"

"It's Zara, Mrs. Fletcher, Lane Barfield's—"

"Of course. I'm sorry, Zara. It's just that you . . . What time is it?"

"Nine o'clock."

The latest I'd slept in years.

"I wanted to make sure you were okay."

"Got home safe and sound."

"It's not that. It's, it's . . ."

"What, Zara? What are you trying to say?"

"Did you reach A. J. Falcone? Had he read the book?"

"He said he hated it. Real piece of work, isn't he?"

"Mrs. Fletcher . . ."

"What's wrong, Zara? Talk to me."

"A. J. Falcone is dead."

Chapter Eleven

I felt my stomach drop, almost dropped the phone with it.

"Something about an accident in his barn," Zara was saying now, "with his horses. He was trampled to death."

My next thought was about Alicia Bond, whom I'd called twice yesterday, leaving a message on her voice mail. She hadn't called me back yet.

"Mrs. Fletcher?"

"I'm still here, Zara. Just trying to sort through all of this."

"What do you think is going on?"

"I don't know."

"Do you think what happened to A. J. Falcone was really an accident? Could it have been connected to Lane's death?"

I held fast to my composure. "Did you ever read Sherlock Holmes, Zara?"

"No," she said after a pause that, along with her tone, told me she found such a question posed in this context absurd.

"Holmes didn't believe in coincidence. He would have believed that three deaths in barely three days in such a circumstance had to bear a connection."

Zara had no response to that; I couldn't blame her. My mind was clearing, the fog of being jarred awake after such a fitful slumber swept aside like wipers sweeping across the windshield in a rainstorm.

"I need you to do something, Zara," I told her. "I need you to do it right now."

"Anything."

"I want all the contact information you have on file for Alicia Bond."

"You think . . ."

"I think she hasn't returned my calls yet. I think she was the other author Lane Barfield coaxed to read *The Affair*. We need to reach her, even if that means alerting the police."

"You believe she's in danger, too?"

"I didn't say that."

"Is it because of this book? Is all this happening because of *The Affair*?"

"I didn't say that, either."

I could hear her breathing and a sound like muffled sobbing on the other end of the line. "I checked all of Lane's files, backup drives, even the cloud. The manuscript is gone. Even in the places, by all rights, it should be. Who could be doing this, Mrs. Fletcher? *Why* would they be doing it?"

"I don't know, Zara."

"You've read the manuscript, haven't you?"

"I'm in the middle of it now," I responded, then veered to another subject to avoid having to elaborate. "What about the author, Benjamin Tally? Have you been able to turn up anything more on him?"

"Nothing," she said, and I could sense her shaking her head. "All trace of him has been wiped from the system, too. I went down to the contracts department myself this morning, Mrs. Fletcher. I figured you could erase an author's existence from our databases but not from people's memories. So I asked around."

"You did *what*?"

"Nobody in Contracts knew what I was talking about. They looked at me like I was crazy. They'd never heard of Benjamin Tally or *The Affair*. At least, that's what they claimed."

"Listen to me, Zara," I said in the sternest voice I could muster. "You're to do no such thing again. Is that clear? You're to do nothing else besides look up the contact information for Alicia Bond, until you speak with me first. Is that clear?" I repeated.

"Yes. Should I go home and call in sick?"

"No, absolutely not. If there really is someone behind all this, you don't want to do anything that draws attention. Just keep coming to work and holding down the fort. It's what Lane would've wanted and, I suspect, will go a long way toward solidifying your position in the company. We need to do this for him, Zara."

"I've got the information you asked for on Alicia Bond, Mrs. Fletcher."

*   *   *

The information Zara had just provided scribbled on a pad before me, I dialed Cabot Cove sheriff Mort Metzger's cell phone number.

"I just left Mara's. Already had breakfast."

"I wasn't calling about breakfast, Mort. Something's happening and I need your help. Call me back when you're behind your desk."

"Does this mean somebody's dead?"

Obviously, he hadn't spoken with Seth yet about what I'd shared with him on the ride from the train station last night. "Several somebodies. But I'm calling about another somebody who might be next."

"I'm just walking into my office now. Hold on."

I did, feeling my stomach twisting into knots, while I waited for Mort to come back on. Over the line I heard a door close, the rattle and squeak as he settled himself in the chair behind his desk.

"Okay, I'm ready."

"Ever hear of an author named Alicia Bond?"

"No. Should I have?"

"Her books were the basis for a crazily successful show on one of the pay cable stations."

"When's that going to happen to you, by the way?"

"Stick to the subject, Mort. We need to find Alicia Bond."

"I assume you tried calling her."

"No response," I said, shaking my head, even though Mort obviously couldn't see me.

"She's famous; what do you expect? And you have reason to believe she's in danger."

"Yes."

"Care to tell me why?"

"Because of a book."

He hesitated. "I'm going to leave things there."

"I've got phone numbers for her, her agent, her manager," I told Mort. "I've got addresses, too. I thought a call from you to the local authorities might enlist their help as well."

"One step at a time, Jessica. I have pen in hand. Give me everything and let me see what I can do."

I began reciting all the information from Zara that I'd jotted down.

Alicia Bond's real name was Margaret Bellucci. She'd eked out a career writing paperback romance bestsellers, until that market pretty much tanked. She became "Alicia Bond" when the first book of her wildly successful fantasy series was published, and she now owned four homes, including her first one, in Santa Fe, which I'd learned about from her bio.

But her primary residence was still located in Marblehead, Massachusetts, so I clung to the hope that she was reasonably close by, which would facilitate a meeting once Mort reached her. I took comfort in the fact that, at the very least, no report had surfaced of any harm having befallen her the way it had A. J. Falcone. Given the level of her celebrity, rare for an author until Hollywood comes calling, the gossip sites and traditional news channels would be all over a story pertaining to any major twist in her life. So no news, in this case, was definitely good news.

I'd never read any of the books in the series or watched the adaptations on cable. They weren't for me. Then again, neither was *The Affair*, and here I was seated on the couch next to a jumble of pages I'd read well more than half of and couldn't wait to get back to. The writing itself might not have been very good, but the story, for all its outlandishness, was utterly intoxicating. So maybe I needed to broaden my horizons, even try my hand at something capable of doing for readers what *The Affair* had done for me.

If only it were that simple. The fact was, laying the absurdities of the manuscript aside, there was something about *The Affair* I couldn't quite put my finger on. Occasionally, the *New York Times Book Review* asked me to pen a review of a book by a fellow mystery writer, and I always found myself wondering where a particular story originated. Something about *The Affair* had me wondering the same thing. I can't say why exactly, and there was no way to find out at this stage, but I felt the answer to that question was another piece of the puzzle that needed to be found.

My phone rang, Mort calling me back just under an hour after our conversation.

"Tell me you found Alicia Bond," I said as soon as I answered.

"Yes and no. Maggie—short for Margaret, as she's still known to her friends and associates—has been spending almost all her time at her home in Marblehead."

"Is she there now?"

"No."

"Damn!"

"You didn't let me finish, Jessica. She's not there, because she's *here*."

"Here *where*?"

"Maine. Hiking the woods of Acadia National Park, where she reserved one of those cabins in the middle of nowhere. According to her agent, who I was able to get on the phone, it helps clear her head. Kind of a ritual before she plunges into her next book. She left Marblehead yesterday and she planned on going dark the whole time."

"Explains why she never returned my calls."

"You ever consider doing something like that, retreating to the woods before you start your next book?"

"Since when did you figure me for channeling my inner Henry David Thoreau?"

"I was only asking, Jessica."

"Anyway, I have my own ritual. Almost the same thing."

"What's that?"

"I ride my bike to the ocean and back."

"Well," Mort said, after chuckling, "you don't want to ride your bike all the way to Acadia National Park and we won't get there fast enough by car."

"You install a transporter device in your office since the last time I was there, Mort?"

"No," he told me, "but I've got the next best thing standing by."

The next best thing turned out to be a state police helicopter. Mort picked me up twenty minutes later and we drove to a small airport a half hour away, getting there just after the chopper had landed to pick us up.

Mort was right. The drive to Acadia would've taken four hours; the helicopter ride took barely forty minutes. And there was a landing pad used occasionally by the park service within walking distance of the cabin Alicia Bond had reserved for her retreat. Had we driven, we would've had to hike a considerably greater distance to reach her, which, I suspected, was the whole point in the woman's mind.

I've never understood the notion of clearing one's head. For me, that's what happens when I write, so I have no need to seek it out before I write. I find my inspiration in the process itself, not in some remote cabin where I'd sit staring at the walls, accomplishing nothing more than wanting to leave.

As Mort and I walked across the tarmac toward the chopper, I tried not to think about how much I hated riding in helicopters. Anyone who tells you it's no different from driving or flying, even in a small airplane, is lying. It's pretty much a bumpy, jumpy, jarring trip, full of bounces up and down that make your stomach feel as if it somehow got left behind. I got nauseous every time I rode in one and had taken to swallowing Dramamine just to manage the worst of the symptoms. But I'd forgotten to take one today and didn't want to be left groggy in any event, given the task before us.

Climbing aboard, though, made me instantly regret my decision. I felt myself getting queasy as I buckled myself into the seat. Mort climbed in after me, regarding me with a wry look across the seats facing each other in the back of the cabin.

"I thought you were over that."

"Getting sick? Since when does anyone get over airsickness? At my age, I've outgrown everything I ever will, Mort."

"*Our* age, you mean."

"Except you don't turn yellow on helicopter rides."

"Which reminds me," he said, reaching into the pocket of his uniform jacket, complete with a sheriff's badge, "here you go."

And he handed me one of those airline barf bags.

Chapter Twelve

Acadia National Park was beautiful from any angle, but especially from above. The forty-seven-thousand-acre marvel of the Atlantic coastline was marked by deep forests, rock-strewn beaches, and ice-crusted granite peaks like that of Cadillac Mountain, the highest peak within twenty-five miles of the entire East Coast, stretching well above the nearest contenders. Locals and tourists who frequented Acadia to mix with the abundant wildlife often stayed over at the seaside town of Bar Harbor, its trendy restaurants and shops forming an odd juxtaposition to the pristine national park. Call it the spoils of nature versus the spoils of shopping.

The chopper's cruise over all that natural beauty almost relieved the nausea that had left me closing my eyes and taking regular deep breaths to avoid having to use Mort's barf bag. It didn't help that Mort wouldn't leave me alone.

"None of this makes sense, Jessica. I think you've finally cracked up and are living out one of your books."

"So I killed Thomas Rudd and then arranged for a horse to trample A. J. Falcone."

"Well." Mort frowned. "You did have a motive for killing Falcone."

"What's that?"

"He sells more books than you."

I readied the barf bag. "I think I'm going to be sick. . . ."

"Your sales aren't down that much, are they? Also, there's nothing in the official police report that mentions murder in the Rudd investigation."

"Not yet," I countered, finding it odd that Artie Gelber had opted to have that wrinkle in the case omitted.

"And I spoke to the police who investigated the scene at Falcone's ranch. Unless somebody turned a horse into a hit man, it was an accident."

"You're so gullible, Mort."

"You mean somebody did turn a horse into a hit man? That's a neat trick, even for your books. Are they getting that stale?"

I let him see me feign a near heave. "Keep at it, Mort. Keep at it."

"I'm sorry about your publisher. Seth told me," he said instead.

"Ever heard of the book *The Name of the Rose* by Umberto Eco?"

"I think I saw the movie. Sean Connery, right? Set during the Inquisition."

"That's the one. Both centered on a book that by all indications kills everyone who reads it."

"I don't remember that part."

"Anyway, it turned out the pages were poisoned to protect a secret the book contained."

Mort nodded, either understanding or pretending that he did. "And you think this book your publisher purchased for a ton of money *kills* anyone who reads it?"

"I'm reading it and I'm still alive, although not for much longer if we don't land soon."

"Any good?"

"I can't put it down."

"Anybody say that about your books anymore, Jessica?"

"When's your term up as sheriff again?"

"I'm appointed, not elected. Talk to the mayor and board of selectmen, as soon as we get home after finding this Alicia Bond, Margaret Bellucci, or whatever her real name is."

"It's Margaret Bellucci," I told him, still holding the barf bag at the ready.

"Bet she sells better than you, too, doesn't she? I do believe we have a pattern emerging here."

"Thomas Rudd didn't sell better than I."

"Thomas Rudd blew himself up."

"No, somebody made it *look* like Thomas Rudd blew himself up."

Mort stopped to ponder what I'd just said. "Or maybe somebody left those clues behind on purpose to get you to believe exactly what you're spouting off now."

"Got a theory as to why they'd do such a thing?"

"I'm still working on that."

"Right, convincing."

"More convincing than a book that kills, Jessica, whether because of what's on the pages or what's in them."

The state police helicopter angled its descent for the landing pad on Mount Cadillac in the forestlands of Acadia National Park. I took the opportunity to dramatically toss the empty barf bag into Mort's lap. "Looks like you need that more than I."

"And why's that?"

"Because me proving you wrong is going to make you sick."

I turned out to be only half-right.

The landing pad turned out to be a good mile's walk from the nest of isolated cabins where Alicia Bond, aka Margaret Bellucci, was staying. No easy trek through woods as deep as the ones in which we found ourselves, especially climbing a steep uphill grade. I had dressed properly in slacks and the lace-up Timberland boots I wore in winter. But nothing could prepare me for the bite of the stiff wind and, worse, the effects of the altitude on the breathing of someone not used to being above sea level. The beauty of the natural landscape we were trudging through diminished in the face of the toll the exertion was taking on me.

I'd read on the Internet that even before she became

publishing superstar Alicia Bond, Margaret Bellucci had been an accomplished outdoorswoman, having scaled some of the tallest peaks in the world and spent time in the farthest reaches the globe had to offer. I'd read that's how she'd come up with the concept for the fantastical land portrayed in her mega-selling series of books. She'd become the rare recognizable literary star, and the rugged nature of her hobbies only added to her mystique.

"You need to stop?" Mort asked, not bothering to cloak the concern in his voice.

"If we stop now," I said, heaving for breath a bit, "we might as well stop every ten feet."

"In which case we should reach Alicia Bond's cabin sometime tomorrow."

"So let's keep going."

We hadn't brought canteens, leaving us with only the bottled water we'd packed, three bottles between us. I stopped checking my watch after twenty minutes that saw us cover half the ground to the cabin the writer who now called herself Alicia Bond had rented. But the forest floor leveled off a bit after that and we began to make better time and I found myself no longer needing to pull myself along by grabbing tree branches for support.

Finally, Mort and I caught our first glimpse of the cabin his GPS had led us to. If Alicia Bond's people had been right about her precise whereabouts, our quest was almost over, with a less taxing, but more precarious, trek downhill back to the helicopter still ahead. I cringed at the thought of something keeping us here after nightfall, unable to imagine managing that effort in the dark, absent flashlights.

But the plan was to collect Alicia Bond straightaway and bring her back with us to civilization. It may sound strange, but I was really looking forward to discussing *The Affair* with her. Had she come away from her read the same way I was coming away from mine? Had she been similarly enraptured and entranced by the plight of young characters on the run, and the concept behind that even higher than this mountain upon which we were about to find her?

Mort eased an arm to keep me behind him as we mounted the cabin steps. For the first time in all the years I'd known him I think, I saw him hitch back his police jacket to free his pistol to draw more readily should he need to. Channeling his inner John Wayne again, no doubt, just as he had when he rose from his chair to keep a drunken Thomas Rudd at bay three days ago.

Had it been only *three days*? The intensity was unrivaled by anything I'd ever experienced. Three deaths, a manuscript I might well have the last copy of in existence, a writer known only by his pen name, and that mysterious bald-headed man I remained certain had been watching me on the train from New York to Boston. That was enough story to fill any three of my books, never mind one. Which in the last moment before Mort knocked on the cabin door brought me around to a notion I hadn't sufficiently considered before now:

What if somebody didn't want *The Affair* to be published?

I'd avoided that question because it led to a hundred more. Like some vast infinity mirror where there was no end, only a continuous repetition of the beginning.

"Mrs. Bond," Mort called, rapping on the polished plank door. "It's the police, Mrs. Bond. Please open the door."

"Wasn't a park ranger supposed to meet us here?"

"I thought so," Mort said, giving Alicia Bond a few more moments to respond and then sweeping his gaze about as if he expected it to capture the park ranger miraculously appearing out of the woods.

"She's not married. Try calling her 'Ms.' instead."

Mort looked miffed. "You think that's why she's not answering the door?"

"Just try it."

"Ms. Bond," Mort said, pounding harder on the door. Still nothing.

"Any more brilliant ideas?"

"Try her real name."

"Ms. or Mrs.?"

"Mrs. Monica Bellucci is divorced."

I slid over to the nearest window, which was covered by curtains, then another, which wasn't. I peered inside and glimpsed what looked like a—

That was as far as I got in my thinking.

"Mort!" I meant to say quietly, but it came out in more of a shriek.

"What?" he asked, shoes pounding atop the plank porch, which smelled of pine.

I pointed toward the window, watched Mort cup a hand over his brow to better focus on the interior. He turned toward me from it, rotating only his neck.

"Well, at least we know what happened to the park ranger."

The ranger lay with his limbs askew on the floor, bullet holes in both his chest and his head. Same with Alicia Bond, who lay half on and half off the bed. A trio of kerosene lanterns, the only witnesses to what had happened here, flickered in rhythm with our movements.

"The ranger was shot outside and dragged in here," Mort said, kneeling by his body. "He's got pine needles and ground brush all over his clothes. A bit of exploration and we can probably find the exact spot where he was killed."

"We?"

"You didn't just come along for the ride, Jessica, did you?"

I looked at the walkie-talkie clipped to his belt as he stood back up. "Who are you supposed to call about this?"

"It's park ranger jurisdiction. For all intents and purposes, they're the law in these parts."

I looked down at the body clad in green uniform and jacket. "Not right now."

Mort followed my gaze. "When it comes to serious crimes, the FBI has jurisdiction," he said, and reached for his walkie-talkie.

True to his word, and because neither of us wanted to stay cooped up with the bodies, Mort showed me the spot, about sixty feet away, at the edge of the clearing in which the cabin rested, where the park ranger had been killed. I imagined the man putting up his hands as his killer approached, the two shots that followed punching him backward and knocking him to the ground. Based on the limited blood spill, he was probably dead by the time he hit it or moments after. Whoever had killed him and Alicia Bond were clearly professionals, well trained and practiced at this.

Something that was in keeping with *The Affair*, in the form of the army of killers pursuing Pace and Abby.

Was I cracking up, living in a book instead of writing one? Was all this even happening?

"We'll be on our way as soon as we square things with the FBI," Mort said suddenly. "We don't want to be up here after dark, and with these winds building, we don't want to be forced to spend the night."

"We certainly don't," I agreed, feeling a need more than ever to finish that manuscript, perhaps to see what else awaited me.

"To repeat your earlier question: What in that book could have caused all this?" Mort asked me.

"I said that? I didn't just form the thought in my mind?"

Mort shrugged. "Maybe we both did. Maybe that's why I remember you saying it."

A twig or something snapped nearby, and he went for his gun, quicker than I'd ever seen him do anything. Only then did I realize he'd already unfastened the safety strap.

"Jumpy, aren't we?"

"I don't think we missed the killer by much; the author and ranger haven't been dead for more than two hours."

"You think the killers might still be about?"

"Depends if they wanted to see who might show up."

"In which case, they would've probably still been inside when we got here."

"Hey, my imagination isn't quite as developed as yours."

"Oh no?" I looked at his hand still lingering close to the butt of his pistol. "Have you actually drawn that outside of the range?"

"This?" he said, following my gaze. "No."

"What about another gun?"

He took a deep breath but didn't seem to finish it. "I was in Vietnam, Jessica."

I could feel my eyes bulging out of my head. "You never mentioned that before."

"I never mention it at all. And, by the way, I haven't been to the range since I became sheriff of Cabot Cove. I've done enough shooting for a lifetime, without sharpening my skills on cardboard."

I could tell that was about as far as Mort was going to go with this, and I couldn't blame him. It had gotten appreciably cooler, the midafternoon warmth beginning to bleed from the air, when Mort and I turned our eyes upward toward a helicopter that must've been carrying investigators dispatched by the FBI in Boston descending toward the landing pad and disappearing below the tree line.

"Won't be long now," Mort said, but I wasn't exactly sure what he meant.

We were there for three more hours, coming dangerously close to sunset, to the point that Mort borrowed a pair of flashlights from the FBI agents to help guide us through the forest that rimmed the mountain back to the plateau that held the helipad. The agents inspected the entire cabin in painstaking fashion, grousing over both jurisdictional issues and the challenge of getting a crime scene unit to the scene.

Mort and I had already discussed the fact that we couldn't reveal the true reason behind our coming here, could make no mention of all that had transpired previously that had led to this point.

"So," an agent asked us, chewing on a mint I realized was a Rolaids tablet when he twisted another out of the pack and popped it into his mouth, "this was a social call?"

"The victim and I shared the same publisher," I said, telling the truth.

"I asked what brought you up here." The agent's gaze fell on Mort. "With the local sheriff in tow."

"We weren't actually coming up here strictly to see Ms. Bond," I said, making up the lie on the spot.

"No?"

I let him see me grab Mort's hand. "We came because she recommended this spot, another cabin just over the ridge."

"And you came by helicopter?"

"Comes with the job," Mort said without hesitation, hand stiff in mine.

The agent didn't look at all happy with our answers, but he also had no reason to hold us any longer, since we clearly weren't suspects.

"Did Alicia Bond have any enemies?" he asked before dismissing us.

"I couldn't say."

"Because you didn't know her well enough?"

I turned my gaze back on the cabin. "Apparently not."

The agent nodded and walked away without saying another word, and moments later Mort and I were on our way back to the helicopter, flashlights sweeping about to cut through the twilight.

"Want to hold hands again?" Mort asked me after we settled into our trek, his eyes checking our surroundings for far more than exposed roots.

"Only if we get your wife's permission. Tell her I have a thing for war heroes."

He bristled a bit at me calling him that. "There'll be hell to pay if she finds out we're having an affair."

"Is that a fact?"

"Well, it would make a pretty juicy rumor."

I rolled my eyes. "I can see Evelyn Phillips's headline in the *Cabot Cove Gazette* now."

"Gossip travels fast in a small town."

"Gossip travels fast everywhere, Mort. The twenty-four-seven news cycle has brought the world into everyone's bedroom."

"Not sure if I like the view. Meanwhile, I just want to see if I've got this right, Jessica," he said. "You believe two other authors who were given the manuscript, an author who accidentally stole it, and the publisher who discovered it are all dead?"

"That sums things up neatly. But you didn't need me to tell you that."

"No. I need you to tell me if you're afraid you might be next."

Chapter Thirteen

Of course I was. I don't have a death wish and I wasn't born with the proverbial danger gene. I sometimes get myself in trouble and put myself at risk when I try to help someone. Here I guess I was helping Lane Barfield; if there was more to his suicide than met the eye, circumstances yet undiscovered, I owed it to him to continue investigating.

It all came back to that manuscript; the murders of Alicia Bond and the park ranger seemed to confirm that, leaving very little doubt. The ranger must have stumbled upon the scene, perhaps after Alicia Bond had already been shot, but more likely before, her killers lying in wait when he'd stumbled upon them and paid for the terrible timing with his life. The very definition of the wrong place at the wrong time. The ranger did carry a revolver, but we'd found it still in its holster with the safety strap fastened.

I was scared and glad to be scared, because the primary effect of the fear was to make me even more determined to find the people who now posed an undeniable threat to my life. Living alone, I was terribly close to banishing the fear of death from my psyche. I guess coming upon as many bodies as I had at crime scenes had left me inoculated against the way most viewed and feared death. Personally, I fear killers getting away with murder much more. Hemingway once said that the world is a fine place and worth fighting for. My refusal to accept evil in the world was my version of that fight. A lot of times the impetus for such came from some personal motivation, but beyond that it was about seeing justice done. That might sound like a cliché, but I honestly believe it, and it's as close to a life mantra as I've got.

People often asked me how I became a writer. I tell them it dates back to a day in my childhood when I found on the side of the road a dead dog that had been hit by a car. Whoever had killed him hadn't bothered pulling over to see if he could be saved or to check his tag for a phone number. I found that number and called it myself as soon as I got home.

I think that was the hardest thing I'd ever done, so hard that it wasn't enough to cover the dog with my coat and call its owners. I had to find out who'd struck him with their car, so I began walking up the long street I lived on, checking the front bumpers and tires on each and every car for blood, fur, or some other indication that its owner was the guilty party. Even though my search continued all the way to dark and then after it with the help of a flashlight, I never did find that car.

The death of that dog became my first case, and to

this day I believe it's the source of my fascination with mystery and seeing justice done, even though I never found the culprit. I wonder if things might've been different if I'd found a car with blood and fur on its front bumper or tires all those years ago. Would that have ended my obsession with crime before it even started? Had every investigation I'd undertaken since, both in fact and in fiction, been nothing more than my subconscious trying to find the person who left that dog on the side of the road?

Questions better posed to a therapist, I suppose. I've never visited one myself, for two reasons, mainly: First, the process of writing serves as my therapy, and second, I've always believed all writers are inherently crazy, eccentric at the very least. You might say that, other than hit men and assassins, mystery writers are the only people who kill for a living.

"I'm going to post a man outside your house," Mort said as we walked back to his car after landing at the private airfield outside Cabot Cove.

I noticed construction workers laying two new runways and extending an older one. Efforts were also under way to fully renovate and expand the terminal, further indication of the outside world leaving a larger and larger mark on what once had been our quaint little village. Much of the work here was scheduled to be completed before the start of what promised to be Cabot Cove's busiest summer ever. I'd heard from the town's top Realtor, Eve Simpson, that every single summer rental property she managed was already spoken for, whereas most years early May would find Eve with at least a third and as much as half to fill. We were fast becoming trendy, a land-based Martha's Vineyard or Nantucket and, God help us, New England's version of the Hamptons.

As I said, God help us.

"You told me that already," I said to Mort.

"That I was going to put a man on your house?"

I nodded. "But you never told me you were in Vietnam."

"You never asked."

"It's not something likely to come up in conversation."

"My point exactly, Jessica. I didn't tell my wife, either, until after I married her. It was a long time ago and better left alone."

"If you say so. It's just that I've never pictured you as anything other than the sheriff of Cabot Cove."

"There are a lot of days I feel the same way, like I never had a life until I got here. Maybe I have you to thank for that."

"How's that, Mort?"

"I've been involved in more murder cases in this job than all twenty-five years I spent with the NYPD. I lost count a long time ago. I heard the board of selectmen are entertaining a proposal to rezone your house into a neighboring town, because you're driving property values down."

"Not a bad idea, given that ordinary people can't afford to live here anymore."

We reached his SUV just as thunder rumbled somewhere off in the distance, a cool breeze the first indication of the cold front forecasters said would be coming through, dragging a storm behind it.

"Let's get you home before the storm comes, unless there's somewhere else you'd rather I drop you."

"Home's fine," I told Mort. "I've got some reading to do."

But Mort wasn't finished yet.

"Who else knows you have a copy of the manuscript?" he asked once we'd pulled out of the airport, driving straight into the flare of lightning on the horizon.

"Lane Barfield's assistant."

"That's it?"

"Well, besides you, Harry McGraw."

"No one else?"

"None that I can think of," I said, racking my brain. "Oh, and Seth Hazlitt, of course."

"Is there anything you don't tell him?"

"I told him the same stuff I told you."

"Except I'm the sheriff."

"And he's my doctor."

"Yeah," Mort groused, "murder is bad for one's health."

Mort stayed with me at my house until my babysitter for the night, the officer I affectionately called Deputy Andy, arrived in his cruiser and parked it at the end of my driveway to discourage anyone who might be driving by from doing anything more than that. I programmed his number into my cell phone so I could reach him easily.

Deputy Andy's arrival seemed to bring the storm along for the ride. It had been building since we'd left the airport and now the lightning and thunder came in full force, accompanied by a howling wind and driving rain that rattled the windows and made the big house feel as if it were lifting off its foundation around me. I've never feared or hated storms the way a lot of people do, even the occasional raging Maine blizzard. I loved nothing more than using the storm as an excuse to read, hopefully something intense and scary to complete the mood.

The Affair certainly qualified there.

Mort's very real concern over my potentially becoming the next victim of this manuscript for murder left me wondering how anyone else could've learned I had *The Affair* in my possession. There had been no phone call or e-mail with an attachment, as had likely been the case with both A. J. Falcone and Alicia Bond. Lane hadn't been expecting me to show up at his office when I did, and he handed me the manuscript on a whim, an untraceable hard copy instead of an e-mail attachment that left a trail. The only person who knew that was Zara, and I certainly had no reason to suspect she was complicit in any of this.

I was about to dig back into the manuscript when my phone rang, a number I didn't recognize with a Manhattan area code lighting up in the caller ID.

"Hello?"

"It's Herb Mason, Jessica," my trusty accountant said in greeting.

"Oh, Herb, I didn't recognize this number."

"It's my office, and I don't think I've ever called you from my office. Anyway, I have some news about this royalty issue you raised."

"Good or bad?"

"I'll leave that to you. I ran a comparison check with the statements of other authors this firm handles. Bottom line: There is no issue."

"Meaning . . . ?"

"Meaning the royalties for the digital editions of your books jibe with the statements issued from other imprints. There's no anomaly here at all, and I imagine a detailed forensic audit of your publisher's records would come to the same conclusion."

The news sunk in quickly, filling me with a hefty measure of relief. I hated even considering the notion that Lane Barfield might have been engaged in some form of financial malfeasance and now found myself feeling guilty I'd suspected him. I'd been a fool for listening to the drunken claims of Thomas Rudd; then again, if I hadn't at least listened, I wouldn't be poised to uncover the truth behind Lane's death, and Rudd's, for that matter.

"Thanks, Herb," I heard myself saying.

"It's me who should be thanking you, Jessica, for the crash course I needed to get on digital publishing. Your world has really changed, hasn't it?"

"Hasn't everything, Herb?"

I hung up, my thoughts veering back to how anyone could possibly have known I had a copy of *The Affair* in my possession. I couldn't chase from my mind the presence of the bald man on the train and couldn't say why, either. I should've forgotten all about him when there'd been no sign of him on the train to Portland or in Boston's South Station, before I made the transfer. But he clung to my memory, something about the way he looked at me and then switched his seat to move closer.

I felt like Pace and Abby in *The Affair*, my enemies lurking behind every darkened corner.

"How?" Abby asked me. "He's the president. It's the White House. It's impossible."

"You forget I've been trained to kill."

"You'll have to get close enough first."

"And for that I'll need your help. You are still his daughter."

"He wants me dead."

"I repeat, you are still his daughter. He still loves you."

She looked at me like she found that funny. Then her expression turned to anger, frustration, or, more likely, both. "You don't understand," Abby said, her tone reeking of condescension. "You can't understand."

"You're right. I don't understand, I can't understand, because I wasn't raised by a mother and a father."

Abby nodded. "You really think you can do it? You really think you can kill the president of the United States?"

"That's the plan."

I'd picked up right where I'd left off, and the pace of the manuscript refused to let up. No lulls, no slow spots, the motion constant. For Abby to live, her father, the president of the United States, needed to die. So Benjamin Tally had turned us into her accomplices, rooting for Pace to succeed and ready to cheer once he did. I seldom had to face such moral dilemmas in my own books, but life was full of them, if not defined by them. The mark of great popular fiction is that it adds just that kind of subtext.

But I wasn't reading *The Affair* for subtext. I was reading it because I was starting to think that somewhere inside this manuscript, mired within the content, was the reason why Thomas Rudd, A. J. Falcone, Alicia Bond, and perhaps even Lane Barfield had been murdered. I stopped for a moment, to collect my thoughts, sort through the more technical aspects outside of Pace and Abby's taut exchanges that might hold the clue to what I was looking for. Say Benjamin Tally was a Washington insider and this book was a roman à clef, a novel about real life overlaid with a facade of fiction.

Maybe I'd find the secret it was hiding in the next section of the manuscript, I thought, reaching that penultimate moment when Abby and Pace are about to infiltrate the White House.

"You mean the tunnels beneath the White House are real?"

Abby nodded. "The Secret Service took us on a tour the day we moved in. The tour came with a history lesson but I wasn't paying a lot of attention to that part. I remember something about the British burning the original White House in 1814 and the tunnels being built under the one I used to live in to make sure the president could escape in the event of an attack."

"Makes sense," I said.

"Anyway, the tour included showing us where one of the tunnels spills out. I'm pretty sure I could find the spot that's located somewhere in Lafayette Park."

"Pretty sure?"

"It's obviously camouflaged so it could never be used to sneak in. And it's not like it's a regular door with a knob and a lock. Even if I can find the exit, I'm not sure we'll be able to open it."

"Leave that to me."

"And you'll kill my father?"

I nodded. "If it's the only way to save you."

Abby's stare turned distant. "If I tried to just go back home, I'd disappear, like the ones who didn't make it where you grew up."

"It was an old farm. And they actually called it the Farm."

"Ironic, given they were raising a different kind of crop."

"Maybe that was the point."

"How'd you fool them?" she asked me.

"By always doing what I was supposed to. Playing the game."

"I tried that, too. It worked until I overheard the truth about what my parents had done."

"We all have our breaking points," I told her.

I had to keep reminding myself I was reading for more than pleasure. But if there were any clues as to what had led to four people being killed, five including the park ranger, I was clearly missing them. Could it have something to do with how Abby and Pace ended up infiltrating the White House? I hadn't gotten to that yet and there was still a big chunk of the manuscript left to read, so the clues could be anywhere.

I read quickly for a stretch, getting to the part when they were inside the secret escape tunnel beneath the White House, steering toward it instead of away.

Abby recalled the spot in Lafayette Park where the emergency tunnel beneath the White House spilled out as soon as we got there. Turned out a secret doorway had been included in the construction of the monument to Major General Friedrich Wilhelm von Steuben. It took me a few minutes, especially since I didn't want to draw attention to us by shining a flashlight for too long in the darkness. The door wasn't meant to open from the outside, but I managed to create enough of a gap along the granite frame to free the latch and push it inward.

It took every bit of strength I had to make it budge and almost as much to seal it again behind us once we were inside the tunnels I had thought were a myth. The winding, circuitous route beneath the White House smelled like a place nobody ever used, because nobody ever did. I tried to keep Abby directly behind me, shielded by my frame, so in the event there were security cameras they would pick up only me. If we were found out and they came for us, the plan was for her to run. Even if my road ended here, I could still buy her the time she needed to escape again.

But my road wasn't going to end here. As we wound our way through the serpentine swirl of the tunnel beneath the most secure building on the planet, I started to realize there must really be some kind of cosmic plan out there. This day, this moment, was what I'd been raised for. To save myself by saving someone else. To find value in what the Guardians had turned me into.

I never wondered who my real parents were. What was the point? I was never going to see them again. Even when I managed to get out, I harbored no aspirations of tracking them down and trying to resume a life I'd never really had. My parents had surely moved on.

And now I had, too.

For the first time since starting the manuscript, I skimmed ahead, unable to wait any longer to get to the part where Abby confronts her father, the president. I didn't believe Pace was going to kill him, which heightened the level of suspense even more.

Finally I reached the section I'd been racing to find, sat up straighter on the couch, and tightened the pages on my lap into a neat pile before reading on. I didn't care how they'd gotten into the Oval Office, where they found the president, Abby's father, hunched behind the historic desk nursing a bottle of bourbon. I cared only about what happened once they got there, the confrontation I'd been long awaiting finally here.

I watched the president rise and face Abby, his daughter who wasn't really his daughter, and lock stares from across the Oval Office. The two of them standing like statues, each waiting for the other to move. I stayed where I was; I owed it to Abby to leave what came next to her and then back her up any way I could.

"I want to know who my real parents are," she said in a soft, flat tone.

Her father swallowed hard, making me think of the fact that I had no parents, fake or otherwise, to go back to. The Guardians were my parents and I wasn't going back to them. In fact, in my mind coming here tonight was about destroying them. How many boys had they killed during my tenure? Was I spared the same fate only because they believed I was a success story, top of my class?

"Make me understand why you did this," Abby said, her voice turning harsh. "Make me understand why you sent those men to kill me, your own daughter. But I'm not really your daughter, am I?"

"These people who tried to kill you, they're the ones calling the shots. They always were from the beginning." He stopped, then started again immediately. "Get out while you still can. Run away and keep running."

His eyes fell on me. He looked as if he had something to say but spoke no words in my direction, before Abby chimed in.

"And I'm supposed to believe you? After all this, I'm supposed to take you at your word?" She shook her head. "Sorry, Dad, that ship has sailed. You're the goddamn president, commander in chief. Call the army, the navy, the air force, the marines. Declare war on these SOBs."

The president stepped close enough to reach out and touch Abby, but he stopped short of doing so. "Who do you think runs the military? The FBI, the Secret Service?" He shook his head, a beaten man. "I can't stop them now. No one can stop them now."

"We'll see about that," I said.

I'd reached that point where my conscious mind had surrendered, no sense I was even flipping pages anymore. The real world no longer existed. There was only Pace, Abby, the Guardians, the president, and what sounded like a plot to take over the government, the country. I couldn't wait to reach over and grab a fresh stack of pages from the top of what remained of the manuscript.

And that's when the lights died.

Chapter Fourteen

A single plug-in emergency light snapped on in the hallway that divided the kitchen from the living room, a second one snapping on in the upstairs foyer, neither making much of a dent in the darkness that had descended upon me. Suddenly, the unrestrained fury of the pounding storm revealed itself beyond the windows curtained by rain under the deluge.

I could see well enough to make my way toward the front window of my house and peered out toward the Cabot Cove squad car parked at the end of the driveway. A flash of lightning revealed a shape behind the wheel, Deputy Andy standing vigil, but I couldn't tell if he was awake or conscious. I hit his number on my cell phone, but it rang unanswered, making me fear the worst. If the loss of power had been caused by men dispatched by whoever was behind the deaths of A. J. Falcone and Alicia Bond, maybe Lane Barfield and Thomas Rudd, too, then I might be walking straight into their arms if I rushed outside to Deputy Andy. Maybe that was what they wanted me to do.

Then I heard the patter of footsteps in the kitchen and realized that wasn't their plan at all.

I discerned two distinct sets and had the presence of mind to tuck the final third of the manuscript, which I'd yet to read, beneath the couch, leaving the rest of the pages scattered on the cushion. Hopefully, my intruders would see those pages and gather them up without ever thinking there were more. Maybe that was all they'd come for, and they'd spare me once they had the pages in their possession.

Fat chance, given I was a risk for the same reason their other victims had been: I had read the manuscript, had the clues that might explain whatever plot *The Affair* threatened to reveal. Whoever Benjamin Tally was, he had somehow included something all too real in this commercial, surefire bestseller. Perhaps he'd done that inadvertently; perhaps he hadn't. It didn't matter right now and I fully suspected that Harry McGraw's search for the real Benjamin Tally was futile, since Tally was likely dead now, too.

Once the remainder of the manuscript was safe, I padded quickly toward the stairs in my stocking feet, the shadows of movement just curling past the wall the intruders would have to pass on their way from the kitchen. They'd clearly gained entry through the back door and I didn't need to rush outside into the storm to know they must have dealt with Deputy Andy beforehand, which explained why he hadn't answered his phone.

I didn't have a gun, didn't have any weapons upstairs any more than I did downstairs. I took the cell phone from my pocket and dialed 911, then returned the phone to the pocket of my sweater to muffle any voice that answered my call.

I made it upstairs, having already rejected any possible flight through a second-floor window. There was no tree branch I could conveniently grab hold of, and any drop from that height would surely leave me incapacitated, or potentially even do my intruders' job for them.

I figured I had fifteen, twenty seconds at most to do something, anything. I entered my bedroom but didn't close the door, so the room would look exactly like the others up here. Sooner or later, at least one of them would poke his head in ahead of coming through. If I could incapacitate him, that would leave me with only one to deal with, doubling my odds of survival.

What's two times zero again?

I could hear shoes grazing the oriental runner that wound up the stairs, grabbed the first potential weapon I spotted—my favorite leather belt with the heavy brass buckle. I stationed myself just to the right of the open doorway, satisfied nothing that might betray my presence was visible from the hallway or upstairs foyer.

The single emergency light up here cast just enough light to splay an approaching shadow across the jamb, so I squeezed the doubled-over belt tighter, with the heavy buckle hanging low beneath my waist. When the shadow took on the elongated shape of a man, I lashed out with the buckle, spinning toward my target to push more force into the strike.

The buckle impacted against the man's temple through the ski mask he was wearing. It stunned him, sent him reeling, making him vulnerable enough for me to pounce, if a second, nearly identical figure hadn't been directly behind him. I tried to bring the buckle up and around again, but the second figure snatched the leather of the belt out of midair and launched himself onto me.

I felt myself being twisted around, weightless against the force of his brute strength. His gloved hand closed over my mouth and nose. I smelled rank perspiration and unwashed clothes before he succeeded in closing off my air. I fought back with everything I had, pinwheeling with him across the room.

"Get her down! Get her down!" I heard the attacker I'd struck with the belt buckle cry out.

Before the one holding me could do that, though, I managed to shove his gloved hand into my mouth and bit down with all the force I could muster. My teeth sank through leathery fabric damp with sweat, and I heard him gasp in pain when they finally found flesh. He jerked away, leaving me free for a moment with the glove caught between my teeth. But he came after me again before I could even spit it out, his bare hand going for my collar.

Again I fought back, but I still hadn't caught all of my breath. I felt powerless under the force of his strength and momentum, shoved backward and down until I was doubled over atop my bedcovers in the last moment before the second man covered my face with a pillow.

I regained consciousness and realized I couldn't move. My first thought was that I'd been drugged, but as my senses cleared I realized I'd been tied to the chair in my bedroom.

Just as Thomas Rudd had been in the kitchen of his Tribeca apartment before his killers rigged the gas explosion that had killed him.

I struggled to free my arms and legs, thinking again of Rudd, but that seemed only to tighten my bonds. Whoever these men were, they clearly knew their way around knots.

Then I smelled the smoke. I caught it wafting in beneath my bedroom door and thought I could feel the heat building beneath my stocking feet on the floor.

They'd left me alive so I could perish in the fire they'd set, another strange death that would never be adequately explained. I thought of poor Alicia Bond and figured shooting her had never been the plan, until the park ranger showing up unexpectedly altered her killers' original intention. I wondered what they'd really had in store for her, in keeping with a gas explosion, a suicide, being trampled to death, and now a house fire. All deaths that would eventually be shrugged off for lack of evidence, especially since the one thing that bound the victims together was a manuscript that for all intents and purposes no longer existed. The only copy left of *The Affair* would soon burn away to nothing, the secrets it held gone forever to form a collective epitaph for the victims those secrets had claimed.

I screamed and screamed for help, stopping only when the smoke started to pool and thicken. I tried to scream again and ended up with a lungful of coarse smoke that left me coughing and retching. I didn't know if it was my imagination that conjured the heat of the flames building downstairs, but I was sure I felt it nonetheless. Just as there was no mistaking the rising amber glow in the crack between the floor and the bottom of the door as the fire gained strength, soon to consume this floor.

The smoke was going to kill me before the fire got its chance, my breath starting to clog in my throat as I somehow formed the thought that Jessica Fletcher, mystery writer and amateur sleuth, had been done in by a mystery she couldn't solve. That didn't seem fair.

Consciousness came and went in fits and starts, whatever strength I'd originally mustered to thrash against my bonds sapped. Every breath I chanced poured blistering heat down my throat and left me coughing anew. My last thought before I passed out, strangely, was that I wasn't coughing anymore, because I couldn't breathe at all. I felt myself thrashing again, more death throes than desperation, and realized my eyes were burning horribly even though they were closed.

I tried to scream one last time, to no avail, as I felt myself lifted upward, rising straight toward the ceiling. All that was missing was the proverbial bright light.

Then I realized it was a pair of powerful arms that had hoisted me, not some heavenly force. I felt jolted and jarred as feet pounded down the stairs, carrying me on through the building red heat of the downstairs that made me feel as if I'd pressed up against the side of a hot oven. But then there was the feeling of coolness and the blessed soak of rain pelting my superheated skin like a fire hose. I felt something soft, spongy, and wet and realized the same set of powerful arms had lowered me to the grass.

I was finally able make my eyelids flutter open, my vision blinded by the deluge that slackened just enough to reveal a blurred shape kneeling on the grass, then sharpening in clarity to reveal a figure not quite instantly recognizable in memory, but almost:

The bald man from the train.

Chapter Fifteen

"Sergeant Ben McCreedy," he said, formally introducing himself while still kneeling over me. "Lieutenant Gelber sent me," he said. "I've been watching you since you left New York."

Good old Artie, I thought. *He must've figured there was more to this than I was telling him and wanted to make sure it didn't get me killed, as it almost had.*

"Well, it paid off," I said, my words ending in a deep, throaty cough that expelled smoke visibly from my lungs.

"Just don't tell him you noticed me on the train," McCreedy said, managing a tight smile.

"It'll be our secret."

He coughed some smoke from his lungs, too. He was an imposing figure even while kneeling, his big, V-shaped frame brightening in the expanding glow of the flames that were consuming my house. The scream of sirens was getting louder, and all three of Cabot Cove's fire engines swung onto my street in single file, closely followed by a trio of Cabot Cove police vehicles.

"Let's get you somewhere safer," McCreedy said, positioning his hands to carry me again.

I tried to angle away from him. "I can walk. Just help me up."

"You're not hurt?"

I looked back toward my beloved home, more of it being consumed by flames every moment.

"Oh, I'm hurt all right," I told him as he helped me up. "I'm plenty hurt. Just not physically."

My knees nearly buckled under my own weight, but McCreedy stopped me from falling and held fast until my footing had stabilized. He continued to support me while I wobbled across the lawn closer to the street.

The fire department's arrival and efforts to douse the flames seemed to happen in the very same moment. They had built a tremendous reputation within the community and prided themselves on having never lost an entire house to fire, since the move from volunteer to fully paid staff had happened on a different watch. The smoke thickened under the floods of water they unleashed upon it, the color changing from near black to gray and finally to white. I tried to breathe and realized it hurt my throat to draw in air. My whole mouth stung, including my tongue, and not from spicy food this time. I looked toward Ben McCreedy and figured my face must similarly be streaked with grime. The slowing rain had probably cleaned at least some of it off, picking up again just in time to aid the efforts of the firefighters in saving as much of my house as they could.

All the memories, the keepsakes and possessions . . . Everything I valued was contained within those walls, the sum total of so many years and experiences. Starting to catalogue the depth of that list brought tears to my eyes and bottlenecked the breath in my throat. I don't think I ever realized what it meant to be "choked up" until that moment. As I watched stubborn flames spouting from my smoldering home, I could barely swallow, speak, or breathe. It literally felt more like a nightmare than reality, and I actually thought in that moment that I might wake up and find none if this was real.

Except for *The Affair* . . .

There seemed to be no way for any of the manuscript, even the final third I'd tucked under the couch, to have survived. But I couldn't be sure until the firefighters and Mort's people searched inside. I clung to the hope that at least some of it could yet be salvaged, given that this might well be the last copy of the manuscript in existence.

In my dazed state—I was clearly suffering from shock—the lag between sound and sight seemed especially pronounced. I watched Mort screech to a halt just free of the fire trucks, saw him climb out and jog my way, before I recorded the sound of his SUV door slamming.

McCreedy stepped forward to introduce himself. "Sergeant Ben McCreedy, Sheriff. NYPD."

"NYPD," Mort repeated, looking my way. "Artie Gelber?"

"Artie Gelber," I acknowledged.

"See," Mort started, addressing McCreedy again, "what your boss and I have in common is spending an inordinate portion of our time keeping Mrs. Fletcher here alive." He gazed toward the house the fire department was still pouring water against to douse the flames. "I'm sorry, Jessica. Now, let's get you into my car until the paramedics can check you out."

Those paramedics were currently tending to Deputy Andy, who'd been found slumped unconscious, but thankfully alive, behind the wheel of his squad car. Maybe the men I'd battled upstairs had meant to kill him but failed. Maybe he'd just gotten lucky. I doubted killing a cop was a line they wouldn't cross.

Mort always referred to his department-issue SUV as a car, too. He climbed into the back with me and closed the door, Sergeant McCreedy left searching the front yard and porch for any evidence the intruders might have left behind. Both the front and back doors were pretty much invincible; Cabot Cove might be peaceful and bucolic, but a single woman living alone can never be too careful. While the intruders had managed to jimmy the locks, McCreedy had had to break a window to gain entry. And he hadn't realized anything was awry from his position outside until he saw the first of the flames sprout on the first floor, accounting for his entry after my attackers had already fled.

The fire department had already gotten the fire under control to the point where barely any flames remained in view. Just smoke that made my home look as if it were shrouded in thick fog. The air, even in Mort's SUV, smelled of char and ash, something bitter and sharp, laced lightly with the scent of chemicals from burned wires, fabric, and carpets.

He handed me a handkerchief. Not until I dabbed my eyes with it did I realize I was still sobbing. Or maybe I'd stopped and started again.

"I don't know what to say, Jessica," Mort said, trying to soothe me. "I know how much the old place meant to you. I can't imagine how I'd feel in your place."

"Houses can be rebuilt, Mort," I said, trying to sound a lot braver than I felt.

"You get a look at who did this?"

"They wore masks."

Mort looked toward my smoldering house again. "The book?"

I managed to shrug, the life fluttering back into me, and then shook my head. I'd just lost the house I'd lived in more than any other, but I found myself thinking of *The Affair*, which I'd never get to finish.

Mort stole a glance at McCreedy, who continued to walk the property with his gaze angled downward. "I'm guessing you never said a word to Artie about this book."

"I didn't know then what I know now. But he must've suspected I was up to something."

"Of course, since he knows you as well as I do. You've got your share of tells, Jessica. It's not hard to figure when you're holding something back."

I shrugged again. "Good thing in this case, since it's what led him to put McCreedy on my tail."

"So Artie Gelber knows nothing about these murders," Mort said.

"He knows about Thomas Rudd and Lane Barfield, but not A. J. Falcone and Alicia Bond. And before I left New York, Rudd's death was only deemed suspicious and Lane's was considered a suicide."

"Not anymore."

"Not by connection with the others, no," I acknowledged.

"How much of that book did you get through before . . ."

"I had about a third to go," I said when Mort's voice tailed off.

"Enough to give you any notion what its part in all this might be?"

I didn't want to tell him I was so enraptured by the story that I might've missed the clues I was supposed to be looking for. "All I can think of is that it's some kind of roman à clef."

"A made-up story that's not so made-up?"

"Very good, Mort. I'm impressed."

"I did go to college, you know."

"I didn't know they taught literature at cop school," I said, trying to sound lighter than I was feeling inside.

Living on my own for so long has left me loath to become a burden to anyone. I wanted to put on as brave a face as I could so Mort, and eventually Seth Hazlitt, wouldn't worry and dote on me out of obligation. The quick response and miracle work by our fire department left me thinking my beloved home might yet be saved, albeit with an extensive rebuild. In the meantime, I could check into Cabot Cove's five-star hotel, Hill House; since it was the off-season, they might even have one of the suites available for an extended stay.

Not the worst place to live for a time, and, I have to admit, I've always been a sucker for room service.

A knock on Mort's window almost made me jump out of my soaked clothes. I turned with him and saw a familiar face pressed against the glass:

Seth.

He'd brought his doctor's bag and insisted on giving me a quick once-over right there in the back seat, freeing Mort to go back to supervising the investigation of all that had transpired. Fortunately, Cabot Cove's fire chief, Dick Mann, was a retired arson investigator, and I was sure he'd be entering the smoldering, sodden interior to do a thorough inspection that might yield some indication of who my attackers might've been.

"Tell him to look for the book," I said to Mort before he closed the door behind him, adding exactly where I'd hidden the rest of it when I heard the intruders' footsteps.

"The book you told me about?" Seth asked as my eyes tracked his penlight from side to side.

I nodded.

"Don't move your head while I'm examining you."

"Then don't ask me any questions while you're examining me."

"Consider it a cognitive exam," he said, trading the penlight for a stethoscope. "Take a deep breath, please."

I did.

"Another," Seth ordered, moving the stethoscope to another part of my chest. "Good. Now turn toward the window and breathe normally."

I did and felt him press the stethoscope tight against my slowly drying sweater.

"Well?" I asked, when he seemed to be finished with his examination.

"You'll live, at least long enough to come see me for a more thorough checkup tomorrow."

"Do I get a lollipop?"

"I save those for my patients who aren't almost burned to death. Your heart's strong and your lungs seem clear. But smoke inhalation can wreak some pretty significant havoc with the nervous system, so we'll want to run some tests tomorrow to be on the safe side."

"I hate when doctors say that."

"What?"

"'To be on the safe side.' Translation: I'm afraid there might be something seriously wrong with you and I want to find out how long you have to live."

His expression grew stern as he packed up his bag. "There is something seriously wrong with you, Mrs. Fletcher, that being your penchant for living out your fiction in reality, ayuh."

"Well, Dr. Hazlitt, in this case the reality is my publisher bought a book his company seems to have no record of, written by an author who doesn't seem to exist."

"I think we'll add a mental exam to the regimen of tests tomorrow."

"Look at what's left of my house and tell me if you think I'll pass. Earlier today Mort and I found the body of another author in Acadia National Park who'd been given the manuscript. She'd been shot, along with a park ranger."

"And then they try to barbecue America's favorite mystery writer."

"I'm hardly America's favorite mystery writer."

"I was trying to boost your spirits, and it certainly sounds like whoever's behind all this is escalating."

"The question being," I added, "who are *they*?"

"I think you should go on a long vacation somewhere far away."

"Exactly my plan, only I don't think Hill House is as far away as you had in mind."

"I was thinking more like Mars."

"Too cold this time of year."

"But at least you'd have little green men for company." Seth's expression tightened. "You're not going anywhere, are you?"

"I told you, Hill House."

"You know what I meant, Jessica Fletcher."

"Just like you know I can't let this go."

"I think you were a pit bull in a past life," Seth told me.

"A dog? Really?"

He frowned. "A mother brought her son to my office once who'd been bitten by a pit bull."

"That's not unusual."

"Maybe not, but this time the dog's teeth were still sunk in. The boy's mother had killed the dog when she couldn't get it to release him, and its jaws had locked in place. I separated it from the poor kid in the back of her minivan."

I looked at him across the seat. "Is there a point to this story somewhere?"

"Ayuh. Sometimes you pay a price for not letting go."

Chapter Sixteen

Mort conferred with Chief Mann, whose initial assessment was that my beloved home remained structurally sound and had suffered primarily smoke and water damage. The fire had been contained almost entirely in the living room area on the first floor, the fast response of the fire department having prevented the total loss that likely would have been the case had they arrived only five minutes later.

House fires spread that fast.

Mort questioned me again about the masked figures. Though my mind had cleared since we'd first spoken, I couldn't remember anything else about them that might be helpful, although there was something lurking at the edge of my consciousness, something about the hand I'd bitten, but my mind was still too frazzled to recall what that was.

"What about the manuscript?" I asked, practically holding my breath.

"I was saving the best for last," Mort told me. "The good news is that the couch you hid it under was pretty much burned up, but the frame withstood the worst of the flames and did a decent job of shielding the pages from the flames."

"Decent?"

"That's the not-so-good news. The pages are virtually intact, but both charred with ash and water-logged, as well as clumped together like salt in the summer. I'm going to let them dry out as best they can in the sheriff's department conference room, and then we'll have a better idea of how salvageable they might be." Mort coughed out some of the smoke that still filled the air like a thick cloud, dissipating much too slowly to suit me. "So, like your house, things could've been a lot worse."

I followed his gaze to my smoldering home, still spitting embers, and felt a pang of both sadness and loss.

"Look at the bright side," Mort continued, trying to make me smile. "You said you needed some new clothes."

"I wasn't counting on an entire wardrobe, Mort."

A suite, as it turned out, was indeed available at Hill House of Cabot Cove, our own quaint hotel. Hill House was several steps above the local bed-and-breakfasts, blessed with a rustic demeanor and charm all its own. No two rooms were alike, and entering the premises was like stepping back in time. The big wooden door opened into a spacious, airy Victorian lobby that featured ornate furniture spread atop elegant carpeting, along with a genuine oriental rug. In anticipation of my arrival, a uniformed officer stood vigil just inside the door not far from the front desk, which was actually a counter, currently staffed by an anxious-looking clerk whose name I couldn't recall.

Seth Hazlitt had accompanied me and I was grateful for the company, though I didn't need any help carrying my luggage—given that the only clothes available to me were currently on my back and a sodden mess. At this hour, there was nothing open to begin the process of rebuilding my wardrobe, and I was thinking I'd have to make do by wrapping myself in towels for a time, until the desk clerk graciously offered me whatever I could use from the lost and found. I salvaged a pair of fashionable athletic pants and a fleece sweatshirt from the pile, along with assorted sundries that would get me through tomorrow at the very least.

Carrying an armful of garments and toilet articles the front desk clerk had supplied, I followed Seth through the comfortable sprawl of the spacious lobby, passing a sitting area and built-in bookshelves, toward a lavish stairway featuring a hand-carved railing that spiraled toward Hill House's upper levels. The guest rooms I recalled retained a measure of the original charm, along with some furnishings, from the hotel's origins as the family home of a wealthy sea captain who'd run an entire fleet of merchant ships.

Much of the Hill House staff, of course, knew me

all too well from a number of murders that had occurred there over the years that I always seemed to
end up investigating. Of course, since it was the
off-season and the hotel had only a few other guests
staying the night, if anyone joined that number tonight it would almost surely be me.

That set my thinking back to consideration of where
I could take this particular investigation. Beyond the
hope that private investigator Harry McGraw could
somehow learn the true identity of Benjamin Tally, the
man who'd written *The Affair*, I didn't have much,
other than the content of the manuscript.

Assuming the clues I was looking for were actually
contained in those chapters. Since I hadn't finished
the book, though, I was still missing the final revela-
tions that would include why the president himself
was in danger, too. Why it fell to Pace and Abby to
save him instead of kill him there in the Oval Office.
I admired the turnabout I'd been in no way expecting,
but I was frustrated by the fact that unless the pages
the fire department had found charred and sodden
could be salvaged, I'd never know all the answers.
What it was that marked anyone who read *The Affair*
for death.

Sitting there in the bedroom in my Hill House hotel
suite, the flat-screen television tuned to a news station
with the sound muted, I had reached an impasse. I
didn't believe in writer's block, but that's what this felt
like. A big obstacle thrown in my way that prevented
me from going any further. All I could do was—

I finally remembered something from earlier in the
night, an elusive image that had been lurking at the

edge of my memory. In focusing on something else entirely, I'd freed my mind to recall whatever it could about the attack that had nearly cost me my life. It conjured an image, a mark on the back of the hand I'd bitten into straight through the glove. I hadn't registered the mark based on the brief glimpse I'd gotten when he groped for my collar, had probably dismissed it as a smudge or shadow. But I registered it now, realized it wasn't a smudge or a shadow at all.

"A tattoo?" Mort said the next morning at Mara's, where he'd joined Seth and me for breakfast.

I nodded. Seth had picked me up at Hill House and driven me straight to his office, where I'd passed a battery of tests. Seth looked almost disappointed, as if he'd hoped to find something wrong with me he could treat.

"I'm buying you breakfast to celebrate." He beamed nonetheless.

"You buying breakfast is something to celebrate in itself."

I was so glad to be alive that my home being rendered uninhabitable by the fire wasn't bothering me nearly as much as I thought it would, especially since it had been deemed structurally sound. If nothing else, that left me even more determined, now that they'd tried to kill me, too. I already had ample motivation in the fate of Lane Barfield, not to mention Thomas Rudd.

"I'm sorry I couldn't remember it last night," I said to Mort.

He looked at me through the steam rising off his

coffee. "Understandable, Jessica. You'd just barely escaped being burned alive."

"There was that."

"What do you remember about this tattoo?"

"The general shape, the fact that it was black, I think."

"You think?"

"The room was dark. They'd cut the power and the only light was from that emergency plug-in thing in the hallway."

"But if you saw it again . . . ," Mort prompted.

"I'd definitely recognize it. Almost definitely, anyway."

He exchanged a glance with Seth, who was seated next to me, neither of them fancying the prospects.

"Could be nothing, ayuh," Seth offered.

"But it's all we have, and these could've been the same men who killed Alicia Bond and that park ranger at the very least."

"How's that help us?"

"It doesn't, necessarily; it just makes identifying that tattoo all the more vital. And if I could find it in a book or something . . ."

"Lots of tattoos out there, Jessica," Seth noted, his expression as dour as Mort's. "Probably enough to fill a whole shelf of old-fashioned encyclopedias, never mind a single book."

"I'll find it," I insisted.

"How? You lost your computers in the fire."

Mort saying that stung, given how many years of work, experiences, and correspondence were contained on those hard drives. Everything was backed up to the Cloud, of course, so I'd be able to reconstruct the data once I had a new computer. My actual collection of photographs, the artwork I'd collected over so many years, the only keepsakes I had left of my late husband, Frank—none of those could be reconstructed, except in memory.

I started to choke up again, thinking there was so much I was going to miss, things I saw every single day and had come to take for granted because they were always there. I was so fortunate that our fire chief's initial assessment and prognosis was that the house itself was structurally sound and could be rebuilt, restored to its original condition almost without exception. Except for those keepsakes. The paint, wallpaper, carpeting, hardwood floors, cathedral ceilings, and art deco moldings could all be restored to reasonably close to their original state. But the house would never be the same again, because of what wasn't hanging on the walls, cluttering the counters, and battling for space on this table or that. I imagined moving back in wouldn't feel much different from moving into my suite at Hill House, in its general coldness and lack of character, having lost what was built up over more than a quarter century of living.

"It'll give me something to do," I said to Mort and Seth.

"That it will," Seth agreed.

"Hopefully," Mort added, "keep you out of harm's way."

"How's Deputy Andy, by the way?"

"Already itching to leave the hospital. Almost as lucky as you."

"Really? What—did his house burn all the way to the ground last night?"

Mort seemed to disapprove of my tone, but I was sure he understood. "He suffered a severe concussion, but he'll be fine."

"Why not just kill him?"

"Because that would've removed all semblance of doubt. A woman burns alive, it could still go down as an accident. A cop gets killed in front of her house, it's double homicide."

This was a different side of Mort, a professional, polished side typical of a seasoned investigator that I glimpsed only in the midst of the investigations I kept finding myself in the middle of. "When did you become so good at this stuff?"

"Since I learned it all from you." He chuckled. "By the way, I love your outfit."

Doris Ann, our librarian, hugged me as soon as I stepped through the door of the Cabot Cove Library, wearing a fresh set of gym clothes I'd pulled from Hill House's lost and found the night before. Next on my list was getting some clothes to tide me over for a few days, before embarking on a more extensive rebuild of my wardrobe. I was a clothes hoarder, seldom throwing anything out, which gave me something else to miss. I was sure there'd be plenty more losses that hadn't occurred to me yet and was glad everything wasn't hitting me at once.

"Oh, Jessica, I'm so sorry," she said, nearly shutting off my air, she squeezed me so tight.

"I promise I'll never miss another meeting of the

Friends of the Library," I quipped after we finally separated.

"That isn't funny. *This* isn't funny."

"I'm still here, and very grateful for that much."

Doris Ann looked as if she was going to hug me again, so I took a step backward, recoiling slightly. "In any event, I think it's time you considered moving someplace where nobody knows you."

"Think that would solve all my problems?"

"I'm thinking Norway or Sweden, one of those Scandinavian countries. Because of the low murder rates."

"Less opportunity for me to get in trouble, in other words."

"Well, yes, Jessica. Tell me you haven't thought about it."

"Murder?"

Her taut glance scoffed at my attempt at levity before her words followed. "What would you do if you lived someplace where nobody got murdered?"

"Write more books, I guess. Speaking of which, I need to use one of the computers to look up tattoos."

"Please tell me you're not thinking of getting one." Doris Ann flinched, her revulsion real.

"I was thinking of an *M*," I said, pointing upward toward my forehead. "Like in *The Scarlet Letter*, only not an *A*."

"Don't tell me: *M* for 'murder.'"

"What else?"

I spent hours on the computer, most of the day. So much that I had to get up and walk around the library's Periodicals Room, where our computers were housed, just to get the blood moving again and work the stiffness out of my joints. I often had to remind myself to do the same when I got on one of my writing binges, when I just couldn't stop.

But this feeling was nothing like that.

Seth was right about the number of tattoos that were out there. So many passing by me on-screen as I scrolled that the colors bled together in my mind, and the snakes, which seemed overwhelmingly popular choices, seemed to coil out from the machine.

Talk about a waste of time.

But I had to feel like I was doing something, that I was at least trying. Anything to distract myself from all I'd lost in the fire, the number continuing to multiply the more time cushioned the shock.

My favorite pair of slippers . . .

My hairbrush . . .

All my books, my beloved books . . .

Some of these items could be salvaged, rid of water and smoke damage by restoration companies that specialized in such things, but far from all of them, and plenty had burned up or been burned beyond the capacity for restoration. Each passing moment brought a memory of something else I'd lost forever, something else those two masked men had taken from me. And if the murders that had preceded the attempt on my life weren't motivation enough for me to uncover the secrets held by the manuscript behind it all, now they'd made it personal, turned it into a race. I had to get them before they got me. The base simplicity of that stoked a fire inside me mixed equally of fear and rage, a dangerous and fraught combination.

I'd been involved in any number of real-life investigations, helped solve any number of murders, but never when I knew my own life was at stake, after an attempt had already been made. More than enough motivation to make me begin my search for the tattoo I'd glimpsed on the back of one of the attacker's hands last night.

And I got nowhere.

Nearly six hours passed with me scrolling through pages and pages of tattoos, site after site on the Internet, to no avail. I couldn't find even a remotely close match with what my memory conjured of the back of my attacker's hand from the night before. Had it been just a shadow? Did he even have a tattoo?

My memory had become fogged with the clutter of lost items and cherished possessions that now existed only in my memory. I couldn't trust it anymore to fashion an accurate rendering of the tattoo.

I trolled the screen for another fruitless ninety minutes, trying other keywords in my searches, and then scrolling through old mythic shapes and drawings in search of something from ancient culture that might yield some clue. Given the potential, if not likely, military background for my attacker, I then turned my attention to both tattoos and comparable shapes either drawn from something connected to war or popular among soldiers.

I was striking out there, too, when I realized Lane Barfield's assistant, Zara, had by now likely heard about both Alicia Bond's murder and the fire that had nearly claimed my life. She must be going crazy, worried sick, perhaps fearing for her own life. I needed to tell her I was fine. I needed to warn her that those fears she might have been harboring were well-founded.

I pulled my cell phone from my bag and hit Lane's office number. It rang six times, went to voice mail.

"Hi. You've reached the office of publisher Lane Barfield," Zara's voice recited. "At the tone, please leave a—"

I hung up and found her cell phone number among my outgoing calls, tried that one.

"Hi. It's Zara. At the tone, you know what to do."

I did indeed.

"Zara, it's Jessica, Jessica Fletcher. I just wanted you to know I'm okay. We haven't spoken, so I—Just return this call, please, as soon as you can. I want to make sure you're okay, too."

I hung up and waited the obligatory moments for her to call back, on the chance she hadn't gotten to the phone fast enough or she needed to get someplace where she could talk. The phone didn't ring. Zara didn't call back.

I tried to return my attention to the screen, but a dread fear had filled me. Zara should've been in the office, should've answered her cell phone when she saw my number.

Something fluttered in my stomach before I felt it tighten. All of me tightened.

I called Harry McGraw.

"Heard you took up smoking," he greeted me.

"Mort or Seth?"

"Spoke to both of them. Didn't want to bother you, because then I'd have to add the call to my billable hours."

"I've got something else you can bill me for."

"Hope it's more challenging than finding who really authored a book, based on no more than a title page."

"How fast can you get to Lane Barfield's office, Harry?"

"Depends why I'm going there."

"I need you to check on his assistant. Her name is Zara. I'm afraid she might be in danger."

"Zara?"

"That's her name."

"Whatever you say, Jess."

"Just make sure she's safe and call me as soon as you've got something."

I heard him let out a heavy sigh. "You know, I do have other clients."

"Really?"

"No. I'll get right over there. And, Jess?"

"Yes?"

"Why am I your favorite detective?"

"Because you never let me down."

"Exactly. And I'm actually making some progress on Benjamin Tally."

I couldn't believe it. "You're kidding."

"I have my moments, most of them senior, but occasionally I stumble into something. They say if you leave a chimpanzee behind a keyboard long enough, he'll type all of Shakespeare's plays. Call me the ape of the private eye world."

"Just call me as soon as you get to Lane Barfield's office."

I hung up and tried to go back to my search for the

tattoo I'd glimpsed the night before, but I couldn't pay attention to the screen anymore. I'd say that I'd just wasted a whole lot of time, but I didn't have anything else to do, and at least the effort had made for a decent distraction from my woes.

I made sure I had everything stuffed into my bag and then walked back toward the main desk, where librarian Doris Ann was checking out some books for a trio of children, something she enjoyed more than anything else. I stopped to bid her farewell.

"Any luck?" she posed.

"Nope."

"Oh well . . . Anyway, Jessica," she said, pushing some stray stringy hair back behind her ear, "if there's anything I can do to help you, anything at all . . ."

Her voice tailed off, no reason to say anything more. I looked up to thank her and noticed on the side of her face a dark squiggly mark that seemed to rise out of the temple. I almost lost my breath.

"Doris," I managed, "is that a tattoo?"

Because it was identical to the mark on the back of my attacker's hand.

Chapter Seventeen

"That?" said Doris Ann, surprised and maybe even a bit embarrassed that I'd noticed. "That's just an old scar."

"But it looks—," I started, leaving it there.

"I know." Doris Ann nodded. "Thanks to a condition called post-inflammatory hyperpigmentation."

"Huh?"

"Scarring turns the skin rough, due to an increase in collagen bubbles coupled with the lack of hair follicles and sweat glands," she recited, as if I wasn't the first person to notice what looked like a dark, jagged scab permanently marring her skin. "That creates discoloration within the skin itself, especially as we age, with the damaged tissue taking on a darker shade, even black. Normally, I cover it up with makeup, but I was too lazy this morning."

"I need to call Mort," I said, groping about in my bag for my phone. "And Seth."

* * *

Because Doris Ann couldn't leave the library unattended, Seth and Mort said they'd come over straightaway. Seth normally booked appointments only through three o'clock, leaving the rest of the day for emergencies. Since today had produced none, he was available. Since this was an active investigation, Mort was under no such restrictions.

They arrived together.

"What's so important you dragged me away from my golf game?" Seth asked me, striding in just ahead of Mort.

"You don't play golf."

"But I'm thinking of taking it up."

"Not at the new fees the country club has posted, you're not."

"What is it you want us to see?" Mort wondered.

"Show them," I told Doris Ann.

"That's almost identical to what I saw on the back of the man's hand last night," I explained, as Doris Ann tilted her face to the side and held her hair back to expose the scar, or whatever she had called it.

Seth was giving it a much closer inspection than Mort. "Post-inflammatory hyperpigmentation," he pronounced, quite professionally. "It's caused by an excess of melanin in the damaged tissue. That's what causes the discoloration. Most scars inflamed like this are spotted, freckled, even raised slightly. Very few achieve this dark a shade."

"Well, I saw another one last night."

"You're sure?" Mort said, turning toward me.

"I'm sure."

"Can I start breathing again now?" Doris Ann joked.

Seth backed away and she fanned her hair back into place.

"What was the name of that television show where a doctor solves crimes? I think it was Dick Van Dyke?" he asked me.

"*Diagnosis: Murder*," I told him. "Why?"

"Because it's time I helped you solve a crime. You hear that, Mort?" he continued, his gaze shifting.

"I heard it, Dr. Watson. Now tell Mrs. Sherlock Holmes here what's on your mind."

Seth chimed right in. "A common treatment for post-inflammatory hyperpigmentation is hydroquinone, which is a skin-bleaching agent meant to counter discoloration and lighten skin's overall appearance, but hydroquinone comes with an extremely high toxicity level. That means it can cause severe damage to the skin, including blistering, burn marks, new discoloration, and extreme tightness. Hydroquinone is available over the counter, but because of its side effects dermatologists have begun prescribing some new prescription creams and pills that have achieved comparable results without the risks."

"So," I said, thinking out loud, "if I'm right about the attacker from last night suffering from the same condition as Doris Ann, then he could be using one of these prescription medications."

Seth nodded. "Very likely so."

"I stick with the cream," Doris Ann interjected. "Don't like taking pills unless I absolutely have to."

"Could be your attacker is taking both," Seth

elaborated, "especially given how pronounced your description of his post-inflammatory hyperpigmentation was."

I looked toward Mort. "Any way we can get a list of all patients prescribed these particular drugs?"

He frowned, clearly not enamored of the prospect of that. "Well, I'd have to call in the FBI, which would require some additional explanation. But since they're investigating those two murders in Acadia, I imagine they'd be most receptive to the request."

"Doesn't mean that they'll share their findings with you, Mort."

He didn't look particularly bothered by my comment. "I've got a friend I can call."

"Someone you served with in Vietnam?" I said, as if to remind him of the rather large piece of his personal history I'd learned of only the other day.

"As a matter of fact . . ."

"Wait," Seth said to Mort, our exchange just seeming to register with him, "you were in Vietnam?"

Cooperation or not, it would take some time for the FBI to assemble such a list. Given that the murders, and the attack on me, had all occurred in the Northeast, Mort said he'd ask the Bureau to start their search with this region, since it was slightly more likely than not that my attacker was from someplace reasonably close by.

Seth had to jet off to check on some of his patients at the hospital but insisted on dropping me off at Hill House first. Once inside my suite, I sat down with phone in hand, prepared to call Harry McGraw, when

I saw I had six missed calls from him. No texts, since Harry hadn't quite mastered that skill yet.

"Where have you been?" he snapped, answering before even the first ring was complete.

"We might have caught a bit of a break in the case from this end."

"Good, because there's nothing on this end, and I mean nothing."

I felt that same flutter in my stomach; it was rapidly becoming familiar. "Zara?"

"She didn't come into work today. Never called anyone to explain why or say what was wrong."

I didn't bother commenting on that. "What about her apartment? Did you check that?"

"Am I a detective?" Harry asked, making himself sound irritated.

"Last time I checked."

"Then of course I checked her apartment. Give me some credit. And give me more for actually getting inside."

"Don't tell me you picked the lock."

"I could tell you, Jess, but it would be a bald-faced lie. I can barely get my key to work in my own building, never mind picking a lock. But I am pretty good at selling building superintendents a bill of goods. A long-practiced skill us private eyes pride ourselves on."

"What'd you find, Harry?" I asked him, dreading the answer.

"Same thing I found in the office: nothing. No sign of Zara. No note, no sign of forced entry. A closet packed with clothes and more jewelry than my four ex-wives combined."

"You only have three ex-wives," I reminded him.

"I like to plan ahead. The way I'm seeing this is that Zara took the day off. Maybe spent it at the movies. Maybe she headed off to the Hamptons to walk the beach or Atlantic City to check out the boardwalk, houses destroyed by a hurricane nobody else remembers, and the only casinos in history to ever lose money."

"You finished?"

"With my report, yeah."

But I wasn't ready to let him go yet. "What about Benjamin Tally? You said you were making some progress."

"And that's all I'm willing to say for now."

"Don't do this to me, Harry."

"What?"

"Hold something back."

"I don't have anything to hold back, Jess. When I have something to hold back, you'll be the first to know because I won't tell you. But here's some advice I won't charge you for: Get out of town. Don't tell anyone where you're going, and just drive someplace."

"I don't drive, remember?"

"Call Uber. No, don't call Uber, because then they could find you."

"I'm at Hill House, which is safer than anywhere else I could go."

"I'm sure you felt that way about being home last night, and look how that worked out."

"Tell me when you're close to finding Benjamin Tally."

"I am close, Jess, just not close enough. I need another day."

"Nice work, Harry."

"That's what you're paying for, little lady."

I tried Zara's cell number again, resolved to call every fifteen or so minutes until she answered. That left me wondering what she'd make of having dozens of missed calls from me when she emerged from the movies or wherever she was. But I should have called her yesterday, as soon as I was back in Cabot Cove after Mort and I had found Alicia Bond's body. I should have called to warn her that she, too, might be in danger. Maybe if I had, she'd be safe now. That possibility would haunt me for the rest of my days, if the worst came to pass, even though I had no way of knowing whether my failure to reach out to Zara yesterday had made any difference at all.

While clinging to the hope that Zara would ultimately answer her phone, I called Chief Dick Mann at home. For years, our full-time firefighters had been supplemented by a volunteer force. As Cabot Cove grew, though, the town budget added funds to allow for an exclusively full-time force, the brilliance of which I'd now witnessed firsthand. I'd known Dick for more than twenty years now. He'd come to Cabot Cove after retiring as Boston's fire chief for two decades. The fire at my house had already allowed him to display his considerable experience as an arson investigator as well. He enjoyed a national reputation and had been called to many other locales to consult when arson was suspected. He might have come here seeking a quieter lifestyle, but he always seemed to be attending workshops and seminars to keep up with the latest thinking and technology.

"Jessica," he greeted me, "are you all right? Is there anything to do?"

"I'm fine, Dick, and thanks to you my house will be again soon, too."

"Just doing our job," he said modestly. "By the way, these may have been the worst arsonists I've ever encountered. They made no effort at all to disguise what they were doing."

"They didn't care," I told him. "This wasn't about insurance or vengeance; it was about murder. And I'm guessing they expected a local-yokel fire chief instead of the great Dick Mann."

"I'm blushing, Jessica. I'm blushing."

I finally got to the real point of my call. "I wanted to talk to you about the parts of that manuscript you recovered that were salvageable."

"Of course. I picked them up at the sheriff's station and have them on ice."

Dick's remark might've seemed flippant, but I'd learned over the years that the recovery process for documents damaged by a combination of fire and water was varied and complex. One of the tried-and-true methods often employed was freezer drying in a frost-free or blast freezer. This had the effect of removing any remaining moisture, while preventing the decay that was common when air-drying was used as the initial strategy. Air-drying worked fine for water damage alone, but add to the mix charred pages that had been drained of their own moisture content, and the result could well be to destroy what little structural integrity remained. You might even end up with a pile of nothing more than pulp. Vacuum freeze-drying would've been the quickest and surest means to achieve recovery, but no such machine existed in Cabot Cove, and truth be told, I couldn't even advise Dick where the nearest one could be found, short of Langley or the J. Edgar Hoover Building in Washington.

Of course, the real challenge here lay in the fact that most recovery strategies involved bound books, not loose manuscript pages. Outside of any number of water disasters at libraries where precious historical documents had suffered damage, I was unaware of a single effort ever being mounted to save actual paper; the most prevalent approach was to simply dump the seemingly ruined pages in the trash. Fortunately, Mort was all in, thanks to his knowledge of the manuscript's deadly history and our experience in Acadia National Park, and that was good enough for Dick Mann without further explanation.

"Any notion as to whether the print is still legible?" I asked Dick.

"I didn't dare try separating the pages to find out," he explained. "I imagine with the help of an electron microscope or some such, you might be able to make sense of the contents. And you did make plain to me this manuscript held significant value to you."

"It does, Dick. Not necessarily monetary, but you might even say it's vital."

"Sounds like a mystery."

"You have no idea."

"Well, what I do have is knowledge that someone tried to kill you last night, and if this manuscript has any part in that, I'd recommend getting it to the FBI's document lab in Quantico as soon as it's safe to transport."

I'd forgotten all about the document lab. They would have the kind of professional dehumidification and vacuum freeze-drying equipment that offered the highest probability for success. The problem was, such a request would have to come through the likes of Mort or Artie Gelber, in which case the Bureau would obviously want to know exactly what they were trying to restore and why.

"Where's the manuscript now?"

"We made some room between the steaks and chicken down at the station."

Dick must've seen my jaw drop through the phone, because he continued immediately.

"Just kidding, Jessica. We have a freezer dedicated to the preservation of evidence. Your pages are safe and sound. We even turned up the fan to aid the drying process."

"You may want to add an armed guard," I recommended, and imagined watching his jaw drop. "Just kidding, Dick. But I'll let Mort know."

"Good thing we can wave at each other through our office windows."

"One of the advantages of living in a small town."

Our call finished, I began to think again of all I'd read of *The Affair* before the fire, but I still couldn't come up with a single clue within the manuscript's content to explain why five, and very nearly six, people might have been murdered because of it. It was a pulp novel, a commercial thriller, not a political exposé. And if it was indeed some kind of roman à clef, it was beyond me to figure out what true story the author was endeavoring to tell.

Might I have this all wrong? Was I missing something that was right before my eyes?

I was stumped, to say the least, so I started asking myself what my characters, my alter egos, would do if they found themselves in a similar predicament.

I turned on the news with a hotel memo pad in my lap, in case something struck me that I had to write down. That's one of the things about getting older: You learn to write down anything you deem important for fear of losing it forever.

A commercial came on—I think for a laxative, adult diapers, or something like that—featuring a woman about my age pedaling about on a bicycle to show off the fact that she was still in the prime of life. I hated these commercials, as much as I did the ones for reverse mortgages, burial insurance policies, and walk-in bathtubs. The aging of the baby-boomer generation had given birth to a flood of exploitive advertising aimed at our specific demographic, airing almost exclusively from early morning through early evening, for obvious reasons. The only positive thing about this particular commercial was that it reminded me that, except for minor scoring of the roof, my detached garage had been spared any damage. The garage held my brand-new bicycle, which I resolved to pick up tomorrow, once I'd found a spot at Hill House to store it, to enable me to better get around while my house was under renovation. I started to wonder if I might want to take advantage of the opportunity to do some remodeling, add some fresh touches to the old house, a thought I dismissed almost as quickly as I formed it.

I ordered dinner from room service and made sure to check the peephole before answering. Then I flipped through the channels, jotting down occasional notes to myself that amounted to pretty much nothing, before nodding off in the chair.

I woke up to my cell phone vibrating on the table set next to the chair; it hadn't rung because I'd forgotten to turn the ringer back on. I recognized Mort's office number, the time on my phone just past midnight, a political commentary show blaring before me until I muted the television.

"What happened to your beauty sleep?" I asked him, clearing the grogginess from my throat.

"You ruined it, as usual. Sorry to wake you, Mrs. Fletcher."

I sat up straighter. "What is it?"

"I'm picking you up at eight in the morning sharp. I think we may have found your attacker."

Chapter Eighteen

True to his word, Mort pulled up to the Hill House entrance in his SUV at eight the next morning. I'd e-mailed and left a message for the insurance adjuster, saying I couldn't meet him at my house as planned and asking whether we could possibly postpone his visit until tomorrow.

I'd been down in the lobby for a half hour, on the chance that Mort arrived early, so eager to hear what he'd learned from the FBI about my attacker that I'd barely slept.

"Ever been to Somerville?" he asked, after I'd climbed into the seat and closed the door behind me.

"Near Boston?"

Mort nodded. "Home of the Irish Mob. The original Winter Hill Gang, later taken over by the infamous Whitey Bulger. Come on, Jess—you're a mystery writer."

"If you'd been keeping up with my books, Mort, you'd know I don't write about gangsters very much."

"I'm only saying." He shrugged.

"Why don't you say why we we're heading to Somerville instead?"

"Because of Tommy Halperin."

"And what's so special about Tommy Halperin?"

"He's on one of those new prescriptions to treat that condition, the one Doris Ann and the man who attacked you the other night have."

"Post-inflammatory hyperpigmentation," I said, recalling Seth's words. "But what makes you think Tommy Halperin of Somerville might be my attacker?"

Mort pulled out his trusty memo pad, the one that was a virtual twin of the pad Lieutenant Artie Gelber of the NYPD kept tucked in his pocket. "Military background in the Special Forces until he received a dishonorable discharge for unspecified reasons. Later did a stint with the private security company then called Blackwater, and worked as a mercenary for a firm known for building private armies. Last known whereabouts, Sudan."

"So, what's it matter if Halperin suffers from post-inflammatory hyperpigmentation if he's in Sudan?"

Mort flipped his memo pad closed. "Because he filled a prescription for that new drug three weeks ago."

I held the picture of Tommy Halperin in my lap for much of the drive south from Cabot Cove, Mort picking up Route 93, which would take us straight into

Somerville. The shot showed Tommy in military uniform above his vital statistics. He was five feet eleven inches tall, which seemed right for the attacker who'd grabbed me from behind, the one whose glove I'd bitten through. His weight was listed as 185 pounds, and even through the uniform, his frame looked rock hard and chiseled. It was an older picture, of course, and there was no telling if Halperin had remained in this kind of shape, as my attacker from the night before last plainly was.

For some reason, I had the strange thought that a suspected killer shouldn't go by "Tommy." That was a boy's name, not a man's, and I never understood why men went by names better fit for their ten-year-old selves. Then again, the gangster world was full of such juvenile labeling. Mikey, Frankie, Billy, Johnny, Matty, Bobby, Davey—I'd heard them all on the news or seen them in the paper all the time, often followed by a colorful nickname. The nicknames had pretty much gone away, but the childish monikers remained, as if all gangsters possessed some kind of regressive gene that left them prisoners to their ids the same way kids are.

According to the Department of Veterans Affairs, Tommy Halperin had fought on the wrong side of the ongoing civil war in the Sudan. A supplemental report detailed his suspected complicity in the massacre of an entire village; he was accused by a well-known human rights group with enough supporting evidence for the American Justice Department to open an investigation of the firm that had employed him as a mercenary.

Apparently, such behavior wasn't all that uncommon in this world.

Halperin had supposedly disappeared not long after the report had been filed. No next of kin had filed any claim on military benefits or pension he might have still had, explaining why no one in the government had caught on to the fact that a dishonorably discharged soldier turned mercenary who had suffered from post-inflammatory hyperpigmentation had returned home.

Our investigation of that anomaly began at a Walgreens located in a dedicated parking lot shared with a Winter Hill Bank Loan Center adjacent to it in an L-shaped structure. This was clearly Somerville's main drag, or one of them, nestled among other staple stores along a row of storefronts. They were enclosed just a few blocks away by a slew of two- and three-story tenement houses that looked like they'd been lifted straight out of the heart of working-class America. Somerville had been a factory and mill town long before it had gained a reputation as a haven for the Boston-based Irish Mob. As the old saying went, the Italians will kill you, but the Irish will kill you, your family, your friends, and your pets. It was the kind of insular blue-collar community that kept to itself and detested outsiders like us who'd come to pry into local business. The stories I'd read about the infamous, and now imprisoned, alpha gangster Whitey Bulger had him buying ice cream cones for kids and Thanksgiving turkeys for the poor, while strong-arming locals out of lottery winnings and taking possession of convenience stores to launder his riches. Somerville was a place where nobody squealed and everybody called cops by their first names, while never even considering ratting anyone out to them.

"Just us?" I said to Mort, surprised that no local police were waiting in the parking lot to meet us.

"I wasn't sure the locals would have our best interests at heart, given that we're looking into one of their own," he explained.

It felt as if we'd driven two hundred miles back in time. That just wasn't something you heard said much anymore, Somerville seeming to offer a last glimpse of a bygone and forgotten time.

"So we're on our own," I said.

"We're on our own," Mort acknowledged, and into Walgreens we went.

Mort took the military photo of Tommy Halperin and we took our place in line at the pharmacist's counter behind two older women, both of whom knew everyone working behind the counter by name. Few realize that, thanks to the opioid crisis, the DEA now keeps a database of every single prescription of any kind filled in the entire United States; the more dangerous ones are funneled to the FBI. Very few realize that, I suspect, because the outcry against governmental snooping would be enormous.

That explained how Mort had been able to track Tommy Halperin down so quickly, thanks to any number of factors in his profile that made him stand out. First and foremost was his age, given that most who suffer from this condition are older, more like Doris Ann's age. There was also the reasonable proximity of Somerville to New York, Acadia National Park, and Cabot Cove. It made sense that whoever was behind the murders I was convinced were associated with *The Affair* manuscript would hire local talent. And Halperin certainly fit the bill there. Even though he boasted no formal criminal record, he'd been involved in several scrapes with the law that suggested criminal involvement prior to embarking on a career as a mercenary. But all the cases had ended up dismissed when witnesses mysteriously recanted their testimony or failed to show up in court.

We reached the front of the line and Mort flashed the photo of Tommy Halperin to three separate pharmacy techs, all of whom said after taking much too fast a glance at the picture that they didn't recognize him.

"He filled a prescription here three weeks ago," Mort said three different times, receiving three different indifferent responses.

"I'm not saying he didn't. I'm saying I don't remember him."

"I've never see him in here."

"What'd you say the drug was called again?"

The silver-haired pharmacist was too busy to talk to us, so Mort and I busied ourselves by speaking to more Walgreens workers. All of them professed to have never seen Tommy Halperin in their entire lives. Nor, they uniformly insisted, did they know anybody by the name "Halperin" at all, in spite of the fact that various offshoots of Tommy's family had been living in Somerville for somewhere around a century.

Maybe if he went by the name "Tom" or "Thomas" we would've had better luck. As it was, we were getting nowhere, and I started to wonder if Mort's decision not to bring in any of the local police had been the right call.

"Excuse me?"

We both turned in the cold-and-flu-care aisle to find the white-haired pharmacist, Manny according to his name tag, drawing close to us.

"This is the one we recommend," he said, taking a rectangular box of cold medication down from the shelf. "It's the store brand, but equally effective at a much better price."

Then he lowered his voice.

"You were asking about Tommy Halperin?"

"You know him?" Mort asked, pretending to check the label on the medication Manny had pretended to recommend.

"From around the time he was born."

"When was the last time you saw him?"

"Three weeks ago, when he picked up a prescription for his skin condition."

"Then he must not be overseas," I noted.

Manny looked at me for the first time, as if not realizing Mort and I were together. "No, he's not overseas." Suspicion tightened his features. "Is that why you're here?"

Mort managed a slight nod. "Partly."

Manny regarded the CABOT COVE SHERIFF'S DEPARTMENT patch on Mort's jacket. "But you're from Maine."

"Not a long drive from here."

Manny the pharmacist shook his head. "What's Tommy done now?"

"What can you tell us about him?" Mort asked instead of answering the question.

"That I was glad when he left and sorry when he came back."

"Any idea who he works for these days?" I asked, hoping Manny had at least some notion that might point us in the right direction.

He checked both ends of the aisle before answering. "Not that I'd want to mention. I can't be sure, but that's what everyone around here figures, given who really runs this town," Manny said, the bitterness plain in his voice.

"What about where he lives?" Mort said. "Can you tell us that?"

I expected Manny to hedge on that, fearful for his own safety if he gave up information to outsiders. He looked at me, seeming to read my mind, as he pulled up his sleeve to reveal a nasty burn scar.

"He gave me this in the basement of his house after I refused to make some prescription opioids 'disappear' off the shelves."

And then Manny gave us Tommy Halperin's address.

The neighborhood where Tommy Halperin lived, a short drive from Walgreens, was more or less typical of Somerville's blue-collar atmosphere. While I saw any number of renovated homes mixed in among a smattering of others that still carried the stains from the exhaust belched from the smokestacks of long-shuttered factories, there was virtually no new construction. The area enjoyed a staid, homogeneous look, the yards surrounding the mostly two- and three-family tenements uniformly small but well kept. Along some streets we drove on, those houses enjoyed precious little space between them. There were few garages, almost none, and many residents elected to leave their trash and recycling containers between their front walks and driveways, which were often cluttered with cars.

It was a gray day, overcast, with the promise of rain in the forecast. All that was missing for this to feel like 1950 were thick gray plumes rising from long-leveled, shuttered, or converted factories that attested to the town's working-class roots. Somerville was only one of the Boston-area communities that boasted a strong presence and tradition of the Irish Mob. Others included Dorchester, Charlestown, Roxbury, and South Boston itself, where the more generic term "Southie" originated. Every mystery writer knows that the Irish Mob is the oldest organized crime entity in US history, its existence dating all the way back to the early nineteenth century and owing to the wave of immigration that spawned street gangs and ethnic rivalries in cities across the East. But the Irish Mob had flourished and risen to power during Prohibition, which gave birth to the forerunners of the Mullen Gang, the McLaughlin brothers, Howie Winter and his Winter Hill Gang, and, of course, Whitey Bulger.

To this day, these particular neighborhoods didn't cotton much to, and remained suspicious of, strangers. And, I imagined, they didn't actually put out the welcome signs for men in uniform driving police-issue

SUVs. I noticed this fact must not have been lost on Mort, given that he had hitched his police jacket behind the holster holding his semiautomatic pistol.

"Here we go," Mort said, following the GPS map onto the street where Tommy Halperin lived. "You reading this the same way I am, Jessica?"

"That depends on how you're reading it."

"Assuming this thing with that book is as big as it seems, whoever's behind the murders is hiring ex-mercenaries and special operators like Halperin to do their dirty work."

"An army of their own, in other words."

"That's my thinking."

"Mine, too."

Mort snailed his SUV to a halt just past the driveway attached to a three-story tenement matching Tommy Halperin's address. A single car was squeezed off to the left to allow others to park alongside it. A big muscle car I thought was a Dodge Charger, complete with massive tires and windows that looked painted black. Close your eyes and it wasn't hard to picture old Buick Roadmaster station wagons and the like dotting driveways like this years before, vehicles in which entire families were routinely packed with luggage so high in the back that the driver couldn't see out the rear window.

I reached into my bag upon exiting Mort's SUV and his eyes followed me to the car.

"Jessica?"

"Just a minute," I said, crouching by a rear tire of the Charger.

"What are you doing?"

"Nothing, really," I told him, standing back up.

I knew Mort didn't believe me, and I kept my distance while following him up the steps to the front porch. If it turned out Tommy Halperin was my attacker from a few nights back, he would almost surely recognize me, but not Mort necessarily. And I felt certain that police knocking on his door was nothing new for him.

"Stay back, Jessica," Mort ordered, even though I already was.

He opened the storm door and knocked on the wood-frame door inside it, painted the same drab gray color as the rest of the house.

"Police, Mr. Halperin. Open the door, please."

No response.

"We have a few questions for you, Mr. Halperin. Just routine," Mort added, raising his voice to make sure he was heard.

I caught a flicker of motion through one of two twin windows on either side of the door. Something about that motion seemed all wrong, triggering an instinctive response. Before I knew it, I had charged up the last few steps and slammed into Mort, shoving him away from both the door and the window through which I'd glimpsed the figure.

BOOM!

The blast reverberated in my eardrums, accompanied by a shower of splinters and shards blown outward at about the level where Mort's head had just been.

Chapter Nineteen

We tumbled over a plastic table topped with a layer of dirt and grime, taking a pair of light matching chairs over with us to the porch floor.

"Are you all right? Are you all right?" Mort demanded, working to free his gun at the awkward angle at which the tumble had left us.

He couldn't reclaim his feet and free the pistol at the same time, so he first focused on rising. Then he stooped to help me to my feet, drawing his pistol in the same moment the Dodge Charger with the blacked-out windows screeched out of the driveway, its massive tires churning through a cloud of smoke. The car tore away down the street, riding that same cloud, with Tommy Halperin behind the wheel, no doubt.

He'd tried to kill us with a shotgun blast before fleeing, and Mort was left with gun in hand watching the Charger whipsaw around a corner up the street;

he wasn't about to start firing in a densely populated neighborhood where a stray bullet might find its way through a window or wall.

"Somerville Police?"

"Guess we should've called them earlier," Mort said, yanking his cell phone from his pocket while holstering his pistol.

I saw faces pressed against glass in some of the surrounding homes, a few doors opening, and people actually emerging from others.

"Jessica!" Mort called when he saw me heading down from the porch toward the driveway.

I heard his footsteps thudding after me, catching up as I reached the driveway and turned my gaze downward.

"It worked!" I responded.

"What?"

"Old trick I used in a book once," I told him, gesturing toward a thin red line bleeding out of the driveway and following the same path the Charger had blazed up the street. "Nail polish. I put a large bottle under one of the rear tires."

"So it would end up coated with the stuff." He nodded.

I flashed my fingernails. "See, my favorite color. Red."

He shrugged, looking off down the street, as if to follow Tommy Halperin's trail. "Why am I not surprised?"

Mort lurched behind the wheel of his SUV; the engine was revving before I got my door closed and seat belt fastened. His tires were smoking as he spun into a U-turn and, with sirens screaming, took off down the street, following the thin red line of nail polish the Charger had left in its wake.

"You would've made a good cop," Mort said, meaning it as a compliment.

"No, I wouldn't."

"Why?"

"I like people too much."

"I don't like people?"

"I have trouble believing anyone I like is capable of doing something bad."

"Sounds strange given your experience."

"I like keeping things black and white in my books. The real world is much grayer."

"Not as much as you think."

Mort followed the trail of nail polish through the narrow streets and tightly clustered neighborhoods of Somerville until it thinned, dissipated, and then vanished. It made no sense to me why Tommy Halperin would've weaved his Dodge Charger through this warren of roads when heading straight for Route 93 should have made for a much better strategy.

Whatever the reason, we were about to learn it. Mort continued along the route until it brought us down a street perpendicular to the one where the Charger was parked almost in the middle of the road.

Mort veered sharply to the side of the street, threw the SUV into park, and went for his gun.

"Slow down," I said.

"Don't worry. I'll wait for Somerville PD before I approach."

"That's not what I meant. Look closer."

He took off his sunglasses and squinted, eying the blackout glass on the driver's side. "Is that . . ."

"Sure looks like it, Mort: a bullet hole."

We still waited for the Somerville police to arrive before approaching the vehicle. Such displays of patience are hardly part of my nature, but this wasn't the kind of murder investigation I was used to becoming embroiled in, fraught with danger and my own life having already hung in the balance.

Somerville squad cars came in full force from all directions, each officer who emerged from his or her cruiser angrier than the last that a pair of outsiders, one who wasn't even a cop, had stumbled into a murder on their turf. They gave Mort short shrift, the on-scene supervisor asking again and again what had brought him here. Mort's answers remained vague. Meanwhile, the supervisor refused to talk to me initially and seemed intent on pretending I wasn't even there.

While he continued to pester Mort about being out of his jurisdiction and breaking protocol by not informing the locals of his presence in town, I loitered and studied the crime scene for myself. All indications pointed to the fact that Tommy Halperin had been shot by someone either standing outside the car on the passenger side or seated within it. He'd suffered a single wound to the temple by a bullet of a caliber sufficient to blow a golf-ball-sized hole out of the driver's side window, against which Halperin's head was resting. I spared myself a closer inspection of the Charger's cab and busied myself instead with trying to picture what had happened.

Halperin recognizes me standing outside his house and blows a hole in his own door with a twelve-gauge shotgun.

Then he flees, not for the highway but here. To someone, based on the positioning of his Charger, whom he was expecting to pick up.

But his would-be passenger kills Halperin instead of joining him.

The second attacker from the other night maybe, clearly still alive and now on the run.

I made a mental bet with myself that whoever it was would have a background similar to Tommy Halperin's, another man with a military and mercenary background familiar with killing for a living.

I felt the cell phone vibrating in my bag and removed it to see I'd already missed four calls from Harry McGraw, but I managed to answer the fifth just in time.

"So you're not taking my calls anymore," he greeted me gruffly.

"I've been kind of busy."

"How many bodies this time?"

"One," I told him, "with another in the wind."

Harry hesitated. "Wait, I was kidding. You're not serious, are you?"

"I'm standing twenty feet from the body right now."

"Hell of a week you've had, Jess."

"It's not over yet, Harry. Still another couple days to go."

"Not at this rate," he said dryly.

"Thanks."

"You're very welcome. You didn't sign up for my sensitivity plan."

"Sensitivity plan?"

"Costs more, my top rate. On account of the fact that it's so out of character. Just ask my ex-wives and kids."

"Are they ex-kids, too, Harry?"

"Except when they need money. Can you talk?"

I looked around. None of the cops or just-arrived crime scene technicians in yellow windbreakers looked back.

"Maybe they think I lost my dog or something," I told Harry.

"In other words, yes," he said. "Which is good, because I've got something on Benjamin Tally."

"Fingerprints, dear lady."

"I'm all ears, Harry."

"Whose would you expect to find on the title page of that manuscript you gave me?" he asked me.

"Lane Barfield's for sure, and maybe his assistant, Zara's."

"Right on both counts."

"Wait, how'd you match their fingerprints?"

"You mean, because neither's likely to be in the system, right? Simple: I lifted a pen from Barfield's desk and a coffee mug from what's-her-name's."

"Zara. You mean you stole the pen and coffee mug."

"What are you, my moral arbiter now?"

"Just keep talking, Harry."

"So, I get a contact in the NYPD's intelligence unit

to lift any prints he can from the title page and match them to Barfield's and Zara's."

"And?"

"They found a ton of prints matching one or the other, as expected. There were four other sets they were able to lift as well, along with smudges and fragments from several more. Of all those, it turns out one set belonged to somebody in the system."

I realized I was pacing about, so anxious my mouth had gone bone-dry. "Who, Harry?"

"That's where I hit a wall. My contact got frozen out, couldn't access our would-be author's prints."

"That's not good."

"I had the same thought. My contact said he was blocked because he didn't have clearance to access the file."

"And we're talking about an analyst in NYPD's Intelligence Bureau?"

"Last time I checked."

"You call Artie Gelber?"

"He hates my guts."

"No, he doesn't."

"The whole NYPD does. I lead all five boroughs in unpaid parking tickets. Over five figures, when the late fees are factored in."

"So pay them."

"If certain clients would pay their bills, maybe I would."

"You never send me any, Harry."

"I must've lost your address, and now your house burned down. Anyway, you need to contact Artie, because I don't want to be the one explaining to him how we went behind his back."

"Good point."

"So, how are things down your way, Jess? Anybody try to kill you again lately?"

"A little more than an hour ago."

"Fire again?"

"Twelve-gauge."

His tone flattened. "Wait a minute, you're not kidding."

I figured I'd call Lieutenant Artie Gelber later, maybe on the way back to Cabot Cove from Somerville after the dust settled here. The on-scene supervisor, whose name I forgot a moment after he introduced himself, finally got around to questioning me about my part in this, at which point I confirmed Mort's story, leaving the man shaking his head.

"And you're not a detective or investigator of any kind?" he asked, still trying to process all of this.

"No, I'm a mystery writer."

He looked at me skeptically. "Why haven't I heard of you?"

"Anything else?"

"Yeah. Do you know James Patterson?"

I gave Mort my take on things, once we were headed north on 93. He nodded through my analysis, having formed the same conclusions himself. Somerville police canvassed homes on both sides of the block, including the one we believed Tommy Halperin's killer had emerged from. That was the only house where no one answered the door, and a uniformed officer was posted while they waited for a warrant to search it.

We didn't need to stick around to learn what they'd uncover at that point. I had already convinced myself that whoever lived in the house was long gone. Halperin had shown up in a panic at the home of his fellow in crime and the man had killed him in order to avoid whatever baggage Tommy was lugging along for the ride. Maybe he figured Tommy was sure to talk if caught and had killed him to curry favor with the employer he'd now rely on to help him disappear. We'd have to wait for an identity on the suspect before coming to any definitive conclusions.

The fact that these two men were almost surely behind the attempt on my life, and likely the murders of Alicia Bond and the park ranger, didn't mean they were the ones responsible for the deaths of Lane Barfield and Thomas Rudd. And they couldn't be behind the murder of A. J. Falcone, all the way across the country, or Zara's disappearance. That meant whoever was silencing all those with a connection to *The Affair* had a virtual army at their disposal.

"I think we're headed in the wrong direction," I said to Mort suddenly.

"Am I supposed to know what you're talking about?"

"The answer's south, Mort, not north."

"New York?" he asked me.

"No, Washington."

It wasn't the first time I'd formed that thought, just the first time I'd verbalized it, and it left Mort shaking his head.

"Know something?" he said after a pause. "If anybody's ever going to solve the Kennedy assassination, it'll be you."

"We'd have to drive to Dallas for that, Mort. And I was speaking figuratively about Washington, not literally."

"But that's where you think this is headed, even if we're not? Someone in the hallowed halls of power trying to keep some secret worth killing a whole bunch of people over."

I nodded, not bothering to add it was all over a manuscript, when Mort's phone rang over his Bluetooth and he answered the call by pressing a button on his steering wheel. Too bad my new bicycle didn't come with that.

"Mort, it's Dick Mann." The voice of Cabot Cove's fire chief resounded through all the SUV's speakers. "Is Mrs. Fletcher with you?"

"Isn't she always?"

"Your office told me the two of you were together. Means I can share some news with both of you at the same time."

"My house didn't burn down again, did it, Dick?" I asked him.

"No," he replied. "But when I came into the station this morning, that manuscript of yours was gone."

Chapter Twenty

"Missing from the freezer," Dick added.

I felt the air go out of me like I was a popped balloon. I'm not often at a loss for words, but this was one of those times.

"I don't know what to say," Dick said apologetically.

"What about security cameras?" I asked him, finding my voice.

"We do have one but it's been off-line for the past few months. Something else I dropped the ball on, Jessica."

"Dick, whoever did this wasn't about to let themselves be seen anyway."

The fire chief of Cabot Cove chewed on that for a few moments. "I'm starting to get the feeling this manuscript was the reason you almost died the other night."

"Welcome to my world," Mort interjected.

Mort promised to stop by the fire station to investigate further as soon as we were back in town. I then told him about my conversation with Harry McGraw and the fact that Harry might have found the real author behind *The Affair*.

"If you ran some fingerprints through the national database and you drew a blank because of some kind of flagging at some upper level, what would you think?"

"That the owner of those prints was protected," Mort said.

"What does that mean exactly?"

"It's probably a bad choice of words. When a file is flagged, which is a very rare occurrence, it's normally because the person is already a subject of another superseding investigation and that party doesn't want any interference."

"So you're talking FBI, something like that?"

"If you're lucky." Mort frowned.

"What's that mean?"

"It means that you might ultimately draw an explanation out of the Bureau. But if it's NSA, CIA, DIA, Homeland Security, or straight military, forget it, because it likely means you're looking into a person involved in something that has national security written all over it."

"Oh boy . . ."

"Care to share a bit more about this book?"

"Outrageous story utterly lacking in credibility that's impossible to put down and stood an excellent chance of becoming a huge bestseller, until all trace of it disappeared."

I finally filled Mort in on everything from soup to nuts—starting with the murder of Thomas Rudd, followed by Lane Barfield's suspected suicide, all evidence of the manuscript's existence being wiped from the publisher's database, and everything else right up until the events in Somerville.

"This kind of stuff never happens in a J. B. Fletcher mystery, does it?" he noted at the end, referring to the name under which I published.

"I'm starting to think J.B. is a lot smarter than me, Mort."

"Well, you did steal that neat trick with the nail polish from her," he noted. "How'd you know it would work, by the way?"

"I didn't. Do you have any idea how often I tried it?"

"I assumed that was the first time."

"Only the first time it ever actually came in handy."

He shook his head behind the wheel. "You must go through a whole lot of nail polish, Jessica."

With the manuscript no longer in my possession, through the course of the drive north I busied myself with a review, like a mental catalogue of its contents from the first page to the last one I'd read. I'm not talking about specific lines or incidents, so much as the subtext in the dialogue. In essence, I was searching my mind instead of the manuscript for something either Abby or Pace had said that might yield some clue as to what about *The Affair* made someone desperate enough to kill to make sure all evidence of its existence disappeared. Mort could tell I was deep in thought and kept the conversation to an absolute minimum, although he might as well have talked up a storm.

Off the top of my head, there was nothing, absolutely nothing, that suggested some conspiracy or coming action some pseudonymous author had inadvertently stumbled upon. I wasn't sure that even if I did find the real Benjamin Tally, he'd be able to tell me anything more. So I rewound further, not to content but to concept.

A young man trained to be an assassin comes to the rescue of the first daughter, who overheard a conversation that marked her for death.

Okay, that conversation was between her parents, the president and first lady, centering on the fact that she was someone else's child and that she'd been kidnapped from the hospital by the same force behind Pace's training. I could see why that made her a liability in commercial thriller fiction, but what might it have to do with real life? Could something as simple as the book's concept be responsible for all that had transpired?

I couldn't see how. Our actual president and first lady, Robert and Stephanie Albright, had suffered a terrible tragedy when their daughter, an only child, died of an opiate overdose as a teenager, an event that ultimately defined him as a candidate climbing up the ranks all the way to the White House. Conservative polling estimates said the election had been tilted his way by a combination of the sympathy vote and the man's passion for fighting the opioid crisis. In fact, his presidency could be traced back to a single, dramatic moment in the first debate among the candidates of his own party who were running, when he enjoyed a hopelessly low recognition rating.

"I'm tired of losing young American lives on foreign battlefields," a dovish rival who was the front-runner at the time had intoned. "I'm sick of the blood of our children being spilled toward no good end."

"Well," the future president had responded, without waiting for the moderator to recognize him, "as the only parent up here who's actually lost a child, I'd like to know what makes you qualified to tell anybody what end is ever good enough for their son or daughter to die for."

The crowd had exploded, leaping to its feet against all rules of debate protocol, launching Robert Albright to 1600 Pennsylvania Avenue. That remark, that debate, that signature issue, had become what defined the entire campaign. The American people seemed to like having this man in their homes, if only through the television. He spoke their language instead of Washington-speak. An online article covering the day of his daughter's funeral went viral, helping to turn him into an everyman, that rare personality conjured by pop culture who actually had meat on his bones.

There was no suggestion of anything like that in *The Affair*. Or, if there was, almost being burned alive had prevented me from getting to it. The third of the manuscript left unread might well have contained the answers I was seeking and would now likely never find. All I could use was what I'd read so far, and I continued to search for something beyond the tragedy that had turned a small-town congressman into the most powerful man in the world. Something in his presidency, or mired among current events in general, that *The Affair* suggested a salacious take on in true roman à clef fashion.

For lack of a pad, and because I got carsick when I tried to write or read while riding in a car, I made a mental list of what stood out the most to me about the manuscript, in no particular order:

Infiltrating the White House through a secret underground tunnel . . .

A powerful force ordering the president's daughter killed because she'd learned of the existence of the Guardians . . .

The fact that the president was actually doing this force's bidding, was little more than a stooge for their efforts . . .

The fact that this force, the Guardians by all indications, was moving to seize power in a way that would effectively erect a permanent government . . .

I stopped my list there, too mentally exhausted to continue. I had the sense that I was missing something that was right in front of me, something hidden in plain sight. I could almost reach out and touch it, but every time I tried, it slipped from my grasp.

Mort and I didn't make it back to Cabot Cove until after dark. Mort insisted on doing a thorough check of my suite at Hill House before letting me inside.

"I think I might send someone over to check this place for bugs," he said.

"Are you serious?"

"Well, I know they're not called bugs anymore, but besides that, you bet I am, Jessica. This isn't the normal opposition you're used to going up against."

"Which would be what exactly?"

"Killers who lack a greater purpose."

"Mort," I said, feigning shock, "you *have* been reading my books."

"I guess the secret's out, then. Seems like the murders are always based on something personal."

"All the usual clichés, in other words."

"You said it, Jessica—I didn't."

"I don't have to tell you that the vast majority of murders *are* personal in nature, based almost exclusively on preexisting relationships. Strangers almost never kill each other—that's the rule."

"The exception being that greater-purpose notion I just raised. It's pretty obvious that Tommy Halperin and the partner who killed him this morning didn't know Alicia Bond, that park ranger, or Jessica Fletcher."

I nodded, because I couldn't think of a better way to respond. The Somerville police hadn't shared with us the name of the likely suspect in Halperin's murder, and I was sticking to my original assumption that it was someone else with a less-than-distinguished military background who'd hired himself out as a mercenary and was no stranger to killing, either.

As today attested to.

Similarly, I knew searching for any links between these men and the force behind all this would be a waste of time. There would be layers of insulation between them that made searching for any connection an exercise in futility. I was virtually certain that hired hands like Tommy Halperin, his partner, and whoever had arranged for A. J. Falcone's death out west had no idea who they were really working for; you didn't have to be a mystery writer to know that was the way things were done.

Once Mort had departed, I found my thoughts returning to the current president. I had met him only once in person but I had come away very impressed by both his charm and his genuine nature. I knew the first lady far better, of course, since I'd participated in and helped coordinate all those fund-raisers carried out on behalf of efforts to promote literacy. . . . I actually had her personal cell phone number, though I hardly could imagine how I might broach with her a conversation regarding *The Affair*. This was an administration untouched by even the hint of scandal, and whatever in this manuscript had motivated a spate of murders seemed in no way connected to its inner workings.

So what was I missing?

I again bemoaned the fact that the theft of the pages salvaged from the fire would deny me the opportunity to probe that further. Again, I was struck by the sense that what I sought was right in front of me, but I couldn't find it, the equivalent of stabbing in the dark.

Maybe not for long, though. If Harry did have a line on the real Benjamin Tally, if I could coax Artie Gelber into identifying the source of the flagged fingerprints, maybe the manuscript's true author would be revealed.

And he might be the only person who knew the truth.

Chapter Twenty-one

Harry was waiting outside LaGuardia for me in the back of an Uber car. He waved to me from a back door he was holding open, hustling me in before the airport police shooed the car off from the illegal parking spot it had just pulled into.

"Where's your car?" I asked him, climbing inside.

He piled in after me and closed the door, the Uber driver immediately pulling away from the curb. "Towed. The parking ticket gestapo finally found it."

"Where?"

"Parked in the bicycle lane in front of my building."

"Nice way to disguise its presence."

"I thought so."

I'd opted to fly this time, instead of wasting interminable hours on the long train ride, especially with no interesting manuscript to help me pass the time.

"You call Artie Gelber?"

I nodded. "He's expecting us at One Police Plaza within the next hour."

"I'll wait in the car."

"No, you won't, and Artie doesn't hate you, Harry."

"Yes, he does. Wouldn't surprise me if Gelber's the one who sicced the parking ticket secret police on me."

"Not his style."

"Which raises another question," Harry said, flashing his trademark scowl, which made his jowls look like they were about to slide off his face. "What was it that brought your friend Artie to the scene of Thomas Rudd's death?"

"I don't follow."

"He's part of the Major Case Squad, right?"

I nodded.

"So since when is a suspected arson considered a major crime?"

"Good point," I said to Harry, realizing it was something that I'd missed. "What are you thinking?"

"I'm not. I try to avoid thinking at all costs. It gives me a headache, and most of my thoughts don't lead anywhere but someplace bad."

"It led to those fingerprints."

"The title page," Harry said, settling back in his seat. "Front of it yielded a mess of smudges, but prints only identifiable as Lane Barfield's or his assistant, Zara's."

Something about that grabbed my attention, but Harry continued before I could figure out why.

"So I had my guy, who was born an expert in latent prints, run a check of the back. By the way, his services didn't come cheap."

"A bill, Harry. Send me a bill. So that's where he pulled these other prints that got flagged somewhere in the system."

He nodded. "It occurred to me that any number of people could have routinely touched the front of the title page—"

"But only someone actually holding it, reading it, would leave their prints on the backs of pages as well," I finished for him, picturing the way I held loose pages, which was more or less typical.

Harry gazed across the seat at me, pretending to be impressed. "You should think about becoming a mystery writer."

"I was thinking detective."

"According to my bank account, being a writer pays better."

"You're coming in with me to see Artie," I insisted.

"Why?"

"Because I'll double your rate."

He flashed that trademark scowl again. "What's two times nothing?"

"I guess thanks are in order," I said to Artie. "What made you assign someone to watch over me? Was it what happened to Thomas Rudd?"

He looked across the big desk in his office on the Major Case Squad level of One Police Plaza.

"Along with your publisher." Artie nodded.

"Two potential suicides."

"Since there were indications Rudd's was anything but that, I did the math."

"What did it add up to?"

"That you might be next, because of something you weren't telling me."

"There was nothing to tell you at the time."

"And now?"

I thought of the murders of Alicia Bond and A. J. Falcone. Then me narrowly avoiding being roasted alive and then the manuscript disappearing. And I hadn't even gotten to the part about Tommy Halperin in my mind.

"Now's different, Artie," I said. "A whole lot different."

Artie nodded, as if I was telling him something he already knew. "Mort called me."

"Did he?"

"We're starting a club."

"What club is that?"

"The Club for Cops Driven Crazy by Jessica Fletcher."

"Pretty exclusive."

"We're the charter members. After speaking to Mort, I'm thinking about resigning from the club and having you arrested for withholding evidence in the form of that manuscript."

"Well," I told him, "I'm not withholding it anymore."

"Only because it managed to disappear." He shook his head, with his eyes jabbing me like daggers. "What exactly were you thinking, Jessica?"

"That I wasn't sure. And by the time I pretty much was, your man had saved my life and the manuscript was no longer in any condition to do you any good. Besides . . . ," I continued, but let my voice tail off.

"Besides what?"

"If that manuscript contains the motive behind all this, I can't find it."

Artie almost laughed. "And, of course, if you can't find it, then nobody else could, either, never mind anyone in One Police Plaza."

"That was my thinking at the time, yes."

"And now, after somebody tried to drill you with a twelve-gauge, somebody who ended up dead himself minutes later?"

"You run Tommy Halperin through the system, Artie?"

He nodded. "And found pretty much the same thing Mort did."

"Pretty much?"

"The FBI's trying to backtrack his transactions. Somebody hiring him to kill would have to pay him, right? So where's the money? Hey, there's a thought: Maybe if we find out who routed it to Tommy, we'll be on our way to catching whatever Deep State is behind all this. That's called police work, Jessica. It's what we could've already been doing if you'd been up-front with me earlier." His gaze tightened and moved back to Harry. "Instead of using hacks to track down fingerprints."

"Hacks?" Harry repeated, but he didn't push Artie further, turning toward me instead. "You want to ask him or should I?" Harry said, looking at me as if Artie wasn't even in the room.

I knew Harry was referring to Artie's presence at the scene of Thomas Rudd's death, but I wasn't ready to broach that subject yet.

"Ask me what?" Artie inquired.

"What a top cop from the Major Case Squad was doing at an arson investigation."

If Artie was bothered by the challenge, he didn't show it. "Ruling out that it was a major crime. Routine Homeland Security procedure these days with any case involving combustibles."

Harry started nodding and didn't stop.

"Satisfied?" Artie asked him.

Harry stopped nodding. "No, because I've got a feeling there was more."

Artie didn't deny it. He actually smiled slightly.

"There was," he conceded.

"A politician, something like that?"

Now it was Artie pretending that Harry wasn't in the room; he trained his attention on me. "Leave it alone, Jessica. The person's identity has nothing to do with what you're after. Trust me on that."

I pictured some big New York honcho's mistress as one of Thomas Rudd's neighbors or something similar.

One Police Plaza itself, meanwhile, served as the headquarters of the NYPD. A fourteen-story, multiwindowed concrete slab of a building located on Park Row, closed to civilian traffic since the aftermath of 9/11, but not for us since my appointment with Artie Gelber secured us passage through the checkpoint at the end of the block. I seemed to recall lingering public complaints over the resulting security perimeter blocking off such a large swath of residential area at the inconvenience especially of residents. Other than modest refinements, One Police Plaza (or 1PP for short), the perimeter, and the inconvenience remained.

The vertical blinds in Artie's office were tilted just

enough to keep anyone inside out of clear view, at the expense of keeping most of the sun out, too.

"What about the identity of the man whose fingerprints got flagged?"

Artie's glance cheated toward Harry before fixing on me. "You mean the fingerprints somebody unauthorized tried to run through the system?"

"Hey," Harry protested, "he was authorized. All my inside contacts are authorized. That's what makes them inside contacts."

Artie didn't appreciate the flippant nature of Harry's tone. "By unauthorized, I was referring to you."

"Guilty as charged, Lieutenant."

"What makes someone want to risk their career for you?"

Harry's jowls started their trademark slide. "Beats me. I'm broke, a genuine pain in the ass, and my car got towed this morning, which I'm guessing you already know about."

Artie's expression begged to differ as he looked toward me again. "I want to know exactly what it is you're looking for, Jessica, and I want to know why."

I told him everything from the beginning, even though that meant repeating some things Artie had already learned from Mort or Ben McCreedy, the big NYPD officer from the train who'd ended up saving my life.

"Okay," he said, once I'd finished, "you believe all this is about the contents of this missing manuscript, but nothing in those contents jumps out at you."

"Did *The Da Vinci Code* make you think about Christianity differently, Artie?"

"I never read it, but I saw the movie."

"Same thing," Harry interjected.

"What's your point, Jessica?"

"That oftentimes thrillers and mysteries raise something just outlandish enough to make for a great concept but too outlandish to be believed or be even remotely connected to the truth. I'd say *The Affair* follows that model."

"So you're telling me you had things wrong."

"No, Artie, I'm telling you I haven't found what's right yet. That manuscript is the key to all of this—I know it is. I just haven't figured out why, and the only person who can tell me—*us*—why is the author, Benjamin Tally, who we've been unable to identify or find."

"And you figure those were his fingerprints on the manuscript?"

"Back of the title page," I affirmed. "Makes sense when you think about it. Harry was able to identify the prints of Lane Barfield and his assistant on both the front and the back as well. There was only one other set that appeared in both places and those are the prints that got flagged."

"For good reason, Jessica."

"What reason is that, Artie? What makes the owner of those prints so important? Who's protecting him?"

"I am," Artie said flatly. "I'm the one who's protecting him."

"He's in Witness Protection," he continued. "The name he's living under now is Alejandro Chacón. Back when he used to be somebody else, he gave up a whole bunch of MS-13 members to the task force."

"Bad hombres," Harry noted.

Artie looked his way. "I take it back; you really are a good detective. So Chacón serves up these names on a platter and we build him a new identity, get him resettled across the river in Jersey. One of those town house communities that go on forever."

"Don't tell me," I picked up. "You also got him a job working for Lane Barfield's company."

"Turns out he loves books, so pushing a cart in and out of the elevator, delivering this and that, was right up his alley. I forgot to ask him if he's read any of yours, Jessica."

"I'd like the chance to ask him myself. Where is he, Artie?"

"We've got him stashed right here at One PP until we arrange for resettlement. Thanks to you and your hack, he's been compromised. You want him to talk, you better have a signed book or two ready."

Five minutes later, Alejandro Chacón was escorted into Artie's office by a pair of uniformed officers who took their leave but remained posted on either side of the office door beyond. I assumed they'd been assigned to protect the informant my efforts had compromised, potentially placing his life in danger at the hands of the gang he'd given up. The glare he cast at me indicated Artie had made sure he'd been briefed on the circumstances and the mess I'd made of his new life.

"I'm sorry, Mr. Chacón," I said, not bothering to introduce myself.

"That's not my name," he said from across the

small conference table against the far wall away from the window in the back of Artie's office.

"I know and I had no idea my associate and I were risking your safety by running your fingerprints."

"You didn't risk my safety; you risked my life."

"I believe the man who ran the company you worked for was murdered. In both his case and that of one of his authors, it was made to look like suicide. Another author was trampled by a horse, a fourth was shot, and whoever's behind all of this tried to burn my house down after tying me to a chair. And it's all because of that manuscript we found your prints on—the back of the title page, specifically. Could you explain how they got there?"

"Because I started reading it."

I exchanged a glance with Harry. I wondered how he felt about being referred to as "my associate."

"It was sitting on the desk of Mr. Barfield's assistant, the one with the funny name."

"Zara," I reminded him.

"Zara, yes. I was dropping off the usual correspondence around lunchtime maybe two weeks ago, and I saw it there, like somebody had just delivered it."

"But not you," I said, trying to fill in all the blanks.

"I might have in a package or something. But these were loose pages, sitting right there on the edge of Zara's desk."

I nodded, feeling a pang of both remorse and sadness over the fact that Zara was still missing, potentially yet another victim of the secrets the manuscript held. But there was also something else, the same feeling that had struck me before of something awry, like an itch in the center of my back I couldn't reach.

"There was nobody around," Chacón continued. "I just started reading it. Standing up right there, I started reading it. I was maybe a dozen pages in when Zara caught me in the act."

"Was she upset?"

"She asked me what I thought. I said I wanted to read more and asked if I could make a copy. Bold move, given that I pushed a cart around, but I couldn't help it."

I more than understood since the manuscript produced that same effect on me.

"She said she couldn't do it, that I should ask Mr. Barfield myself. I didn't, of course. Figured I'd just have to wait for the actual book like the rest of the world."

"Did Zara say anything else about the manuscript?"

Chacón thought about that. "I don't think so. She startled me and I knocked some of the pages over. I just wanted to put them back and be gone."

"We checked Zara's apartment," Artie said after Alejandro Chacón had been escorted from the office by his keepers. "And the emergency number she left with HR has been disconnected."

A pang of guilt rattled me. I couldn't shake the possibility that Zara had been targeted because she'd aided my efforts to uncover any other author with a connection to *The Affair*. That had produced the names of A. J. Falcone and Alicia Bond, both of whom were now dead. Their murders had followed that of Thomas Rudd—who'd swiped a thumb drive from Lane Barfield's desk because he thought it contained something other than a manuscript—and preceded the attempt on my life.

A question on that note was plaguing me, but I was more concerned with Zara at present.

"What about her parents?" I asked Artie.

"A lot of 'Larsons' in the phone book, Jessica, and that's just Manhattan. We dumped her cell phone records but this was only yesterday, after Mort filled in the blanks. It wasn't a priority at that point."

"Wasn't a priority?"

"Being a missing person isn't a crime, Jessica."

I felt the pang of guilt roll through me again, harder this time. I needed to see this all the way to the finish and do right by Zara.

Artie excused himself to take a call, his eyes seeking me out as he listened to the voice on the other end.

"Sure, I'll tell her," he said, laying the receiver back upon its cradle. "That was Mort Metzger, Jessica. He just heard from the Somerville PD. They've captured the man they believe killed Tommy Halperin."

Chapter Twenty-two

"Is he talking?" I said, leaning forward in my chair. "Mort didn't say."

"Did he say to call him?"

Artie shook his head. "I guess it's my turn today. Share and share alike. Let's see—so far we know a young woman is missing who helped you and, thanks to the hack here working on your behalf, you've ruined the entire life of a key witness to multiple murders. Am I forgetting anything?"

"Do you believe me, Artie?" I asked, feeling uncharacteristically insecure about my conclusions, probably because of the damage I'd done to two lives. So far.

"If you include this Halperin character, six deaths are directly associated with your claims, to go with the attempt on your own life. That said, we have no hard evidence whatsoever that those deaths are linked to a manuscript that, for all intents and purposes, no longer exists. And all we know about that manuscript is what you can tell us, and, by your own admission, you never even finished it."

I nodded, unable to refute a single one of the points Artie was making. I glanced over at Harry, whose jowls were starting their slide again.

"I want to go back to something you said before," Artie said, rising from his chair and walking around his desk. "That Thomas Rudd believed Lane Barfield was stealing from him and that your own accountant confirmed oddities in your royalty statements as well. So what if these two other authors felt the same way? Maybe Rudd also managed to contact them. Maybe this isn't about a missing manuscript at all, and maybe the financial malfeasance stretches much deeper than you think."

"Deep enough to account for hiring men like Tommy Halperin?"

Artie stood over us, making me look up when he responded. "Maybe Thomas Rudd wasn't the first. Maybe he found out about what was going on from one of these other authors."

"Neither would have given him the time of day, Artie."

"You did."

"We went back a long way. He gave me one of my first blurbs."

"Well then," Artie said, scoffing, "I'd better stop smearing his character."

"What about my character?" Harry asked him.

"You don't have any character to smear."

"Which of my ex-wives are you dating, Artie?"

I rose from the chair, pushing up on the arms. "I'm sorry about Alejandro Chacón. I truly am."

Artie didn't look to be in an apology-accepting mood. "A little late for that, Jessica."

"But hopefully not for Zara Larson. Can you get a warrant to search her apartment?" I asked, not wanting to give away the fact that Harry had already given it the once-over.

"Don't need one if there's a reasonable suspicion foul play might be involved."

"At the very least."

Artie checked his watch. "I just happen to have a few minutes."

Harry and I accompanied Artie over to Zara's apartment on the West Side, just beyond the fashionable Chelsea neighborhood, saving us the bother of hailing a cab or getting another Uber car.

"There's something that's bothering me," I said, breaking the silence that had swiftly settled inside Artie's department-issued sedan.

"Something else, you mean."

"It goes back to Thomas Rudd. If I'm right, and all this really is about the manuscript, then somebody killed him because they knew he'd swiped that flash drive."

"Okay."

"So who could have known that besides Lane and Zara? Since at least one of them is a victim, too, there must've been another way whoever killed Rudd got wind of what he'd inadvertently stolen."

"What's your point?"

I hesitated. "Mort wanted to check the hotel room where I'm staying for bugs."

"You think Lane Barfield's office might have been bugged?"

I should've nodded but shrugged instead. "Something sophisticated, capable of recording both audio and video, planted by whoever's wiping out anyone with a connection to the manuscript."

"That's not so sophisticated these days, Jessica."

"It used to be."

"Don't get me wrong," Artie said. "It would take some pretty impressive logistics to manage the task."

"Can you sweep his office to check?"

Artie snickered behind the wheel, glancing at me in the rearview mirror. "Only if you promise to go back to Mort. It's his turn with you tomorrow."

"Hey, how about we grab some coffee?" Harry McGraw piped in, leaning forward in the back seat.

"You buying?" Artie asked him.

Harry gestured toward me. "I'll just add it to her bill."

I exited the car with Harry but stopped short of following him inside the coffee shop. Instead I moved beneath the shop's overhang and called Mort.

"Tell me something good," I greeted him.

"How about you not being here?"

"I heard that, Mort."

"Good. Has Artie arrested you yet?"

"On what charge?"

"Being a pain in the ass. New York has a lower tolerance for such things than Cabot Cove."

"Tell me about the suspect in the Tommy Halperin murder," I requested.

"Pretty much just like we figured: owner of the house Halperin parked his Charger with red nail polish stains on a rear tire in front of. Also, just like we figured, the suspect's background is a virtual twin of Tommy's, right down to the dishonorable discharge and last known whereabouts being overseas."

"Makes you wonder, doesn't it, Mort?"

"Not as much as you do."

But I could tell he'd already considered exactly what I was getting at. "How many more Tommy Halperins are out there?"

"At least one: Francis Malloy."

"Don't tell me: Francis Malloy is the suspect being held in Halperin's shooting."

"But he isn't talking, not even a word uttered since he was arrested at Logan Airport trying to book an overseas flight."

"Can you run his financials, see if there's anything that matches up with Halperin's?"

"Already in the works. I'm thinking of recommending a new bond issue to the town selectmen, by the way."

"What's that?"

"A second police force you can have all to yourself, Jessica."

"Which one are you planning to run?"

"I'm actually thinking of retiring."

"You already did that. It's why you came to Cabot Cove, Mort."

"I was more retired before I came to Cabot Cove. I

guess I should have retired someplace quieter, like Afghanistan."

"Any chance of you getting Somerville to let me interview Francis Malloy?"

Mort hung up.

Zara Larson's apartment was exactly what you'd expect for a young woman starting out on her own in New York City. A three-hundred-square-foot studio with a small breakfast nook and an alcove just big enough to fit a full-sized bed. It had the feel more of an oversized dorm room than of a starter apartment, a thought that stoked further guilt in me, given that Zara wasn't far removed from her college years.

The size and simplicity of the studio made canvassing it in search of some clue as to the young woman's whereabouts, or ultimate fate, a relatively simple task. Especially when you add to that the fact that Zara clearly lived sparsely and frugally. The mismatched furniture strongly suggested items picked up at sidewalk sales or second-, even thirdhand stores. The flat-screen television was a mongrel brand and looked tiny even on what amounted to a tiny wall. I didn't know a lot about computers, but I knew enough to tell that Zara's Apple laptop was several generations behind.

"Well, this tells us something," I said to Artie and Harry while standing over a desk built into a nest of bookshelves.

"What?" Artie wondered.

"When people leave anywhere of their own free

will, even when they want to make it seem otherwise, they take their computers."

"I don't see her phone anywhere," Artie noted. "But there's a charger plugged into the socket by her night table."

"Which tells us whatever happened, happened outside this place. Otherwise, there'd also be signs of a rushed packing job."

Zara didn't have a lot of makeup, but what she did have tucked away in the small bathroom looked undisturbed, further indication foul play was more likely here than her going on the run. I couldn't believe she wouldn't have called me if the latter was the case, given that I would probably be the only person who'd believe her and could help. That made me check my phone, as if by some miracle Zara had checked in while we were standing inside her apartment.

No miracle, I saw, and returned the phone to my bag.

"Something's missing," I said suddenly.

"I thought you said nothing was missing," Artie said, rubbing his hands, encased in plastic gloves, together.

"No, something is. I can't seem to put my finger on what it is."

"Hard to find something that's not here, Jess," Harry noted, clearly wanting to be anywhere but here.

"Humor me and I'll pay your overdue parking fines."

Harry looked toward Artie Gelber. "You're a witness. You heard that."

"Heard what?" Artie asked him.

I gave up. Whatever felt . . . wrong, whatever . . . anomaly my murder sense, as Mort called it, was alerting me to wasn't coming to me. I couldn't stand back and regard the scene objectively, professionally. Every time I tried, the realization that whatever fate Zara had suffered might well have been my fault slammed my consciousness again. I tried to detach myself, tried to see this tiny apartment in the same manner I'd survey any crime scene.

But posing the mere thought of "crime scene" left the guilt reaching for me again. In all the years I'd done my amateur sleuthing, I couldn't remember another time when my efforts had resulted in harm to someone innocent. And if there had been one, I knew I would remember it, just as I knew that if something happened to Zara Larson it would haunt me for the rest of my days.

I felt my guilt recede in favor of determination and resolve, much more welcome feelings. This had gone far enough. Enough people had already died. And I needed a different route to get me to wherever it was I had to be—to sort through the chaos of a manuscript that had gone missing, likely for good.

The Affair was about power.

The Affair was about politics.

The Affair was about Washington.

The Affair was about the White House.

And the White House was where I needed to go.

I told Harry and Artie that I had to use the bathroom. Once inside, I eased the phone from my bag and pressed the contact on my phone that read FIRST LADY.

Stephanie Albright had enlisted my help a few years back to support the cause of literacy at events all across the country. In addition to lending my own efforts to that cause, I was able to recruit a number of popular authors to join in, advancing the first lady's personal passion project in leaps and bounds on a nationwide basis. We'd become friends in the process and she'd repeatedly reminded me that she looked forward to the opportunity to return the favor.

Much to my surprise, she answered after only a few rings, and buoyantly so.

"Jessica, how nice to hear from you!"

"Madam First Lady—," I started to say.

"Stephanie, please. And what can I do for you, Madam Queen of Mysteries?"

"Jessica, please. And I was wondering if you could get me in to see your husband."

Chapter Twenty-three

"The president will see you now, Mrs. Fletcher."

I rose from a chair inside the president's Outer Oval Office, which adjoined the Oval Office, butterflies fluttering in my stomach. I've lived long enough, and achieved enough success, to have met more than my share of dignitaries in my time, even two former presidents. But I'd never had occasion to meet a sitting president in the Oval Office.

Especially under the circumstances in which I was meeting this one.

In the company of three personal secretaries of the president, I'd waited my turn, gazing out through a French-style door at the Rose Garden, which looked entirely different than it did on television, bigger and even more beautiful. I'd also used the small lavatory on two separate occasions to wash my hands, for fear of passing some germ on to the most powerful man on the planet.

"Mrs. Fletcher?"

The prompt from the president's assistant made me realize I hadn't moved an inch after rising from my chair, and I fell into step behind him. I hadn't even figured out what to say to the president yet, how to broach the subject that had brought me to Washington. I'd tried rehearsing any number of approaches on the train ride down here from New York, but all of them sounded lame in my own mind. How do you tell the president about a series of murders somehow connected to an unpublished, and now missing, manuscript? How do you suggest the possibility that something amid that fiction might reflect on something very, very real? Whoever Benjamin Tally really was, I had come to grips with the fact that he was likely dead now, too, that it was ludicrous to think that whoever was behind the likes of Tommy Halperin and Francis Malloy hadn't gotten to Tally as they'd gotten to everyone else associated with this manuscript.

And now I was about to speak to the president of the United States, to ask him . . . what exactly?

I had no idea.

"Mrs. Fletcher?" the president's assistant prompted again.

I realized my heels had ground into the carpet, bringing me to a halt. I had to push myself to get moving again, and I followed the president's assistant through a nearby door that led into the Oval Office. You know the old cliché about finding your heart in your mouth? I had detested it for as long as I could remember. But no more, because that was an apt description of what I was feeling in that moment.

I was more anxious than I was excited, given that this was hardly a social call and I still had absolutely no idea how I was going to bring up the subject of *The Affair*. Winging it had always been my preferred way of doing speaking engagements and interviews; I'm always at my best when I'm being spontaneous and at my worst when I have something prepared. But today was different. Today was about making the most of my time here and leaving with something I could hopefully act upon.

Was I here to warn or advise the president? Was I here to give him a heads-up that something nefarious seemed to be afoot, or to fill my head with more information about the subtext that might be lurking beneath the story? Thomas Rudd, Lane Barfield, A. J. Falcone, and Alicia Bond had already paid a terrible price for being associated with the manuscript, not to mention potentially the missing Zara Larson. I had no idea what my visit today might yield, what I might be able to coax out of the president.

I thought I'd be meeting him alone and was a bit unnerved to find two others present in the Oval Office. The man I recognized as Harlan Babb, a longtime politico who served as chief of staff. The woman might be Sharon Lerner, head of the White House's communications office. They both introduced themselves and we exchanged greetings, some small talk that faded from my mind almost before it occurred, because all of my attention was focused on the president himself.

He had risen to his feet, smiling behind that famed desk. As I moved to take one of the chairs before it, he came around the desk and took my hand in both of his.

"My wife's told me so much about you, Mrs. Fletcher. I can't believe it's taken me so long to meet you. I always enjoy being the second-most famous person in the Oval Office."

The president was known for his humility and good humor, a constantly upbeat personality who exuded a confidence that was infectious. The fact that he'd suffered such a devastating personal tragedy made his optimism all the more pointed. The country embraced him, not just because he had lost a child, but because he had found hope and purpose in that despair.

"I've just been around longer than you, Mr. President," I told him. "That's all. And it's my books that are famous, not me."

"'Destiny represents the sum of our deeds,'" the president quoted.

"Einstein?"

"Michael Newton. Einstein said, 'The high destiny of the individual is to serve rather than rule,'" the president quoted, serving to remind me that he was a true student of history.

I took the chair he offered before his desk. Harlan Babb and Sharon Lerner took seats opposite each other on the matching couches behind me.

I watched as, instead of retaking the chair behind his desk, the president took the one next to mine. I had no idea what the first lady had told him that resulted in this meeting, since she hadn't asked me for a specific reason. One friend doing another friend a favor . . . I guess common courtesy stretches as far as the Oval Office.

"Much more comfortable," he noted. "I'm glad to have this opportunity, Mrs. Fletcher, to thank you for all you've done for my wife. This cause is so important to her and you have no idea how much your help and participation have meant."

"It's the least I can do, Mr. President."

"She mentioned you wanted to see me, insisted that I squeeze you in today—between a pair of prime ministers as it turns out."

"Well, I've never run a country."

"Just as they have never written a book, at least a mystery."

"I believe history's more to your liking, isn't it, sir?"

The president nodded. "In large part because history holds the greatest mysteries of all. Why men took the actions they did and the chain of circumstances that led to those actions. I find real life, human nature itself, fascinating. Mysteries offer a glimpse into the dark side of that nature. I guess that's why I've come to avoid them. Sitting behind that desk," he said, aiming his gaze toward it, "I see all the darkness I want to see."

I let my eyes linger on that desk and the credenza behind it. When you spot something that grabs your attention, it's like opening a mental catalogue where you store it for future consideration. Here in the Oval Office, though, I was struck just as I'd been in Zara's apartment, not so much by what I was seeing as by what I wasn't. And you can't put your finger on what you can't see, other than to label it something amiss, awry.

"I should read more history," I told the president, meaning it. "I wish I'd read more history dating all the way back to my college days in Victorian England."

He chuckled. "The past provides a much deeper appreciation of the present."

"Because it's not dead; it's not even past."

"Faulkner?"

"Faulkner." I nodded.

He stretched a hand over his desk and grasped an oblong glass-encased paperweight and began passing it from one hand to the other. I recognized it as the one John F. Kennedy had fashioned from a coconut shell in the wake of PT-109 being cut in half by a Japanese destroyer and the crew being marooned in the Solomon Islands during World War II.

"Is that the original?" I asked President Robert Albright.

He held it up for me to get a better look. "Absolutely. On loan from his presidential library up your way in Boston. Kennedy used the coconut shell to get a message to the nearest PT base on Rendova and that led directly to his rescue. He later had the shell preserved as a keepsake. I've idolized him for as long as I can remember."

He laid the heavy paperweight back on his desk.

"So, Mrs. Fletcher," the president said, crossing his legs casually, "what is it you wanted to see me about?"

"Research," I blurted out, before I could ponder the question further.

"Okay," he prodded me on.

"Are there really escape tunnels beneath the White House?"

The president laughed, Harlan Babb and Sharon Lerner joining in as if following his cue. "You'd be amazed how often I get asked that."

"Is it true?"

"They may have existed once, but if that's the case, the rising water table swallowed them long ago. So when you hear rumors of JFK sneaking in mistresses through those underground passageways, it would be wise to dismiss them."

"I guess he was looking for a different kind of escape," I said, cringing at my lame attempt at humor.

But the president smiled politely. "Are you thinking of including a romp through those legendary tunnels in your next mystery?"

I took my lead from him, just as Harlan Babb and Sharon Lerner had. "Actually, I came across them in someone else's manuscript."

"Political thriller?" the president asked, expression crinkling in distaste.

"How'd you know?"

"What other book would include a scene like that? Don't tell me, the president turns out to be an impostor."

"Not exactly."

"The president learns he has only a week to live and decides to change the world in those seven days."

"Wow, I only wish. Can I steal that from you?"

"Another one I've heard is out there somewhere: The president is kidnapped and held for ransom."

"How about the president's daughter runs away because she's been targeted for assassination?" I blurted out before I could stop myself.

That was the problem with not having better prepared myself; I'd gotten to the point but had no idea what to do with it. And my statement rendered without forethought felt insensitive, given the tragic loss of his daughter well before he took office.

But the president seemed unperturbed, leaning in closer to me. "Keep going."

"She's rescued by a young man about her age."

"How old?"

"Early twenties."

"Sounds more like a movie."

"I imagine that would be music to the author's ears," I said.

"But you didn't come to discuss his book, Mrs. Fletcher," the president noted. "You came to discuss yours."

If only he knew, I thought.

"Well, sir, Victor Hugo wrote that good writers borrow but great writers steal."

"I thought that was Picasso."

"He appropriated the quote for art."

"In other words, he stole."

"Or borrowed. Semantics," I added.

"Don't tell me," the president said, grinning as he traced the air with a hand. *"Murder in the White House.* Has anyone used that title before?"

"I believe Margaret Truman did, not that it matters.

Titles are like bottles, Mr. President: They keep getting recycled."

"So in this book you read by somebody else, the president's daughter . . ."

"Needs to find the truth to save her own life."

"Classic," he complimented.

I frowned a bit. "I was thinking a bit clichéd."

"Same thing sometimes, Mrs. Fletcher."

I could feel Harlan Babb and Sharon Lerner shifting about on the facing sofas behind me, cognizant of the need to manage the president's time with someone else, likely one of those prime ministers, almost surely settled in the visitors' room, waiting for their audience.

"Have you ever encountered such a book, Mr. President?"

"You mean, like the one you're planning to write?"

"I was thinking more along the lines of that manuscript someone else wrote."

"What's the title?"

"The Affair."

I thought maybe that got a rise out of him, but he rolled right along casually before I could be sure.

"Catchy," the president said, then shook his head. "But I've never heard of it."

I knew my time with the president was drawing to a close. "One of the plot points is a book within the book, and everyone who reads it is killed."

"Sounds supernatural."

"Unfortunately, murder is very natural."

The president reached out and squeezed my arm,

taking an unspoken signal from his keepers that my time was up. Just then, the main door to the Oval Office opened and the first lady glided in, elegant and fashionable as always.

"Jessica." She beamed. "I'm so glad I caught you."

"Madam First Lady," I said after she hugged me lightly.

"Stephanie," she corrected again, then stole a glance at her husband. "You're among friends here."

"You never told me Mrs. Fletcher here was so interesting," the president noted, as Harlan Babb and Sharon Lerner positioned themselves to usher me out. "You've been holding back."

"Why should you get to have all the fun, my dear?" Stephanie Albright quipped. "Come, Jessica—I'll walk you out."

It felt strange to hear the first lady of the United States say she'd walk me out. Could she even do that? I wondered, still in awe of my surroundings.

I accepted the president's hand, his grasp strong and sure. "I can't wait to see how that book ends."

"The one I'm reading or the one I'm writing?"

"The one where the president's daughter hears something she's not supposed to and goes on the run. The one with the nonexistent tunnels."

I considered his polite, temperate, and casual response as I met the first lady halfway to the Oval Office doors, which had been closed again. Clearly, my overt mention of the manuscript's contents hadn't riled him at all. Politicians may all be expert liars—it kind of comes with the job description. Nonetheless,

I had the very clear sense that the president honestly had little or no interest, and even less of a stake, in what I was saying.

"Jessica, would you mind waiting just outside?" Stephanie said. "I'll be along shortly."

"Of course."

Harlan Babb held the door open for me as I approached and closed it again when I had exited. I waited just as the first lady had directed, thinking for a moment I heard raised voices coming from inside the Oval Office, one followed by another and then silence. Moments later, the door opened and Stephanie emerged.

She brushed free some hair that had strayed onto her face and eased a hand around my shoulder. "I hate Washington," she said, as if embarrassed that I might have heard the brief commotion.

"You've said that before, Stephanie."

"And I'll keep saying it until we're living somewhere else. But it provides an incredible platform to accomplish things that, thanks to people like you, we're accomplishing."

"You give me far more credit than I deserve."

"Really? Do you need me to recite all the big-time authors you've enlisted in the cause of literacy?"

I shrugged. "It gives me something to discuss with them at writers' conferences. We're a benevolent lot, always looking to serve a noble cause."

I could see the genuine warmth in her expression. "You were the first celebrity to sign on."

"I'm no celebrity, Stephanie."

"Do you remember how I contacted you?"

I nodded. "My Web site. You e-mailed me. I thought it was a hoax."

"Being the first lady of the United States seems to have that effect on people. But I'm blessed you actually replied."

"I'm glad I did. It's nice to make a difference," I told her, "even nicer to be doing it with you."

She reached out and squeezed my shoulder. "Did you get the list of upcoming events I e-mailed you?"

"Oh, that's right. Sorry I never responded. I already have them on my calendar."

"And your talk with my husband, it went well?"

"It did. I can't thank you enough for making it happen, especially on such short notice."

Something changed in the first lady's expression. It took on a tautness I'd never seen before, producing an effect kind of like that of seeing a woman without makeup for the first time. "You never told me what you wanted to see the president about."

"You didn't ask."

"I'm asking now."

I weighed my options, the seconds feeling like minutes, and opted for the approach I was most comfortable with. "I needed his opinion on something." The truth.

"Something you didn't ask for my opinion on."

"I can't say."

"You needed to see the president of the United States for a *case* you're working on?"

"I didn't say that."

"You didn't have to. You wouldn't have asked for the meeting if something serious wasn't going on. I know you, Jessica. Discretion might as well be your middle name, and you don't ask for favors lightly."

"Stephanie—"

She squeezed my arm tighter; I'd forgotten her hand was still clamped on my shoulder. "Just remember one thing, Jessica. This isn't Cabot Cove; it's not even New York City. It's Washington, an entirely different kind of arena."

"This isn't a game," I told her.

"Figure of speech."

I looked at the first lady more closely, wondering if she already suspected the purpose of my visit, if she knew far more than she was intimating. If she somehow knew about the manuscript. Maybe I should have told her everything then and there. About the murders, the manuscript, and how it might be a roman à clef, indicting the current first family. I couldn't bring myself to do that, though. I wasn't ready. There was too much I still didn't know.

"Jessica?" she said, after I'd started to walk away in the company of one of the members of her Secret Service detail.

I turned back around, met her gaze.

She waited a moment. "Be careful."

I'd taken a cab to the White House, but I felt like walking for a while with no particular place I had to be. I find walking to be the second-best way to relax, after riding my bicycle. How much I enjoy taking a break from writing in the middle of the day to enjoy Cabot Cove's pristine beauty, especially outside of the cluttered summer season. I'd ride the same streets I'd

ridden hundreds, even thousands of times, always noticing something I'd never noticed before. Sometimes
I biked for blocks, other times for miles, secure in the
notion that I could spend the rest of my life never leaving those ten or so square miles. Everything I wanted,
needed, and loved was a bike ride away, except in winter when the streets grew icy and snow piled.

Cabot Cove might be a coastal resort town, the
self-proclaimed Hamptons of New England, but it was
still Maine. That's why I hated winter, for the blissful
bike rides it denied me.

From the White House, I walked through the National Mall, along the Reflecting Pool, around the
Tidal Basin, before finding myself between the US
Capitol Building and Supreme Court, working out the
facts of this case the same way I worked out the plot
points of my books while biking. Along the way, I'd
similarly passed through any number of eras in the
history of the United States, including the Revolution-
ary War, the Vietnam War, the Korean War, and World
War II, and walked by the memorials to Presidents
Lincoln, Roosevelt, and Jefferson, making me appreciate all the more the scope and gravity of what I'd
become embroiled in.

My visit with the president had yielded nothing—
not that I should've expected otherwise. Maybe I'd
entered the Oval Office expecting to see a copy of *The
Affair* on his desk, establishing some elusive connection that would've explained everything. The truth
was that I had come to Washington mostly out of desperation, because I had nowhere else to look for the
truth.

Instead of clearing my head, walking among the tourists, school groups, and families that perpetually roamed these streets confronted me hard and fast with the fact that I was still in danger. I was the last person alive intimately familiar with the contents of *The Affair*. And I couldn't expect that whoever was behind the murders was going to stop just because Tommy Halperin and Francis Malloy had failed to finish the job.

I felt my phone vibrating in my bag and nearly jumped out of my shoes, startling a family snapping pictures on the majestic grounds of the Capitol, and I suddenly felt everyone staring at me. Fighting back against the sense of paranoia, I eased my phone out in a trembling hand and saw it wasn't a call, but a text message that had made my heart jump.

She didn't die of a drug overdose

Chapter Twenty-four

The text had come from a blocked number. It had to be from someone who knew I'd been at the White House, someone who knew about my conversation with the president.

Harlan Babb? Sharon Lerner? The first lady? The president's personal assistant? The president himself?

There weren't a lot of options.

She didn't die of a drug overdose

The text could be referring only to the president's teenage daughter, who'd passed tragically several months before he declared his intention to run for the highest office in the land. Most pundits didn't give him much of a chance, but that had all changed when America saw a man on a stage otherwise filled with politicians. It wasn't so much a matter of sympathy as of empathy. He wore the pain of loss on his sleeve and made no attempt to hide it. He gave the country permission to feel.

But if his daughter hadn't died of a drug overdose . . .

In shock, I finally slipped the phone back into my bag. I didn't feel like completing that thought right now. If the first family's daughter hadn't died of a drug overdose, was it possible that . . .

I just couldn't help myself.

. . . she'd been murdered? Had that been what had set off this spiral of murder that grew out of the existence of a future surefire bestseller that would ultimately reveal that truth to anyone who could read between the lines?

Or maybe they didn't have to read between the lines. Maybe that final portion of the manuscript I'd never gotten the chance to read saw Abby murdered, too. A stand-in for the very real daughter of the president suffering the same fate in fiction her real-life counterpart had in fact. Perhaps the manuscript even made clear who her killer had been through a thinly veiled suggestion.

A secret that couldn't be revealed in any form . . .

That would explain the murders. That would explain why Halperin and Malloy needed to burn my house down in order to effectively kill the manuscript, along with me. Two victims for the price of a single match—three, if you included the truth.

She didn't die of a drug overdose

I stood in the shade beneath a tree on the Capitol Building lawn to compose myself. Collected my thoughts before I eased the phone back out of my bag. Didn't realize I'd pressed the proper contact or even heard the phone ringing until a familiar voice answered.

"Do you have any friends in Washington?" I asked Artie Gelber.

It turned out he did, a whole bunch of them.

"You saw the *president*?" he said, as if not believing what I'd just said. "You're not kidding?"

"I'm not kidding."

"And now you believe his daughter might have been murdered?"

"Not based on what he told me, Artie."

"No, based on this mysterious text you received."

"Not a lot of people know what we talked about."

"But a whole lot know how much you support the first lady's cause of promoting literacy. It's hardly a secret."

"What's your point?"

"That this text message didn't necessarily come from someone who was inside the Oval Office."

"It doesn't matter where it came from," I told him, "not right now anyway. What matters is finding out if the message is true and the president's daughter was murdered."

"Thus your question about any contacts in DC Metro Police."

"I didn't specify police. I'd settle for the FBI,

Homeland Security, the highway patrol, or the ghost of Broderick Crawford or even Efrem Zimbalist Jr. Anybody who can access confidential medical records and open doors at the hospital where the president's daughter died of this supposed overdose."

"Would you settle for me?"

Artie said he could clear his schedule and be on an early train from New York the next morning. Since I hadn't prepared to stay overnight, this gave me an excuse to buy a new set of clothes and assorted sundries, just as I had after moving temporarily into Hill House. I normally love shopping, but not today. The crowds bothered me, leaving me holding my breath every time someone brushed up against me. By the time I left CVS, I couldn't wait to get to the Hyatt, my go-to hotel in any city where I stay, save for the occasional boutique luxury hotel.

Truth be told, my favorite hotels of all time were the old Howard Johnson's, where my family always stayed when I was a little girl, long before rewards points, concierge levels, and Gold Passports. I loved the orange lettering and all the flavors of ice cream available in their coffee shops, which made the best scrambled eggs I'd ever had in my life. They were also the only restaurants where I could get the big green peas with my turkey dinner, served all the time instead of just on Sundays. There weren't many Howard Johnson's left anymore, just a handful, but if there were, I'd probably still be staying in them.

That said, the Grand Hyatt Washington was located in the city's Penn Quarter neighborhood, which was about as convenient as it got. My favorite feature of the hotel was the open-air atrium that spiraled upward from the lobby, centered amid rooms on all sides. That design eliminated the claustrophobic feeling common among most big-city hotels, especially the older ones with their narrow halls and closet-sized rooms. My room featured an atrium view, well worth the extra cost, since it meant there was no exterior window through which I could be watched from the outside world or caught in the crosshairs of a sniper rifle. A thought that never would've crossed my mind a week ago.

Then again, a week ago I would never have believed I'd be in the Oval Office meeting with the president and wondering how he might be connected to a murder conspiracy.

I ordered room service and cruised through the television channels, starting the process over again as soon as I'd tried them all. Flirted with the notion of ordering one of those in-room new-release films but decided to save the twenty dollars and settled on an old black-and-white movie on TCM instead, Jimmy Stewart starring in *Mr. Smith Goes to Washington*.

Of all things.

I've always loved room service, something I guess you never grow out of. I'd just finished breakfast and was working on my second cup of tea when a knock fell on the door.

"Who is it?" I said, eye pressed against the peephole to find Artie Gelber on the other side.

"Guess."

"What's the password?"

"I ought to have you arrested."

I opened the door. "Only you would say that."

He stepped inside my room and closed the door quickly behind him, as if trying to keep out a draft. He looked around with a cop's eyes, I think to reassure himself I was safe and alone.

"You need to call Mort, Jessica," he said, his expression somewhere between somber and grave.

"He's dead," Mort told me, not elaborating further, as soon as I got him on the line.

"Who?"

"Francis Malloy. The Somerville cops went to escort him to his arraignment and found him dead in his jail cell. An apparent suicide."

"Seems to be going around lately. Anything on the security camera?"

"It was off-line."

"Of course it was."

"You want my advice, Jessica?"

"You're going to give it to me whether I want it or not."

"You need to disappear for a while. Let Artie and me sort this out."

"If I don't get to the bottom of this fast, I might disappear for good, Mort. However big we thought this might be, it's even bigger. Oval Office big."

"As long as you don't ask me to arrest the president."

"It's out of your jurisdiction. Artie's, too."

"But not our wheelhouse."

This was the new Mort talking, the Mort I'd never glimpsed before until the past week. I still knew little or nothing about his career with the NYPD, wondered what I'd find if I dug deeper, just as I wondered about his Vietnam experience.

"Where are you staying?"

"The Hyatt."

Mort hesitated. "I've still got some friends in DC Metro from my NYPD days. I'm thinking of asking one to camp out outside your room."

"That's not necessary."

"No? Okay, the lobby, then. Give me any more lip on the subject and I'll head down there myself."

"How could Cabot Cove survive without you?"

"Easy," he said. "With you out of town, things are a lot quieter."

"I think we need to bring the FBI in on this," Artie said after I'd finished my call to Mort.

"Someone there you can trust?"

"A whole bunch of people."

"Implicitly?"

"That narrows the field a bit," he conceded, "but still a decent number."

"Okay, and what are we supposed to tell this decent number, exactly, Artie?"

"How about the truth?"

"A challenging proposition, given so much of it is actually supposition."

Artie looked unswayed by my argument. "That text message is a game changer, Jessica, especially coming right after your visit to the White House."

"You think the FBI will believe the first family's daughter didn't die of a drug overdose, that she was murdered?"

"Not initially, in all likelihood."

"That's my point."

"So what's your plan?"

I had been waiting for that question. "According to all the reporting, Kristen Albright was rushed to Med-Star Georgetown University Hospital's emergency room six years ago this week. She was pronounced dead of what was later confirmed to be an opioid overdose one hour later but was already on life support when the paramedics brought her in."

"Okay," Artie said, waiting for me to continue.

"We need to speak to as many people as we can find who were on duty in the ER that night. Nurses, receptionists, doctors, residents, attendings, janitors—anyone."

"On whose authority?"

"You're still one of One PP's top liaisons to Homeland Security, right?"

"Of course."

"And I assume that job comes with some fancy cross-jurisdictional title."

"Correct again." Artie nodded.

"So technically you're Homeland Security, in addition to NYPD."

"More than technically," he agreed.

"And that means you have license to investigate anything that falls under Homeland's purview."

"Only if it covers a threat to national security, Jessica."

"I think it's safe to say that applies here," I told Artie.

She didn't die of a drug overdose

Artie handed me back my phone with the mysterious text still boxed on the screen.

"Any chance the number can be traced?" I asked him.

"Under normal conditions, I'd say yes. But in this situation, given what we're facing, there's no way it'll lead anywhere worthwhile. If Homeland Security, or the FBI, manages to nail down the number, my guess is it'll lead to an unregistered burner phone that's probably already been discarded."

"I don't like your attitude," I said, glad I was still able to find a semblance of humor in all this.

I was eager to get going, to head over to Georgetown University Hospital, aka Georgetown University Medical Center, to see what we could dig up. This was where my avocation as an amateur sleuth and my day job overlapped a bit, in the sense that we'd reached the stage of a very real case that I couldn't wait to get back to, the same way it was for the ones I make up. That's the way it had always been for me. My work picks up momentum as I go. It gets to the point where hours disappear, time melting away when I'm tearing through those final pages, all the connections falling into place. If only real life worked that way, if only I had that much control over finding the truth behind *The Affair*.

"I'm not telling you anything you hadn't already figured out yourself," Artie was saying.

"I wish you would."

"You know what I wish? That we dump all this into the FBI's lap and head to Union Station and take the next train back to New York."

"We've already been over that."

"Excuse me for being cautious."

"They didn't try to kill you, Artie."

"I think I know that."

"And they killed my publisher. That makes this personal. That's my point."

He nodded, weighing my comment. "Have you ever gone up against anything like this before?"

"No."

"That's *my* point, Jessica."

Chapter Twenty-five

We took the Metro, DC's subway system, to George-town University Medical Center. Founded in 1898, it was one of the oldest academic teaching hospitals in the country and boasted a sterling reputation in all respects. It was located on Reservoir Road Northwest, just beyond the primary Georgetown campus, and easily accessible via the Dupont Circle Metro stop on the Red Line, where a shuttle bus ran every fifteen or so minutes from the stop to the hospital itself.

"We should have taken a cab," Artie groused.

I shrugged, having neglected to note the need to board the shuttle bus on top of the Metro ride. I think we were the only non–Georgetown students on board; to say we stood out would be an understatement.

The hospital itself was a sprawling structure fin-ished in red brick that look lifted from another era en-tirely. After entering the ER, Artie asked me to hold back while he flashed his Homeland Security ID and tried to discern the best person with whom to begin our inquiry into the death of Kristen Albright six years before. Since she was the deceased daughter of the current president and first lady, I was sure the hospital got more than their share of such inquiries, though the vast majority probably came from the likes of the *National Enquirer* and other tabloid-type newspapers and television shows, chasing down conspiracy theories of their own making. There were all kinds of such stories out there, the most outlandish of which claimed that the purported drug overdose was a cover story for the president himself, then a congressman, murdering his own daughter to keep her from exposing an affair that would have doomed his political ambitions. One rumor said the affair was with the then first lady. Another insisted that the dalliance was with a male congressional page, and I seemed to recall a third that insisted space aliens were involved somehow.

Go figure.

I hovered close enough to Artie to hear him inquire about that night six years ago, stating that circumstances had arisen that called into question the veracity of the original diagnosis. He said just enough, and in just the right tone, to let the emergency room receptionist know this was an investigation deemed serious at the highest levels of government.

"Those records are sealed," the receptionist told him. "I don't have the authority to be of any assistance to you."

"That's why I'm here, ma'am," Artie said back to her, "to find somebody who does."

That person turned out to be the head emergency room nurse on duty that night six years earlier, who'd since been elevated to the position of chief administrator of emergency services. Her office was located on the sixth floor in a neighboring wing of the hospital complex. The receptionist called ahead to make sure she was in but, on Artie's urging, stopped short of saying why.

"It's going to be tough to explain your presence," Artie said to me, contemplating the options as we walked along a winding connecting corridor to the hospital's office annex.

"Mort never had a problem with that."

"You ever investigate the potential murder of the president's daughter with Mort?"

"Not recently. And I guess I'm too old to pass as your assistant."

"Only just."

"Can I make a suggestion?"

Alma Desjardins, current chief administrator of emergency services and former head ER nurse, handed Artie back his Homeland Security ID wallet without, as I'd suspected, even casting me a second glance. I'd suggested to Artie that he not bother introducing me at all. I also promised to remain silent, so as not to force the issue. Now that he'd made good on his part of the bargain, it was left to me to make good on mine.

No easy task, of course, given my penchant for butting in.

Alma Desjardins had a big, friendly smile that made me feel as if she were about to invite me to dinner. I thought she must be a pleasant person to work for. Her desk was cluttered with picture frames of all sizes, the ones I was able to glimpse containing a slew of smiling faces captured in group shots, both small and large. And, just as I'd hoped, she cast me a glance and a nod without aiming any inquiries my way.

"What can I do for you, Agent?" Alma asked Artie.

"Actually, it's Lieutenant," Artie corrected. "I work with the NYPD's Major Case Squad and I'm here because a case I'm following up north has potential national security implications."

Alma Desjardins jotted down some notes before looking back up again. "And what kind of case might this be? I assume you can tell me that."

"I can." Artie nodded. "It's a murder investigation, actually several murders."

She didn't bother jotting that down, just waited for Artie to continue.

"Mrs. Desjardins, we have reason to believe that the murders in question may be connected to the death of Kristen Albright several years ago."

Alma laid her pen down atop the pad. "The president's daughter?"

Artie nodded again. "I'm afraid so."

"It was an opioid overdose, as I recall."

"That's correct. And she was rushed here, to Georgetown University Medical Center, where she was pronounced dead."

"How can I help you?"

"You were working the emergency room that night as head nurse—is that correct?"

"It is," Alma replied, like a woman who knew how to answer a question.

"What do you recall about that night?"

"The security people disrupting the entire ER."

"Security people?" Artie quizzed, a mere instant before I was about to blurt the same query out.

"They arrived shortly after the ambulance, maybe even with the ambulance."

Trying to make sense of that, I looked toward Artie. He didn't look back. Had Kristen Albright been the first daughter at the time, the men Alma was describing would've almost surely been Secret Service agents. Since she was merely the daughter of a sitting congressman back then, I had no idea who they might be.

"Were they uniformed police?"

"No. They wore plain clothes. Dark suits, just like you."

"Did they identify themselves as police officers?"

Alma shook her head.

"Were they wearing badges, likely dangling from lanyards?"

Alma shook her head again.

"Could they have been plainclothes Capitol policemen?"

"If they were, they didn't identify themselves as such."

Artie finally glanced my way, looking as baffled by this unexpected turn of events as I was. "What do you remember about that night from the time the ambulance arrived?"

"It was clear from the way the paramedics were working on the poor girl that she was unresponsive.

I'd seen this before, far too many times, and it seldom ends well."

"I understand. But you weren't in the room when she was being treated."

"No, but two nurses and two of our best emergency medicine physicians were. For over an hour, more than enough time to take every measure possible to save the girl. But I knew it was hopeless. Like I said, I'd witnessed the same scene before more often than I care to consider."

Her gaze found me across the desk, as if she was looking for the support of a fellow woman. I clung to my promise to remain silent and I let my eyes meet hers.

"And then?" Artie prompted.

"All routine from that point. One of the treating physicians signed the death certificate and a funeral home came to pick up the body."

I realized Artie had rested his trusty memo pad in his lap and had been making notes the whole time. I hadn't noticed before because I had kept my focus trained on Alma Desjardins.

"So," he continued, "four emergency room personnel treated Kristen Albright after she was brought in, these two doctors and two nurses."

"That's right."

"Anyone else? Another doctor or nurse perhaps? A technician who may have prepared the body for transport?"

Alma shook her head. "After the poor girl passed, those policemen blocked off the room where we tended to her. They didn't let anyone else in until her parents arrived, followed closely by the funeral home to pick up the body."

"The couple came together?"

"Yes."

"And how would you describe them?"

"Exactly as you'd expect from parents who'd just learned they'd lost their only child. 'Grief-stricken' wouldn't do it justice." Alma's expression turned genuinely sad. "I've seen that scene replayed all too often as well."

I couldn't help myself. "How long after their daughter was pronounced dead did they arrive?"

Alma didn't respond right away, as if she was taken aback by my suddenly inserting myself into the interview. "I don't recall exactly, but I'd say around twenty minutes."

I felt Artie staring at me harshly, but I continued anyway. "So that would be eighty minutes after their daughter was brought in. Do you remember how they were notified?"

Artie kicked my leg lightly.

"No."

"What would be the routine approach?"

Artie kicked me harder, hard enough for Alma Desjardins to notice.

"The police normally handle such things. And since they arrived with, or shortly after, the ambulance, I assumed they'd taken care of it."

"Except you can't be sure they were police."

"Who else would they be?" Alma challenged.

I took that as my cue to go silent, before Artie left my leg bruised.

"How many of these plainclothes policemen were there?" He picked up the thread.

"Four inside, but I seem to recall two more taking up posts outside the ER entrance."

"So six in total. And you've dealt with comparable tragedies with comparable dignitaries, or their family members, before."

Alma sighed. "As I've already said, far too often."

"Do you recall a similar security presence for those?" Artie asked her.

"No, never anything like that night. No."

Artie flipped his memo pad to a fresh page and wrote down some more notes. "One more thing, Mrs. Desjardins. Do you still have a record of the two nurses and two physicians who treated Kristen Albright?"

"I'm sure we do. It might take a few minutes, but I can look it up for you."

She started to stand up, suddenly impatient for us to be gone.

"I have one more question, if you don't mind," I said.

Alma sat back down, not minding. But Artie clearly minded enough for both of them.

"No autopsy was performed, was it?" I continued.

"As I said, we turned the body over to the funeral home at the request of her parents, just Mr. and Mrs. Albright at the time. The results of the blood work and toxicology screen later positively confirmed the initial diagnosis and cause of death. We were dealing with grieving parents. There was no reason to put them through more heartache at the time."

I rose from my chair ahead of both Alma Desjardins and Artie. "Of course. And you recall nothing else unusual from that night?"

"Like what?"

"Anything suggesting that Kristen Albright died of something other than a drug overdose, specifically opiates."

Alma shook her head. "No, nothing at all."

"Thank you for your time, Mrs. Desjardins," Artie said, extending his hand across the desk to shake hers.

"My pleasure, Lieutenant. And I can either text or e-mail you the information I find on those two nurses and two doctors who treated the poor girl."

He jotted both his cell phone number and e-mail address on a fresh page he tore from his memo pad and handed it across the desk.

"Thank you, Alma," I said, feeling Artie tugging me toward the door.

"My pleasure . . . Mrs. Fletcher."

"Happy, Jessica?" Artie asked me in the hallway beyond, stopping just short of the same elevator we'd used to get up here.

"That she recognized me?"

"That you could have compromised us. I'm not actually here in an official capacity, in case you've forgotten."

"Says who? You told her you were following up some murders that had taken place in New York City that may—*may*—be connected to the death of the president's daughter. That's the truth."

"True or not, I wasn't here under the auspices of Homeland Security."

"Semantics, Artie."

"You can explain that to my wife if I get suspended without pay."

The elevator door opened. People got out; people got in. We stayed where we were as the door closed again.

"Are you this meddlesome with Mort?" Artie asked me.

"I'm usually worse with Mort."

He scowled, starting to look more and more like Harry McGraw. "Now I know what I've been missing."

All that was missing from his expression were those sliding jowls.

"Tell me what we just heard," I said.

"You need me to repeat it for you?"

"Just the part about six plainclothes security types showing up with the ambulance."

"We need to check with Capitol Police or DC Metro to see if they were part of a detail."

"What kind of detail?"

"The kind that might've been working a nightclub or concert where Kristen Albright was ambulanced from. Or maybe it was a private detail, hired by her parents to babysit her."

"Wonderful job they did."

"You have a better explanation . . . *Mrs. Fletcher*?" Artie asked, imitating the way Alma Desjardins had said my name.

"Go back to that text message I received, the one

that said Kristen Albright didn't die of a drug overdose."

"Which led you to believe it was murder instead."

I nodded. "A theory that much better explains the
six men who looked like cops but wore no badges.
And I'll tell you something else, Artie: Until we speak
to one of the doctors or nurses who actually treated
the girl, we can't be sure it really was an overdose,
can we?"

"'We'?"

The elevator door opened again and this time we
got in, joining a young woman smiling at a picture
displayed on her phone. That made me think of Alma
Desjardins's desk, priority given to any number of
framed photographs she'd surrounded herself with.
I'd caught brief glimpses of a few of them, enough to
know she had a big family, children and grandchil-
dren everywhere.

I was thinking of those pictures when a thought
struck me, a memory of another desk I'd recently seen
and what had been bothering me about it.

"Oh my . . ."

The girl with the phone looked at me.

So did Artie. I wondered if he knew my knees were
shaking.

"What is it, Jessica?"

I held Artie's stare. "Something I just realized about
my visit to the Oval Office."

"Something you saw?"

"No," I told him. "Something I didn't see."

Chapter Twenty-six

After leaving Georgetown University Medical Center, Artie and I headed over to the Starbucks on Pennsylvania Avenue. While he followed up outside with some phone calls based on the contact info Alma Desjardins had forwarded him, I joined a line inside as long as one you might find for a ride at Disney World, emerging finally with a hot tea for me and some kind of iced mocha concoction for Artie.

"Two nurses and two doctors," he said, popping off the lid on his large cup and sniffing the foam. "One of each of whom has a phone number that's been disconnected."

"That's not good."

"It gets worse. I googled all four. The other two are dead, both within a year after leaving the hospital in Georgetown."

"So the four people who treated the future president's daughter when she was brought into the emergency room suffering from a drug overdose *all* relocated and we know that at least two of them are dead."

"That's right."

In spite of everything that had transpired, I was still having trouble believing that. "What are the odds?"

"I'm not a betting man," Artie said. "I'll keep trying to reach the other two, whose numbers don't work anymore. I've already called One PP back in New York to run more detailed checks on all four."

"Wanna bet the other two turn out to be deceased, too?"

"What did I just tell you?"

"And if you were a betting man?"

He flashed that Harry McGraw–like scowl again, jowls not dropping as dramatically this time. "That's one I wouldn't take."

We sipped our drinks, standing there on the sidewalk outside Starbucks, the world continuing to pass by around us.

"I need to ask you something now, Jessica."

"I don't know."

"I haven't asked the question yet."

"But chances are that'll be my answer."

"It's about the manuscript," Artie said.

"Have I thanked you for saving my life, by the way?"

"Only a dozen times, but feel free to thank me again. After you tell me what the missing manuscript has to do with all this."

"Best guess?"

"Best guess."

"An author who goes by the name Benjamin Tally

wrote something that turned out to be too close to the truth."

He nodded, eyes scanning the surrounding area for a place to sit down. "I think it's time you told me everything you can about the manuscript, the abridged version."

"You mean like CliffsNotes?"

"Anything that helps me understand what the hell is going on here."

I summed up the contents of the manuscript as best I could, composing the kind of plot summary normally found in the kind of extended piece I occasionally penned for the *New York Times Book Review*. On the sidewalk we'd found a shaded table belonging to a restaurant where the luncheon rush was just ending.

When I finished, emphasizing what I took to be the most salient points of *The Affair* for our purposes, Artie just sat there, stonelike and expressionless, as if he hadn't heard a thing.

"The Guardians," he said finally.

"I thought that would get your attention. What if they're real, Artie? What if they're the ones behind all this?"

"And this author, Benjamin Tally, just made it all up and happened to get lucky?"

"Well, I wouldn't call it lucky."

"Figure of speech."

"The fact is, the best hope we have that Benjamin Tally is still alive is because he used a pseudonym. The only person who probably knew his true identity was Lane Barfield, and he's dead. In any case, until we find Tally, we won't know for sure."

"I think it's time to put the resources of the NYPD to good use."

"I was thinking more like Homeland Security."

"I'd rather keep the circle as small as possible, Jessica, limited to people I trust."

"Speaking of which, I think it's time I called someone I can trust."

"Anybody I know?"

"The first lady of the United States."

I was supposed to meet First Lady Stephanie Albright at the Compass Coffee on Seventeenth Street Northwest between the Capitol Building and the Lincoln Memorial. The airy, bright, and modern coffee shop and roaster was always packed. Luckily, I arrived ahead of her and managed to snag a corner table for two with a clear view of the entrance, so I'd know when her entourage arrived.

A woman wearing sunglasses, with her hair bunched beneath a wrap, suddenly pulled out the chair across from me without asking if anyone was using it. I looked up, started to protest, then stopped as quickly as I had started.

"Hello, Jessica," said the first lady.

"Stephanie?" I said to the woman, who didn't resemble the first lady at all.

She took the chair she'd just pulled out, positioning it so her back was to everyone else in Compass Coffee. I looked around, seeking out her Secret Service detail.

"I came alone."

I waited for her to continue.

"You said this was about my daughter."

"And that's why you came alone?"

She shoved her chair farther beneath the table, kept her voice low. "When it comes to this subject, I become a mother again, not the first lady."

"Are you in the habit of just walking out of the White House on your own?"

"I made an exception."

There was no point in delaying the issue. "How did your daughter die, Stephanie?"

She looked angered by my question. "You know how she died; the whole world knows how she died."

"No, they don't, and neither do I." I decided not to mention the text message I'd received yesterday yet. "I need for you to tell me the truth, Stephanie."

"I know you, Jessica. I know you well enough to be sure that you're looking for confirmation, not information. Why don't you tell me what you think happened?"

"I don't believe it was a drug overdose. I believe Kristen was murdered. I believe she was murdered because of something you and the president had become involved in. And I believe that's connected to the residence you currently occupy."

"A great plot for a mystery," was all she said, but her voice cracked several times.

"There's more. I think she was murdered as a warning to your husband, because whoever wanted to make sure he became president didn't want him stepping out of line. Is that what happened, Stephanie?

Had he stepped out of line, refused to follow somebody else's plan?"

"Where'd you get such a ridiculous idea?"

I took out my phone, jogged it to the text message
I'd received yesterday, and angled the screen so she
could see it.

She didn't die of a drug overdose

I watched the first lady mouth those words to herself, her lips trembling slightly.

"Who sent you this?"

I hardened my stare. "It's the truth, isn't it?"

"Who sent it, Jessica?"

"I thought maybe you had. Because you were tired
of living a lie, because things had spiraled out of control. Because you saw me potentially offering a lifeline
to help get the truth out and bring whoever's behind
this down."

"You've read too many of your own books."

"Indeed I have, each one as many times as it takes
to get it right. Same thing I do when a real-life case
ends up in my lap. I need to get everything right; the
difference is that I'm not in control. The story's not
mine to change, just to interpret."

"And that's what you're doing here? That's why you
called me?"

"I called to help you," I told the first lady.

"I didn't ask for your help."

"Yes, you did, Stephanie: You asked for my help
when you showed up here in disguise without the
Secret Service. You had an idea of exactly what this

was about as soon as I mentioned your daughter. That's why you came."

The first lady removed her sunglasses. I could tell she'd been crying.

"They'll kill you, Jessica."

"They already tried."

"These are powerful men. You don't understand."

"Help me to understand."

"You mean the whole truth, Jessica?"

"Is there any other?"

"The truth will bring my husband down."

"You can't know that."

"You don't understand," the first lady implored.

"You said that already."

"It's not you, not me, not even the president. You've sealed all our fates, Jessica. We made a deal with the devil and it looks like he's finally come to collect on the debt."

"Who are these people, Stephanie?"

"They got him elected. They set this all up."

I let that comment hang in the air, weighing everything Stephanie had just said with what I already knew. But there was still another mystery hanging out there.

"If neither you nor the president sent me that text, it had to be either Sharon Lerner or Harlan Babb," I said finally. "They were the only other ones in the Oval Office when I met with the president."

"It was Sharon."

"How can you be sure?"

"Because Harlan Babb, the chief of staff, was the one who came to us in the beginning. He's the one who set this whole thing into motion. My husband gets to go from congressman to the most powerful office in the world. All we had to do was cooperate, go along with the plan."

"But Kristen disagreed," I advanced, laying the truth alongside the contents of *The Affair*, "didn't she? She caught on to what was happening and became a liability."

The first lady didn't nod, didn't have to. "How did you figure all this out, Jessica?"

"Because of a book."

"What book?"

"An unpublished manuscript," I said, and proceeded to fill her in on what had brought me to Washington in the first place.

Stephanie Albright didn't look even a bit surprised by any of it; after all, she'd been dealing with these people for some time and was intimately acquainted with what they were capable of. It was her turn to pause now.

"A pseudonym," she said. Finally.

I nodded. "Chosen by someone seeking a way to expose the truth. I'm guessing that's a very short list."

The first lady nodded this time.

"Sharon Lerner?"

"She's been with my husband since the start of his career."

"She knows everything?"

Another nod. "Along with Harlan Babb."

"Call Sharon Lerner, Stephanie."

She took the phone from a bag she'd slung over the chair and pressed a contact name. I could hear the phone ringing, the click preceding the call's going to voice mail.

"She's not picking up."

"Can the Secret Service be trusted?"

"Some, not all."

"Enough?"

"I'm not sure."

I shouldn't have been surprised, but I was. "This goes that deep," I managed.

"As deep as that manuscript?"

"In the manuscript, the first daughter finds a knight in shining armor who saved her life. Then they try to bring down the conspiracy together."

"That's why it's called fiction, Jessica," Stephanie said, her eyes turning watery.

I leaned forward in my chair. "Here's something that's fact: At least two members of the medical team that treated your daughter in the emergency room that night are dead."

Her face turned ashen, all the pigment seeming to wash away. "Murdered?"

"A car accident and a home invasion," I said, recalling the details Artie had later learned.

"Murder," the first lady said.

"We're trying to find the other two."

"Don't waste your time. They're dead, too. It's how these people work."

"The Guardians," I said to myself.

"How did the book end, Jessica?" Stephanie Albright asked hesitantly, as if she was afraid of what my response might be.

"I don't know. Those men tried to kill me before I finished it. Then what the fire department was able to salvage of the manuscript disappeared."

The first lady stared at me from across the table, her eyes wide and full. "I'm sorry, Jessica."

"It's not me you should be sorry for, Stephanie."

"The country, too, if that's what you mean."

"It's not," I told her. "I meant your daughter. I meant Kristen. From this point, everything we do is about her, about what the Guardians did to her."

"The Guardians?"

"What the people behind everything are called in the manuscript," I told her, the lines between fiction and reality becoming increasingly blurred.

Her eyes were looking past me now, past the wall, past Georgetown. "It's my fault. I'm the one who let this happen. I knew what we were getting into and I ended up getting my own daughter killed."

I reached across the table and grasped the forearm the first lady had laid there. "Loading the gun doesn't mean you pulled the trigger. We'll get the people who did. I promise. We're going to get them."

"Did you hear what I just said about them, about what they've done, what they're capable of doing?"

"I heard, and now I want you to hear me. The manuscript changed everything. It's not just you and the president anymore and it's not just me who's picked up their trail. Three different police departments are investigating, including the NYPD with a direct link to Homeland Security. I have a friend in town who's waiting for my call now," I continued. "I trust him completely and there are plenty of people he can trust outside of all of this we can enlist immediately."

"Not based on the contents of a manuscript alone," the first lady said reflectively.

"No," I conceded. "It would take considerably more than that."

"As in me."

"And your husband."

Her expression grew pleading. "You need to come back to the White House, Jessica. You need to lay this all out for the president, the same way you did for me. It's our only hope."

"Where's the president now?"

"Either the Oval Office or the residence. We don't have anything formal on the schedule for this evening."

"What about Harlan Babb?" I asked, referring to the president's chief of staff, the man who'd set all this in motion.

My mind was racing, similar to the way it did when I neared the end of one of my books. The nervous excitement over surmounting the last hump and heading into the home stretch. Finally having a clear idea of how I was going to wrap everything up.

"I'm not sure," Stephanie answered.

"Can we distract him, get him out of the White House if he's there, so you and I can be alone with your husband?"

Stephanie started to nod, then stopped. "I think so. Assuming I can, will you do it? Will you come to the White House? Will you help me put an end to this madness?"

I nodded. "Just tell me when."

Chapter Twenty-seven

9:00. Come to the back gate. You'll be escorted
to the Oval Office. We'll be waiting for you.

My cab approached the White House grounds one
hour after I'd received that text from Stephanie Albright,
after battling traffic awful even by Washington standards at this time of night. But it gave me time to collect
my thoughts yet again, some of which continued to
plague me.

Like what had suddenly struck me in Alma Desjardins's office about what was missing from the president's desk, from the entire Oval Office, in fact.

When I finish a book, or think I have, it's often with
the realization that something is still missing. Giving
the book a fresh read, or just setting it aside for a brief
time, is normally all it takes for the missing piece to
reveal itself, usually in the form of a duplicitous character or a twist that's set up but not acted upon. That

was how I felt right now about this very real, and tragic, story.

Kristen Albright never should have died, didn't deserve to be murdered. But there were greater factors afoot that had grown and multiplied in all the years since. The first lady and the president would pay a steep price for their complicity in her death and their acquiescence to the powerful force that had corrupted them. They would be judged, ultimately, in the court of public opinion. I wasn't sure there was a way for Robert Albright to both save his presidency and expose the monsters who had sought to subvert democracy. And I was prepared to make the best case for the latter with him, rehashing all the additional murders somehow made necessary by the existence of *The Affair*.

The cab dropped me at the Visitors Entrance to the White House just before nine o'clock. My name was indeed on the evening admittance list, and a pair of uniformed Secret Service agents took me to the post of two marines who brought me inside the building and escorted me down the hall toward the Oval Office, where a suited Secret Service agent cracked open the door for me.

Almost there, I took the phone from my bag and was turning it to silent when I received an incoming text message from Artie. I entered the Oval Office, the door closing behind me as I read the message:

Harlan Babb was found dead. Murdered. Artie

I looked up to see the president rising from behind his desk, not smiling as he was when I'd been there yesterday. The first lady rose from the same chair I'd occupied then; she was joined by a second figure in the adjacent chair: Sharon Lerner.

Neither of them was smiling, either.

"Sit down, Jessica," said Stephanie Albright.

"I'll stand, if you don't mind."

"Suit yourself."

"Guess I had things wrong, didn't I?" I said to the first lady.

"You should've stuck to writing mysteries," she told me, "not living them."

"That's quite a statement. Did you ever consider writing a book?"

"Is that supposed to be a joke?"

"Not at all," I told her. "It would make some story. A couple sacrifices their own daughter to attain the power they crave. Forget *House of Cards*; this is a castle of them."

"You have a way with words, too," Sharon Lerner said.

I was hearing her voice for the first time. How I'd let myself be manipulated, accepting Stephanie Albright's word that the late Harlan Babb had been responsible for orchestrating all this.

"It was you, wasn't it?" I challenged.

"I was only the initial messenger," Lerner said matter-of-factly.

"And watchdog, right? Keeping an eye out for whoever's pulling the strings and, I imagine, running the country."

"I'm running the country," the president said stiffly.

"Really? And were you the one who ordered all

these murders to protect a secret an unpublished manuscript came too close to?"

"Of course not."

"Then you're not really running the country, are you, *Mr. President*?"

"We're not the monsters you think we are," Stephanie said, her tone even more matter-of-fact than Sharon Lerner's.

"No? How many more people have to die before I can think that?"

"You don't understand."

"I hate when people say that, Madam First Lady. But you're right—I don't understand. I don't understand how any of you could have learned that *The Affair* even existed, never mind how close it came to the actual truth behind this administration."

I caught the first lady exchanging a furtive glance with the president, a realization striking me with a force that sent literal shivers up my spine.

"Wait," I resumed, "you've *read* the manuscript, haven't you? But how, how did you get your hands on a copy?"

She exchanged another glance with her husband, not as furtive this time. I was the final hole to be filled in, which explained why I'd been lured to the White House.

So I could join Thomas Rudd, Lane Barfield, A. J. Falcone, Alicia Bond, and probably Zara Larson, too.

Stephanie Albright was shaking her head. "You've got things wrong, but you're too stubborn to realize that."

"Really?"

"The great Jessica Fletcher unable to see something that was right in front of her all along," Stephanie said, turning to look at her husband.

I looked again at the famous Resolute desk, presented to President Rutherford B. Hayes by Queen Victoria in 1880, built from English oak timbers salvaged from the British exploration ship HMS *Resolute*, and saw what I'd realized I'd missed from Alma Desjardins's office.

Because it wasn't there to see.

Pictures: pictures of Kristen Albright that, by all rights, should have been in framed evidence. A parent holding fast to the memory of his departed daughter.

Unless she wasn't dead, I thought in that moment. Unless she hadn't been murdered at all.

She didn't die of a drug overdose, the text that must've come from Harlan Babb read.

Not because Kristen Albright had been murdered, but because she hadn't died at all.

"Did she run away or did you throw your teenage daughter out because she didn't fit into your plans?" I heard myself ask the president and first lady, the pieces falling together.

It all made sense now, why *The Affair* was so dangerous to the president and those behind his election and his presidency. In true roman à clef fashion, first daughter Abby had run away, too. Kristen Albright had just done so before her father was elected president, instead of after.

"We're not evil," Stephanie insisted. "We took advantage of a terrible situation."

I just shook my head. "Because a runaway child

would have doomed the master plan, right? So you concocted the whole thing. Invented a drug overdose to enlist the sympathy factor and make Robert Albright the kind of impassioned figure people would welcome into their living rooms, because he was one of them. It would be brilliant, if it wasn't so horrible."

"It can be both," the president of the United States said.

"We were opportunists; that's all," the first lady said in their defense.

"On top of being awful parents, apparently. Instead of doing everything you could to get your daughter to come home, you must've done everything you could to make sure she never came back. What would have happened then, Madam First Lady? How far would you have gone to keep your secret safe? Maybe the people behind all this would have arranged for her to be killed. Maybe you would've gone along with that."

Stephanie cringed at that but didn't bother trying to deny it.

"Do you even know where she is?" I continued, unable to disguise the harshness in my voice. "Did you ever try to find her?"

"I'm sorry, Jessica," she said, no longer cringing. "I truly am."

"No, you're not. It's not possible for someone willing to do what you've already done to be sorry for anything." I looked toward Sharon Lerner, who'd remained sitting, so still she seemed painted onto the scene, her eyes unblinking as they remained fixed on me. "Who are you?"

"Do I need to introduce myself again?"

"I'm not talking about your name. I'm talking about who you work for, who's behind all this. Did someone behind the scenes finally manage to take over the government? Some kind of silent coup with a puppet as president?"

The Guardians, I recalled from the manuscript, again coming frighteningly close to the truth. The murders all made a twisted degree of sense now, why all the people who knew the content of *The Affair* needed to die to keep the secret of who was really running the country.

Thomas Rudd, Lane Barfield, A. J. Falcone, Alicia Bond, Zara Larson . . .

I conjured their names to remind myself how close I'd come to following them. But I didn't intend to follow them now.

Stephanie Albright shook her head, grinning as if she found this whole scenario playing itself out humorous. "Jessica Fletcher, ever so trusting. So trusting you came alone."

"I came alone," I told her, "but I'm not as trusting as you think. That talk we had in Compass Coffee a few hours ago? My phone was on the whole time, our conversation heard by that New York police lieutenant I told you about. Oh, and did I forget to mention he's also the NYPD's Homeland Security liaison? I imagine they're outside the grounds now."

"Waiting for your signal—is that it?" the first lady asked.

She tried not to sound riled, but her tone betrayed her.

"No need," I said. "You're not going anywhere, and

my friend knows everything I do, except the fact that your daughter didn't actually die."

I aimed that statement not at the first lady, but at the president. He didn't respond, remaining impassive, like a child's toy whose batteries were wearing out. Then my eyes fell on Sharon Lerner, looking at me smugly, not concerned at all by the sudden turn of the tables.

"You knew all this already," I said, speaking the words as I thought them. "You already knew about my friend and you know Homeland Security is here or on their way."

"On their way," Sharon Lerner said, her voice sounding hushed. "But this will be over before they get here."

The coldness of her voice, coupled with the intent of her words, sent a flutter through my stomach. "What's it going to be?" I asked her, my anger trumping my fear for the time being. "An accident on White House grounds? A heart attack maybe? A manufactured mugging attack that kept me from getting here at all?"

Lerner smirked.

I turned toward the first lady, rotating my gaze between her and the president. "How'd you get the manuscript that set all this off? Who sent it to you?"

It was the vital remaining unanswered question, the part of this that made no sense.

"It doesn't matter, Jessica," Stephanie Albright managed, not sounding very convincing at all.

I seized on the hesitation, the doubt, in her voice.

"You know how this ends, don't you? Because I'm not really the last one alive who knows the truth: You and your husband are. And how long will it be exactly before you become liabilities instead of assets to whoever's really behind this?"

The Guardians, I thought, recalling the puppeteers from *The Affair.* Whatever Sharon Lerner was a part of must have been very much like them.

"You get it, don't you?" I said insistently to the president and first lady. "You've outlived your usefulness. You're the final two who have to die because of the manuscript—not because you read it; because you lived it." My gaze found Lerner again. "Please don't tell me I'm going to be the fall guy. Please don't tell me you expect the world to believe I came here and murdered the president and first lady. I've never even fired a gun in my life and everyone knows it."

"You mean like this one?" Sharon Lerner said, a semiautomatic pistol gleaming in her grasp, aimed somewhere between the three of us, as she rose from her chair. "Too bad you won't be able to base a book on this, Mrs. Fletcher. That's what you do, isn't it? Base your books on real-life investigations."

"Looks like the opposite was the case this time, only it was somebody else's book. But the ending hasn't been written yet, has it? How do you intend to do away with the only two people left who can expose you besides me?" I said, rotating my gaze between Robert and Stephanie Albright. "What's the plan? A terrorist attack? A bombing that kills the first family in the residence? No, don't tell me—that would spoil the suspense. But the president and first lady have to die. That's the only way this can end. I'm not the only one who won't be leaving the White House alive, am I?"

I'd trained all of my focus on Sharon Lerner, so I wasn't able to gauge the reactions of the president and first lady. Lerner, meanwhile, stepped away from her chair, her next intentions cloaked by the emptiness of her expression. I thought I was looking at a stone-cold killer or, at least, someone with the emotions of one.

"You should have stuck to books," Lerner hissed.

The Guardians . . .

I was going to ask her if the people behind her actually called themselves that, when the president jerked up the famed paperweight on loan from the John F. Kennedy Presidential Library and Museum and flung it in the same swift motion. It plunked into Sharon Lerner's skull with a cracking thud. I watched her empty eyes turn glassy as her knees buckled and she crumpled to the floor. The pistol she'd been holding ended up halfway between me and the first lady.

Neither of us went for it. We were in this together now; at least, I hoped we were.

"She was supposed to hold me here," I told the Albrights, "for whoever's coming. That must've been the plan." I glanced down at the unconscious form of Sharon Lerner splayed on the Oval Office carpeting. "They're probably coming for me now."

The first lady stormed past me, still ignoring the pistol. I thought she was going to push straight through the door, but she locked it instead.

"Think that will hold them?" I asked her.

"It doesn't have to," said the president. "You're right,

Jessica. This has gone far enough. We didn't know about all these murders that manuscript caused. We thought everything was under control."

"It's far from that, sir."

The president looked toward his wife, their stares locking, clearly of one mind on what had to happen next.

"We're getting out of here," he said. "*All* of us."

I watched Robert Albright move from behind his desk to an interior wall and feel about it as if to check for a water leak. His athletic prowess was a well-known fact long incorporated into his biography. I recalled from reading up on him the previous night that he'd actually started at quarterback for his Ivy League college football team, which explained the ease and accuracy with which he'd hurled the paperweight at the now unconscious Sharon Lerner.

His fingertips seemed to dig into a depression. He curled them and pulled, a segment of the wall receding into a swath of darkness.

"It's true," I heard myself say.

The legendary tunnels beneath the White House were real.

Chapter Twenty-eight

"Lucky for us tonight," the president said, opening the door all the way.

Moments later, a moldy smell of age and long-trapped air filled the Oval Office and flooded my nostrils.

Stephanie Albright brushed past me and stooped to retrieve Sharon Lerner's pistol from the floor. For a moment, I thought she was going to train the pistol on me; then she aimed it safely downward after flicking the safety back on.

"We need to hurry," she said. "We're in this together now."

I thought I heard footsteps converging on the Oval Office from the hallway beyond, caught the flicker of movement outside the windows behind the president's desk.

"Let's go, Mrs. Fletcher," the president called to me.

I moved behind the first lady toward the secret passageway that led into the tunnels beneath the White House that no one really believed existed. The president flipped some switches on a landing, illuminating a narrow stairway that spiraled downward into the depths of the earth itself.

Maybe bringing me along revealed the true character of the first couple, who had allowed themselves to be swept away on a tide of political ambition. I've heard power does that to people in general and Washington does it in particular. In fact, by all rights Washington seemed to encourage the realization of such ambitions through any means necessary. The Albrights were guilty of taking advantage of a family crisis, turning a daughter who'd run away into one who'd tragically died. In the process, an event that could've ended the future president's political career ended up providing the very foundation of his campaign.

As I followed the president down the steel stairs, which wobbled a bit under our collective weight, I wondered if the force behind Sharon Lerner had approached Albright in the wake of his daughter's disappearance, suggesting the exploitation that had ultimately propelled him to the White House. I wondered if that same force might have actually been responsible for Kristen's disappearance; indeed, perhaps she hadn't run away at all but had been kidnapped and disposed of to help convince the president to accept that force's help. His political career would've otherwise been over, and by Washington standards, his actions might've even qualified as acceptable behavior.

The light splayed by bulbs recessed into the finished ceiling of the tunnels was murky at best, revealing clouds of dust kicked up by our presence. I had no idea how well the tunnels were maintained or precisely where they led, other than what I'd learned from reading *The Affair*. Something continued to plague me about the manuscript, something I couldn't quite put my finger on. The puzzle wasn't complete yet, as much as I wanted it to be. There was still a piece missing.

The pistol Stephanie Albright was holding caught some of the light spraying downward and bounced it back. She had mentioned once learning how to shoot a gun to defend herself well before she got to the White House, where being under constant Secret Service protection changed the entire nature of self-defense. The fact that we'd ventured down here alone, instead of the first couple trusting the Secret Service to protect them, confirmed for me that there were strong elements that couldn't be trusted even within their protective cadre. Whoever was behind this hadn't left anything to chance, and why should they? They were seeking to control the most powerful person in the world, to be free to alter the balance of power as they saw fit and to force the enactment of policies that best served whatever their ends were. They had assumed Robert Albright to be nothing more than a willing puppet, and he likely had served in just that capacity, until the moment he hurled John F. Kennedy's coconut paperweight into the head of Sharon Lerner.

Stephanie Albright was pressed close to me, bringing up the rear. Her perfume, the same one she'd worn for our meeting that afternoon at Compass Coffee, smelled sweet and fruity, vaguely like a combination of linen and fresh citrus. Still clutching the pistol, she swung her gaze back toward the tunnel's origins when we both heard something like a door slamming.

"They're coming," she said to her husband.

At the front of our three-person convoy, the president picked up his pace, until a rolling gray blanket stopped him in his tracks.

Rats . . .

An endless stream of them, visible as specks of motion on the flattened surface of the plank flooring. Rummaging forward, stopping to sniff the air from their hind legs before settling back down and scurrying over our feet and pawing at our legs. The first lady looked like she would have shot them all, if she'd had enough bullets.

Over the squealing of the rats, we all heard far heavier feet tramping our way from back beneath the Oval Office. What looked like flickers of flashlight beams sliced through the darkness, distorted by the winding bends along the tunnel's length. I imagined the original tunnel footprint had indeed been laid two hundred years ago, when the White House was reconstructed, that the tunnel had been dug to steer around the heavier pockets of limestone and shale that couldn't be hammered out with a pickaxe. What a formidable construction challenge this must have posed at the time, I considered, as we trudged on, our progress slowed by the growing wave of gray and black swimming about at floor level and climbing over itself.

"Your perfume," I said to Stephanie Albright,

realizing what was whipping the creatures into such a frenzy.

"What?" she said, kicking at the rats, only to have more of them fill the vacated spots.

"Rats are attracted by smell and sweetness."

They continued to cluster, slowing our progress and steadily shortening the distance between us and the pursuers back up the tunnel. The flickers were becoming less fissures in the darkness and more hard glimpses of focused beams.

Closing in on us, certain to catch up before we could push through the black wave that continued to thicken at our feet.

"Do you have it with you?" I blurted toward the first lady.

"What?"

"That bottle of perfume."

She switched the pistol she was holding to her other hand and fished a glass spray bottle from the designer bag slung from her shoulder.

"It's not your scent, Jessica," Stephanie Albright said, handing it to me.

"No," I said, glancing toward the dark rolling, chirping blanket at our feet and ankles, "but it's theirs."

I prepared to hurl the perfume bottle back toward the pursuers closing in on us, then thought better of it and looked toward Robert Albright.

"I think you'd better do this."

The president accepted the bottle from my grasp and flung it lightly back in the direction from which we'd come. Just a flick of his wrist and it was soaring through the air, lost to the darkness. Then we heard the distinctive crackle of glass breaking and, almost instantly, the black wave seemed to move as one toward where the perfume bottle had shattered. A lumbering, rolling blanket that smelled of spoiled ground and wet burlap. I don't know why I hadn't noticed the smell before, or why it seemed worse in their wake.

We clung to the hope that the rats descending on our pursuers up the tunnel would buy us the rest of the time we needed to reach the exit. The way I recalled it from *The Affair*, we must be past the halfway point at the very least.

The bulbs recessed into the ceiling flickered as the tunnel shook lightly. I felt my heart seem to lurch in my chest at the fear the tunnel was about to collapse, then felt the rumble of a Washington Metro train thundering along a tunnel that must have been built below or adjacent to our position.

I started breathing easier and was further reassured by a chorus of chirping from the rats, which had formed a massive moving obstacle in the path of our pursuers. Slowed them enough that I no longer caught glimpses of the flickers from their flashlight beams radiating forward down the tunnel in our wake.

The tunnel swerved one way and then the other before settling into a steep rise that tested both my endurance and my shapely, but thankfully flat, shoes. Still, I was out of breath by the time I drew behind the president on a narrow ledge that finished in what looked like a steel security door.

"Open it," I implored.

"I already tried," said Robert Albright. "It's stuck."

The flashlight beams began to flicker and then flash again, our pursuers having surmounted the obstacle formed by the rats. I wished I could have lent something to the president's efforts in trying to yank open the exit door from the tunnel, but I would only get in his way.

The first lady, meanwhile, was standing poised on the steel landing in a shooter's stance, Sharon Lerner's pistol aimed toward the final bend in the tunnel our pursuers would soon reach. She looked steady and sure, no shakes or quivers, a woman utterly composed in the face of a grave threat. In that moment, I no longer saw the woman whom I'd assisted with countless fund-raisers supporting literacy. All of it, I knew now, had been a sham, her daughter's death manufactured to further her husband's political ambitions. Stephanie Albright herself was a sham, a facade, doing nothing more than playacting a role she'd helped write herself.

Her steely conviction as she steadied her aim at the source of the flickering lights made me wonder if she had been the driving force behind the charade that had propelled Robert Albright to the presidency. They had both conspired with the force that had raised them to power to suit its own ends, but I had the distinct feeling that Stephanie had been running the show, managing the machinations for the two of them. I suspected her husband had been following her lead all along. As much as he'd wanted to become president, she had wanted it more.

The lights brightened, shapes growing into shadows behind them. The first lady fired the pistol once and then again. The light beams jumped, then froze in place, our pursuers holding fast behind the cover of the last bend in the tunnel before it gave way to the upward grade that had brought us to the exit door that the president was still trying to jimmy open.

The flashlight beams brightened anew, our pursuers risking an advance Stephanie Albright swiftly chased back with three more shots. What kind of pistol was this? How many bullets did it hold in its magazine and how many were left? Assuming fifteen and a full magazine meant she still had ten remaining.

Behind us, her husband kept pulling on the stuck latch, a metal-on-metal scratching sound accompanying his efforts as the heavy door ground against its frame, beginning to give. I was watching him make a bit more tentative progress when the first lady fired another two times and then let loose two more bullets after a brief pause.

Leaving her only six shots, give or take.

I glimpsed the strain of exertion on the president's face, a shoe braced up against the frame now to add to his leverage. The seal had been broken, an inch of the door now protruding beyond the frame, lengthening incrementally by the second. I heard a thud, a rattle, saw him recoil, and spotted a squarish doorknob that had broken off in his hand, a rectangular hole revealed beyond it.

The president tried to push his fingers into the breach to find something to latch on to in order to jerk the door open the remainder of the way, his hand too big to manage the task.

But mine wasn't.

I heard Stephanie Albright squeeze off two more shots, only four or so bullets left to keep our pursuers at bay, as I eased up to the door and pushed my much smaller and more nimble fingers into the hole vacated by the doorknob after the president yanked his fingers out. I remained silent, knowing he'd grasp the point of what I was doing, and felt him grab my shoulders for leverage, bracing himself against the railing.

I found a jagged edge, twisted and mangled by his efforts, which had ultimately left the knob in his hand. I was able to fasten my narrow, lithe fingers around it and pull with a single hand.

The door moved, not much but a little. It moved more when I pulled again, and kept moving, more and more of the edge showing. The jagged metal was cutting into my fingers and I could feel the warmth of blood dripping down from them. I recorded the pain but didn't really feel it, the motivation I needed found in the next three shots the first lady fired, leaving her only one.

Click, I heard.

Make that none, I thought, as I clenched my teeth and grimaced, finding better purchase on the jagged metal edge inside the hole at the expense of my already torn fingers. I didn't even register the pain anymore. I just pulled.

And pulled.

And pulled some more.

The first gunshots fired our way came as the door gave inward with a final heave, letting the fresh air spill inside, along with a flood of lights from just beyond the jamb.

More of the men behind the murders that had dominated the past week, I thought, as I surged out just ahead of the president and first lady to avoid the spray of bullets that was closing in on us from behind. I dropped down a few feet off what seemed to be the base of a statue. Still blinded by the powerful beams, as I started to raise my hands in the air, I knew it was over.

"Jessica!" I heard a familiar voice bellow.

My eyes finally cut through the glare of light and found the familiar face of Artie Gelber before me, his gun drawn, a virtual army of uniformed and plainclothes Washington, DC, police flanking him on both sides.

"Go!" he ordered.

And they surged through the open doorway, weapons blazing. The gunfight raged on as I collapsed into Artie's arms.

Chapter Twenty-nine

"I'm sorry I ruined your suit," I said to Artie as the paramedics finished bandaging the hand I'd used to get the heavy exit door open the rest of the way.

We had emerged in Lafayette Park, through General von Steuben's statue, the same way Pace and Abby had entered the tunnels to gain access to the White House in *The Affair*. I couldn't help but smile at the irony of that, in spite of all that had just transpired.

Artie glanced toward his shoulder and the beginning of the blood trail I'd left all over the fabric. "I'll expense it out."

He turned his gaze back toward the big door that spilled out onto a grassy, tree-lined patch of land. A number of dark-clad gunmen, some wearing suits, had already emerged in the custody of the police, and now I watched a pair of stretchers follow them in testament to the aim of the cops who'd accompanied Artie here.

Secret Service personnel under Artie's direct supervision had already taken charge of the president and first lady, cordoning off a separate area for paramedics to check them out. They wouldn't be going anywhere tonight without a heavy complement of guards, and not back to the White House until it was fully cleared and deemed safe. I had no idea what the Secret Service knew, or even suspected; I knew only that more of what had transpired would emerge in the coming days. How much exactly, I had no idea.

Secret Service supervisors made several attempts to approach me, only to be shooed away by Artie on each occasion. He clearly wanted to be the first one to hear my story in order to determine the safest strategy for us to pursue, as far as how best to release the narrative we'd managed to piece together. I could only imagine what he was thinking—speculating, at that point.

"You're not going to believe it, Artie," I said the next time our eyes met, thinking of my exchange with the Albrights up in the Oval Office before we'd made our escape. "You're not going to believe any of it."

"When I'm around you, Jessica, I've learned to believe anything."

"Well, Mort and Seth won't believe it."

"What about Harry McGraw?"

"I'm not sure he'd even listen."

His eyes cheated toward the tunnel exit, then fastened again on me. "Care to provide some notion of what exactly happened?"

"Even a notion would take too long to explain, and this isn't the best place to try. I think I need to have a drink."

"I didn't know you drank at all."

"Not yet. I'm rethinking that right now." I followed his gaze toward the final stretcher being carried out from the aftermath of the gunfight that had followed the police storming the door in our wake. "You never did tell me how you knew where to wait for us, that this was where the tunnel spilled out."

Artie grinned. "Simple, Jessica: That's where you told me it was in that manuscript."

We met two days later at Harry's favorite place, the Tick Tock Diner, but arrived an hour ahead of him so Artie could fill me in on things he didn't want Harry to hear.

"All this is still being sorted out," he started, "and I'm mostly out of the loop at this point."

"Give me the broad strokes," I told him.

"Sharon Lerner is cooperating and talking up a storm, giving up the entire network behind all this."

"Any names I'd recognize?"

"I'm sure there are, but it's the ones nobody recognizes that are the scariest. I wish I could say I was surprised, but this is just politics as usual to the nth degree." Artie stopped and then started again. "Virtually everything you said has been confirmed, Jessica. Pat yourself on the back for cracking another case."

"One the world will never hear about," I noted.

"Not the truth, anyway. And I'm fine with that, as you should be, too."

"Depends on what happens next."

"Hypothetically?"

I nodded. "Hypothetically."

"All the principals behind this are going to disappear. No arraignments, no plea deals, no interrogations, no court appearances, no formal arrests, no mug shots. Nothing that can be linked in any way to what happened a few nights ago and what started years before that."

"So what happens to them?"

"They'll be transported somewhere warm and tropical, where they'll likely never be heard from again."

"Guantanamo?"

It was Artie's turn to nod.

"Are you confident they've all been rounded up?"

"Not yet. But I will be."

"Which raises one final question."

"The president and first lady," Artie said, posing the question for me.

"Not a question, but that's the gist."

"It's also above my pay grade," Artie said.

"Best guess?"

"We're coming up on the next presidential election."

"That's not a guess."

"Yes, it is," Artie said, leaving things there before elaborating further. "You think the country could handle the whole truth, Jessica?"

"I think the guilty deserve to be punished, and that includes Stephanie and Robert Albright."

"'Justice' is a relative term, Jessica," Artie noted.

"That sounds strange, coming from you."

"They did save your life."

"I've thought about that."

"And?"

"I'm sure they had their reasons."

"And those are?"

"Well, one reason in particular, connected to the one part of this that's still hanging out there, a part I realized I had wrong all along."

He leaned forward in our booth. "You've got my attention."

"I think I'd like to remain elusive, too."

"How about a hint?"

"This needs to end where it started."

He thought only briefly. "The manuscript?"

"I never did finish it."

"But it's gone, Jessica."

"Only the pages, not the story."

Befuddlement claimed his features as Harry Mc-Graw slid into the booth next to me, already signaling for his regular server.

"What'd I miss?" he asked us.

Kingdom Books was located in Waterford, Vermont, amid rolling hills layered atop unspoiled land that stretched as far as the eye could see. It was one of my absolute favorite stores this side of Otto Penzler's Mysterious Book Shop. Kingdom's "Otto" was actually a couple, Beth and David Kanell, who'd built a store founded on mysteries because they loved them. It wasn't all that close to Cabot Cove as sharing a New England location might have suggested, but I still made it a point to get down there for an event every time I had a new release, and for the paperback reprint.

But that's not why I was there. Today, and for the last three days, I'd come to Kingdom Books because Beth and Dave had recognized someone I'd described to them. I was sipping a tea Dave had made for me, and browsing the noir section of the stacks lined with new and used mysteries, when I glimpsed her entering the store. I caught David's look and then his nod, moot because I'd already recognized her.

I waited until she reached the section of the store devoted to thrillers. The Kanells had told me she did that on every visit, a few times a week. Never leaving without buying at least one of the books she'd sampled over coffee in one of the store's cushy chairs. I approached so my frame was between her and the door.

"Hello, Zara," I said to Lane Barfield's assistant, Zara Larson, "or would you prefer Kristen?"

I didn't know what reaction to expect from Kristen Albright, who'd turned herself into Zara Larson, but it wasn't a smile.

"How'd you know you could find me here?"

"You put Waterford, Vermont, as your hometown on your application to work for Lane."

She shook her head. "I must've forgotten that. I came here once with my parents when I was a little girl. Never stopped loving it."

"With good reason. And since I knew you loved books . . . ," I told her, glancing about the store to make my point for me.

The way Zara gazed at me next seemed to put more distance between us. "You're even better than I heard. It must be nice to live what you write."

"You should know, given that you wrote *The Affair.*"

I waited for a reaction, continued when none came.

"See, Zara," I said, using the name I knew her by, "I must not be as good at this as you think I am. If I were, I would have figured out that all the murders—Lane, Thomas Rudd, A. J. Falcone, Alicia Bond, and nearly me—had little or nothing to do with the contents of the manuscript. It was all about who the author was. You reappearing on the scene, as a bestselling author no less, would have brought down your parents. The people behind them couldn't let that happen. But even that wasn't enough for you, was it? You wanted to stick it all in your parents' faces, exact your revenge." I paused, studying her reaction. "You sent them a copy of the manuscript, didn't you? That was your real revenge, even more than publishing it."

She might have trembled slightly—that was all—as if comfortable with her actions and resigned to the consequences they'd unleashed.

"People died," I continued, "innocent people, because of what you did, what you wrote. You'll have to live with that for the rest of your life."

She looked away, maybe toward the door to judge the distance, then turned her gaze back on me. Her hair was longer and worn in a different style. She had lost some weight and her complexion had the kind of sallow shading of someone who didn't spend much time in the sunshine and fresh air.

"I didn't mean for that to happen," Zara Larson,

born Kristen Albright, said. "I didn't know what I was writing was so close to the truth. I made it all up. And I never expected anyone to be able to trace the manuscript to Lane Barfield. I took precautions, used a UPS Store instead of the mail room."

"UPS Stores have security cameras, Zara. Did you really think the people behind this wouldn't pull out every stop they could to find who sent that manuscript to the White House?"

Zara lapsed back into silence, giving me time to again consider the text message that had come from the late Harlan Babb: She didn't die of a drug overdose. I had indeed mistaken the intent of his message, thinking he'd meant to imply that the president's daughter was instead murdered. In fact, the message had been to imply she hadn't died at all, but had run away. I had ultimately figured that much out, but not the fact that Zara Larson was both Kristen Albright and Benjamin Tally, until later.

"When did you begin to suspect the truth?" she asked me.

"I should have, after paying a visit to your apartment with an NYPD detective. It had something starkly in common with your father's desk in the Oval Office: not a single family picture, none at all. And how could there be without exposing your true identity?"

"What else?"

"I should have suspected the truth then," I told her, "especially when the only remaining identifiable prints on the manuscript's title page belonged to you and Lane Barfield. Since he clearly wasn't the author, that left only you."

"There is that," Zara acknowledged.

"You would've made a good actress, Zara. Your performance in the office was brilliant."

"That's because it was genuine, Mrs. Fletcher. I've wanted to be a writer my entire life, and working for Mr. Barfield, living in that world every day, gave me the courage to try. I've never enjoyed anything more than writing that book."

"It would have been a huge bestseller," I told her.

She turned back to the shelves, seeming to study the various titles of Robert Ludlum as she responded, then suddenly swung back toward me, expression so taut I could see the first impressions of age lines on her face. "I knew my parents were involved in something I wanted no part of, with people who were in a position to help them gain the only thing they really cared about," she said, the bitterness palpable in her voice.

"Power?"

"Nice guess."

"It's not a guess. It's a fact. The subject of pretty much every book in this section. So which is it, Zara? Was running away or writing the book your real revenge?"

"Running away allowed them to kill me off in pursuit of what they truly wanted."

I nodded. "You helped them more than you can possibly realize."

"Stupid me." Zara looked at me in the context of the store and started to move away. I moved with her to the J. B. Fletcher section of Kingdom Books. "I dream of having a shelf like that someday, just like my parents dreamed of something else." Her gaze and voice grew imploring. "I didn't mean for all those people to get murdered, Mrs. Fletcher. I had no idea the people behind my parents would go that far."

"I don't think your parents did, either, for what it's worth."

"It's not worth much." She shrugged.

"I can help you with your career, Zara, your dream. Introduce you to the right agent, maybe the right publisher. I believe you're a victim here to a large extent as well."

She regarded me suspiciously. "What's the catch?"

"Zara Larson needs to go away. Kristen Albright needs to reappear."

Her gaze narrowed, her expression twisting into a mask of befuddlement that deepened those thin lines. "That would destroy my parents."

"I know."

Her expression lengthened in realization, her eyes showing all of the whites. "Which I'm guessing, then, is the point."

"It's also the best strategy, maybe the only way, for you to stop living a lie . . . Kristen."

"It seems I don't have much of a choice here," she said, cringing at my use of her real name.

I just looked at her, watched her expression as a strange realization, something like surprise but not quite, blossomed on her face.

"You're writing the ending for this, aren't you?" Kristen Albright asked me, shaking her head. "You're writing the ending you want the story to have."

"I'm writing the ending it needs."

"It's not a very happy one."

"Not all stories call for that."

Kristen Albright tightened her gaze upon me. "The book had a different title originally: *The President's Daughter.*"

"Why'd you change it?"

"Because it stopped being about me. I got lost in the story."

"It was always about the president's daughter, Kristen, no matter what you called it."

"You'll make me famous, Mrs. Fletcher. You'll make it so the whole world will know who I am and what I've done."

I let her comment hang in the air for a bit before responding. "As I said, not all stories come with happy endings. But I do have a question for you, Kristen: Since you never actually lived with your parents in the White House, how'd you know the tunnels were real and that the exit was built into General von Steuben's statue in Lafayette Park?"

She shrugged her narrow shoulders. "I made it up."

"Really?"

The daughter of the president of the United States nodded.

"Well," I said, "I guess sometimes truth really is stranger than fiction."

Read on for an excerpt from the latest
Murder, She Wrote Mystery,

MURDER IN RED

Coming in May 2019 from
Berkley Prime Crime

"Well, Jessica, at least I wasn't murdered."

The quote read by the priest presiding over Jean O'Neil's funeral received a smidgen of laughter from those who packed Cabot Cove Community Church. Jean had been the local librarian from the time I moved to our town and was fond of greeting me with lines such as "What will it be, Jessica—more books on poisons?" She'd retired a few years ago when her multiple sclerosis finally grew too bad for her to continue negotiating the stacks.

In lieu of a eulogy, Jean had penned brief snippets directed at any number of town staples. I thought mine would take the cake, until Sheriff Mort Metzger's— "Well, Mort, I guess I'm going to get away without paying those parking tickets after all"—got a louder laugh.

Meanwhile, the snippet for Seth Hazlitt, Cabot Cove's resident family doctor, raised merely a collective giggle: "I think you can cancel my next appointment, Seth." But then, "Sorry, I don't have a forwarding address to send my bill" got a louder reception.

I hate funerals, but then again, I don't know anyone who likes them. Jean's was different in the sense that she'd beaten the odds at every turn: first by outlasting the dreaded disease's debilitating effects and then by drastically outliving her expected life span. She'd even enjoyed a final renaissance of sorts, thanks to an experimental new treatment provided by the Clifton Clinic, aka Clifton Care Partners, a state-of-the-art private hospital that had opened just outside town and was about to celebrate its first anniversary. Billed as a "rejuvenation clinic" as well as a hospital, the Clifton Clinic had drawn a steady flow of outsiders to our once bucolic town year-round, further roiling those of us who remembered what it had been like when we could greet everyone in Cabot Cove by name.

I learned a long time ago that you can't fight change; even the beloved home I'd shared with my late husband, Frank, was undergoing extensive renovations in the wake of a fire that had nearly claimed my life. Funerals always make me think of Frank, which I suppose is why I've come to detest them so much. Frank and I practically raised our nephew Grady, which meant he grew up witnessing my fits and starts of writing back in my days substitute teaching high school English. It had been Grady who'd plucked my first manuscript, *The Corpse Danced at Midnight*, almost literally from the trash and given it to his girlfriend at the time, who happened to work for Coventry House, the imprint that would ultimately become my publisher.

And if it weren't for him, I'd probably still be filling in for others instead of filling in the plot holes I inevitably found through my rewrite process.

Listening to the priest wax on with more of Jean O'Neil's witticisms left me feeling I should invite Grady and his family up for a visit soon. It had been too long since I'd seen them, especially young Frank—named after my husband, and more like a grandson to me, given that his namesake and I had raised his father through a great measure of Grady's youth. And he so enjoyed blaming some of the business scrapes he'd gotten himself into over the years, pursuing this scheme or that, on having a fertile imagination to match mine.

Thinking of Grady and his family also made me realize it had been too long since I'd spoken with George Sutherland, the Scotland Yard inspector who was the only man I'd ever actually dated since Frank's death, though I'm not sure our get-togethers were dates so much as two friends enjoying a mutual attraction and each other's company.

In other words, dates.

Since Jean had no family, the Friends of the Library had taken on the task of arranging her service and funeral arrangements, and decided against a wake or memorial in favor of a reception to follow her burial in Cabot Cove's local cemetery, which was part of the National Historic Register. As chair of the Friends, I had the official greeting responsibilities, which I was dutifully performing outside the church when I spotted Mimi Van Dorn approaching.

"Wonderful service, Jessica," she said, taking my hand affectionately. "I'm sure it would've made Jean proud."

"Thanks, Mimi. I sure do miss her."

Mimi looked around the front of our old church, shaking the platinum blond hair from her face. Once her natural color, it now came courtesy of a bottle. Mimi was older than I, but you wouldn't know that from her appearance. She joined the Friends of the Library as soon as she moved to Cabot Cove nearly a decade ago, and we quickly bonded over our mutual love of books. Not just reading, but the need to support the printed page and, especially, libraries. I recall a particularly contentious town council meeting where we needed to beat back a proposal to relocate our beloved library to make room for yet another high-end housing development. But she gave such an impassioned speech that the council members flirting with voting for the proposal abruptly changed their minds.

"I leave you with this, ladies and gentlemen," Mimi had concluded, turning to face the standing-room-only crowd. "This isn't just a choice between books and buildings, words and wood; it's also a choice between dreams and developments."

Mimi won me there and we'd been close ever since. She was one of my best friends in town, having taught me how to play bridge, canasta, and pinochle, though gin rummy remained my favorite. She had come from old money and had settled in Cabot Cove long before it became fashionable to do so. We seldom, if ever, talked about our personal lives, but rather about our preferred books over the years. We rarely agreed, which seemed to draw us even closer. I've bonded with people over many things, but never over anything as effectively as books.

"Well, I intend to make a sizable donation to the library in Jean's name," Mimi said. "Perhaps to name a new collection. What was her favorite genre?"

"Anything but mystery," I told her.

"I'm being serious here, Jessica."

"So am I. She was a fan of classical fiction and looked forward to the day, she used to say, when I finally wrote a real book."

"You're joking."

"Maybe, but only in part. She used to read my books only to offer me critiques of what she deemed the more relevant parts, all of three or four pages normally. She did that for all forty-seven of my books, and I'll miss her doing it when number forty-eight comes out."

"A clever way of letting you know she'd read them." Mimi nodded, dabbing her eyes with a folded-over handkerchief, more to keep her makeup in place than out of grief.

Mimi hadn't seemed to have aged in the years I'd known her; if anything, she looked younger. I knew how vain she was about her appearance, just as I knew how averse she was to use the surgical methods to which many women resorted. She'd become a health fiend in recent years and an obsessive follower of new diets meant to assure eternal youth. We'd first met when she caught me jogging along the sea and then again when I was riding my bicycle through town. She thought I'd eschewed driving to get more exercise until I confessed it was because I never learned how to drive.

"But I heard you had your pilot's license," she'd remarked.

"I do, thanks to my late husband, Frank, who taught me how to fly."

"But not drive? Really?"

"Not a lot of accidents up in the air, Ms. Van Dorn," I said.

"So long as you don't run out of fuel," she'd quipped. *"And call me Mimi."*

"I'll see you at the reception, then," Mimi resumed today, angling away from me to cross the street toward her car, parked away from the funeral procession.

Most of the rest of the crowd had moved toward the parking lot that adjoined the church. I saw Mimi reach the street and noticed she'd dropped her handkerchief on the grassy strip we'd been standing on. I stooped to retrieve it, rising to see her half-stopped in the middle of the road, speaking heatedly into her cell phone.

As an SUV, an old Jeep Cherokee, suddenly wheeled around the corner, picking up speed, headed directly for Mimi.

I lurched into motion, charging into the street and practically leaping into Mimi just before the Jeep would have struck her, the two of us locked in an uneasy embrace as we spun to the other side of the road, squeezed between two parked cars.

"Jessica," a white-faced Mimi managed to utter, stiff and pale with shock.

"One funeral for the day was enough," I said, forcing a smile even though I was shaking like a leaf.

I walked off toward the car belonging to the Friends of the Library member who'd be driving me to the reception to get things prepared. Turning my gaze backward to make sure Mimi was okay, I spotted her back on her phone, yelling at whoever was on the other end of the line. Then I peered down the street, as if expecting the old Jeep Cherokee to come roaring back.

But it had disappeared.

Ready to find
your next great read?

Let us help.

Visit prh.com/nextread